PRAISE FOR *T*

"A dangerous town carved ou
who can name spirits and tan
save the natural world: *The Na*
and the w

—Eliot Schrefer, New York Times bestselling author of *The Lost Rainforest*

"Absorbing, masterfully crafted, and brilliantly original, *The Namer of Spirits* is an illuminating story about friendship, courage, and the power of words."

—Jenny Goebel, Green Earth Book Award-winning author of *Out of My Shell*

"A luminous and essential story for all ages. I was swept away by the lovable characters, magical world, passionate quest, and wise guides. *The Namer of Spirits* reflects current ecological issues in a way that offers readers understanding, hope, and the courage to take action. Everyone should read this."

—Laura Resau, Américas Award-winning author of *Tree of Dreams*

"A rich, multi-layered story with a subtle ecological message, and a cast of characters who had my heart from page one, *The Namer of Spirits* is simply spellbinding.

Teachers and librarians who are searching for well-written fiction to pair with environmental non-fiction need to snap this one up! Highly recommended."

—Darby Karchut, Colorado Book Award-winning author of *Del Toro Moon*

THE NAMER OF SPIRITS

OWL HOLLOW PRESS

Owl Hollow Press, LLC, Springville, UT 84663

Library of Congress Cataloging-in-Publication Data
The Namer of Spirits / T. Mitchell. — First edition.

Summary:
The perils of deforestation and the magic of friendship are explored through a fantastical adventure involving giant mistcats, tempestuous forest spirits, and a girl with a special gift for speaking the words that shape what things become.

ISBN 978-1-945654-82-4 (paperback)
ISBN 978-1-945654-83-1 (e-book)
LCCN 2021944998

For Cailin—like Ash you see the truth of things and always speak your heart.

And for Addison—for showing me the power of naming.

Part 1

Warning Bells

Every child who grew up in the village of Last Hope knew what the warning bells meant.

One bell, rung from a watchtower, meant that a storm had been spotted. Usually such storms came from the west—the direction of the cloud forest beyond the wall. Storms rolled over the tops of trees in the distance like giant bulls charging toward the village.

Two bells meant that dao fora warriors had been seen, skulking among the cloud forest underbrush or racing through the trees on their mistcats. When two bells were rung, wall soldiers readied their muskets, and any workers in the fields beyond the wall hurried in through the gates as quick as their legs could carry them. Even those within the village would take shelter when two bells were rung, in case the dao fora shot poison arrows over the wall.

But three bells meant something much worse. Three bells, rung from a watchtower, was the warning signal everyone listened for, because three bells meant an illwen had been spotted coming toward the village.

When three bells were rung, soldiers left their posts and ran for the longhouse, along with all the villagers, because no wall, musket, or amount of bravery would keep a monstrous, rampaging illwen out. All that the soldiers and villagers could do when illwen attacked was take shelter within the sunken stone walls of the longhouse and wait for the angry forest spirit to pass.

That's what village children were taught to do since they were old enough to walk. And that's what plantation workers and squatters learned to do as soon as they arrived in Last Hope. Even if they didn't know how to speak the common tongue, they knew to drop whatever they were doing and run to the longhouse when three bells were rung.

Which is why, on this hot spring day, when twelve-year-old Ash Narro heard a warning bell sound from the watchtower by the forest gate, she froze and did what all villagers did—she waited to hear if another bell would follow.

Ash's father, Garrett Narro, stood nearby, holding a broom. He'd been sweeping up debris from the previous night's illwen attack. Broken branches and leaves littered the front porch of his general store, along with dirt and rocks that had blown against the storefront. The store itself, and the rooms above it where Ash and her parents lived, had been spared. Still, there was plenty to clean up. Illwen almost always appeared during a storm, and for the past several months all the storms had been dusty and dry, bringing vicious winds but no rain to end the drought.

A second bell sounded from the forest gate watchtower. The whole village became quiet as a frightened rabbit as people waited to learn what threat had been spotted. Ash held her breath.

No third bell sounded.

The north, east, and south watchtowers soon picked up the warning, each sounding only two bells.

Ash let out her breath and looked to her father. He kept staring across the village square at the forest gate watchtower where a lookout shouted to soldiers on the ground. More soldiers ran from the barracks to the gate. The jingle of their buckles echoed across the square.

"Open the gate!" called the lookout.

"Jumping frogs," grumbled Garrett Narro. "What now?"

"Are dao fora attacking?" asked Ash.

Her dad shook his head. "They wouldn't open the gate if dao fora were attacking."

"Then why did they ring two bells?"

Garrett shrugged and went back to sweeping the porch. He was the sort of person who rarely troubled himself with questions he didn't have answers for.

But Ash wasn't that sort of person—not in the least. She had a mind that constantly wandered into hidden places. People often scolded her for daydreaming and getting carried away by "flights of fancy," although Ash never saw it as such. Rather than imagining things, she thought of it as paying attention to things that no one else noticed and seeing what could be—the way a weed could be a flower once you noticed its beauty. Everything had hidden possibilities, and if she listened closely enough, she sometimes heard whispers of what those possibilities might be.

Now, for instance, she heard several possibilities whispering around the gate. She couldn't make out what the soldiers said, but they seemed excited about something. Dao fora warriors must be near—otherwise the watchtower wouldn't have rung two warning bells. Yet the soldiers didn't appear frightened. Maybe the dao fora came in peace. They might have even brought gifts. Ash tried to envision what sort of gifts dao fora warriors would bring. Beautiful birds? Precious gems? Tame mistcats? She watched the gate, eager for it to open.

Her father cleared his throat. "There are plenty of sticks that still need picking up."

Ash stooped to gather broken branches, but her thoughts stayed on the gate.

Lately, dao fora warriors had shot at plantation workers and squatters who'd strayed into the cloud forest. Perhaps the lookout had called for the gate to be opened because a wounded squatter needed to be let in. But if that was all, why ring two warning bells?

She carried the sticks she'd collected to the pile by the porch and started to break the longer ones in half across her knee.

"Ouch!" One stick refused to break. Her knee throbbed. Ash propped the stick against a rock and stomped on it, but it didn't even bend.

"Aren't you a strong stick," she said.

The stick hummed in response.

It was a sound Ash felt more than heard—a tingling that ran up her spine and collected at the back of her head, calling to her. The stick wanted a name. Not a common name, like the ones people used to describe things, but a true name—the sort of name that revealed what something could be. The sort of name that no one else seemed to hear but her.

Ash studied the stick. It was slightly thicker than her thumb and long enough to serve as a good walking stick. She tried digging her nails into the silver bark but couldn't even scratch it.

Ironwood, she realized, amazed.

Ironwood trees were rare and extremely strong. The only one she'd seen in the area grew in the webworm plantation fields beyond the wall. How did the stick get here?

The more she considered the stick, the more the hum of possibilities deepened. She cocked her head and tried to listen to the wood, but all the commotion at the gate made it hard to concentrate.

Garrett Narro finally set down his broom. "Stay here," he told Ash. Then he strode toward the crowd gathering around the gate.

Ash set the stick with the others in the pile. The moment she let it go, the hum became a whine.

"Guess you don't want to be left behind," she said. "Me neither."

She glanced at where her father had gone. He'd nearly reached the crowd by the gate. Her friend, Rosa Baker, headed there as well. Ash hadn't talked with Rosa in over a week.

"Come along." She picked up the stick. "Let's see what all the fuss is about."

"Clear the gate!" shouted the watchtower officer.

Four wall soldiers pressed the villagers back, while two more lifted the heavy timber and swung open the gate door. Ash squeezed between people's hips and shoulders to get a better view.

A skinny boy stumbled through the opening a moment later, followed by two squatters. One of the squatters held the end of a rope that had been looped around the boy's neck. He shoved the boy forward, then yanked the rope.

Villagers gasped and stepped back, afraid of the boy even though he was tied up. Wall soldiers poured into the gap and cleared a path to the square.

The boy wore the strangest clothes. Crude leather pants covered his legs and a cloak the greenish-gray color of tree moss hung from his shoulders. He wasn't wearing a shirt. Swirls of red clay decorated his chest, and a woven leather band lifted his long black hair back from his face.

Ash's pulse skipped. The boy resembled descriptions she'd read of the forest people who shot arrows at squatters and plantation workers. A real live dao fora!

Mayor Tullridge blustered through the crowd. "What's the meaning of this?" he demanded.

"We caught him sneaking around the wall, trying to attack the village!" said the man holding the rope.

Ash didn't know the man's name. Squatters were always coming to the village, claiming they'd been granted land to farm by the governor himself. But since there wasn't any farmland left in the village, new arrivals often had to resort to clearing parts of the cloud forest beyond the wall to farm, or "squatting" as villagers called it.

The second squatter looked related to the man holding the rope, only younger. His dark hair had white tufts of webworm silk stuck to it from walking through the plantation fields. Both squatters beamed with pride at having captured a dao fora. The younger one carried the dao fora boy's bow and a quiver full of arrows.

The strangest thing about the dao fora boy was that he didn't look worried about being captured. In fact, the corners of his mouth turned up in a curious smile as he looked around. Except for his odd clothing, he hardly seemed like the fierce, murderous warriors Ash had heard soldiers tell stories about. He looked like a kid, not even as old as her. He was skinnier than her too.

The squatter holding the rope shoved the boy toward the center of the village square. Villagers created a circle around him, trying to get a good look without getting too close.

"Why, he's just a scrawny child," said one woman.

"Don't be foolish," grumbled another. "Dao fora always look young, on account of them having no beards. They're small, too, but that doesn't make them any less dangerous. Ones who looked younger than this killed my brother, bless his soul."

Soon villagers fell into arguing about what to do with the boy. Some wanted to tie him to a wall post or hang him by his ankles to scare off other dao fora. Others thought this cruel, but even they didn't want to release him. If they let him go he'd just hide in the forest and shoot poison arrows at them. Or he'd send more illwen to attack, just like the one that had torn through their village the night before.

Eventually, Mayor Tullridge announced that they'd hold the boy prisoner until his fate could be determined. This solution led to new problems since they couldn't decide where to keep the boy. The village had no jail. Anyone who committed a crime was forced to work without pay in the webworm plantations beyond the wall, but people figured the boy would escape if they took him beyond the wall since that's where he'd come from.

Finally, someone pointed to the empty rabbit cage in front of the general store and suggested keeping the boy there.

Ash looked to see what her father thought of this plan. His brow furrowed, the way it did when he went over shop figures that didn't add up, but he didn't protest. No one else had a cage as sturdy as his, with thin metal bars that rabbits couldn't chew through.

The two squatters shoved the boy into the cage while Ash's dad got a padlock for the door.

The cage wasn't large, but the boy was small enough that he could crawl around inside if he didn't lift his head too high. At least it was better than being tied to a post in the blazing hot sun. Or being hung off the wall by his ankles.

"There," said the older squatter. "As long as we've got one of theirs, they won't dare send more illwen to attack us."

"Unless they don't control the illwen," someone else said.

"Everyone knows the illwen come from the forest where the dao fora live," argued a farmer. "They're the ones sending those monsters here, and if they do it again we'll show 'em what we've got."

The crowd moved into the shade of a fig tree near the square to get out of the midday sun. The sweltering heat, on top of the ongoing drought and the recent illwen attack, had everyone in a prickly, fearful mood.

Instead of following the crowd, Ash crept closer to the cage to inspect the boy.

She'd never seen one of the dao fora up close before. She'd heard people talk about how, long ago, dao fora used to come into the village to trade goods at her parents' store, but that all ended after dao fora attacked some squatters in the cloud forest. Then soldiers built the wall to keep the dao fora out.

These days, dao fora only came near the village to shoot poison arrows at people. Dao fora raids had killed several people caught outside the wall, including Rosa's dad. People claimed that the dao fora were why the illwen attacks had increased, although no one knew for certain if this was true. And even if it was true, no one knew how dao fora managed to command such wild,

destructive forest spirits. Telling an illwen wh
like telling the wind where to blow.

The boy sat cross-legged on the ground, watching
ers. Ash didn't think he looked like a killer. He was just a scrawny kid who seemed surprised that all this fuss was over him.

Suddenly, he scrambled back to the far end the cage. Ash stepped closer to see what had startled him.

The boy's gaze followed a black-and-yellow caterpillar inching along one of the cage bars.

"Are you avoiding *that*?" asked Ash, pointing to the caterpillar.

The boy made no response, but his gaze didn't leave the caterpillar.

"It's only a webworm." Ash picked up a leaf and coaxed the caterpillar onto the edge. It seemed like an ordinary webworm to her. The little black-and-yellow caterpillars were common as dirt, especially in the webworm plantations beyond the wall where rows upon rows of jujube trees had been planted for webworms to feed on so workers could harvest the silk they spun. She turned the leaf to keep the webworm from falling off. Then she held it out toward the boy. "It won't hurt you."

He scrunched his nose as if the caterpillar smelled bad.

Ash had never met someone so peculiar—smiling at the wrong times and avoiding the wrong things.

She set the webworm on a nearby bush. She didn't like the way they munched up all the leaves on plants, and she thought the silky tents they spun looked like mold rotting the forest, but she didn't want to kill the creature. It might have a name—maybe one that other webworms knew—and named things couldn't be replaced.

The boy eyed her warily when she returned. Ash held her hands up to show that the webworm was gone. "See? There's nothing to be afraid of."

"Ash! Get away from him!" snapped Rosa Baker. She'd left the crowd by the fig tree and strode across the square toward the store. "Don't you have any sense? He's dangerous."

"He doesn't look dangerous."

"That's how they are," said Rosa. "He'll kill you as quick as look at you. Step back."

Ash set her jaw. She hated being told what to do, especially by Rosa. They were nearly the same age. It used to be that, when they played, Ash came up with the games and told Rosa what to do. But the last time Ash asked Rosa to play, Rosa claimed she was too old for Ash's games.

"I'm not scared of him," said Ash.

"You should be."

"Why? He hasn't done anything. He could be lost. Or maybe he's the son of an important chief and he came to offer us a peace treaty. There might be others in the forest waiting to bring us birds and gems if we listen to him and treat him kindly."

The boy watched them with an inquisitive tilt to his head.

"This is no time for your silly make-believe," said Rosa. "He's one of *them*. Now stop being childish."

"I'm not childish. Surely some dao fora are nice."

Rosa's expression darkened. "*Nice?* What's wrong with you?"

Ash knew why Rosa was upset. After all, dao fora warriors had killed her dad. But the boy in the cage was just a kid. Chances were he had nothing to do with what had happened to Rosa's dad. Couldn't Rosa see it was wrong to keep a kid in a cage?

"I'm not the one who's behaving unreasonably," said Ash.

Rosa looked fit to burst. “So you’re taking *his* side? I can’t believe this.”

“All I’m saying is that you don’t know him. Or why he’s here. He might have gotten lost and he came to the village for help.”

“My brother’s right—you don’t have any sense,” said Rosa. She stormed back to the crowd milling in the shade.

Ash wished there was something she could say to call Rosa back, but no words came to her. She didn’t think she should apologize—everything she’d said made perfect sense. Nevertheless, a thread of doubt remained. What if Rosa was right?

Her thoughts skipped back to when Rosa’s dad had been carried through the forest gate. They’d been playing in the village square together that day, and they both saw the soldiers bring him in.

At first Rosa’s dad had looked comical, carried on a sling held by four puffing men. A slender, feathered arrow stuck out of his leg. It was just one arrow, and barely any blood showed around the wound. Rosa’s dad even joked with some of the soldiers. Later, his lips turned blue and his heart stopped beating.

Ash examined the boy again. Was he a killer? Should she fear him and hate him like everyone else did?

A smile played at the corners of his mouth. This time it wasn’t a curious smile. It was a warm, inviting smile that didn’t appear remotely threatening.

There must be a name for someone who smiles like that, thought Ash.

In response, she heard a whisper. *Friend of Strangers*.

Left Behind

Ash kept her room a very particular way. It wasn't a large room, but to Ash it was a kingdom, and like any kingdom it had several regions.

There was the region of her bed with its two blankets, and the region of her shelves with five books and a kerosene lantern that gave off a warm yellow glow. There was the region of her door with the hooks on the back where she hung her stormcoat and school clothes. There was the region of her window, with the nearby chair where she liked to read. Lastly, there was the region of her dresser.

Half the dresser held her clothes. Ash didn't have many clothes, so the other two drawers contained things that were important to her. One drawer held rocks, ribbons, coins, buttons, feathers, and other odd items she hadn't found names for yet, but that she thought she might. And the top drawer was reserved for her most precious things—her named objects.

Currently, this drawer stood empty.

Ash had packed her named objects into Wayfarer, her carpet-bag, the night before when the winds had picked up. It was a good thing she had, too. If she hadn't, she would have needed to stuff her named objects into the bag *after* the warning bells sounded because there was no way she'd leave named objects behind during an illwen attack.

She hadn't unpacked Wayfarer yet, and she decided not to given how the wind outside was starting to gust. Besides, she had more pressing matters to attend to.

Ash lit the lantern and trimmed the wick to give the brightest light. Then she lay the ironwood stick across her lap.

In the lamplight, the smooth, cool bark resembled the silvery tint of a pewter cup. The stick tapered to two knobby twigs at one end that branched apart like a Y.

"Hello again," she said. "You're welcome to stay with me if you like."

The hum she'd heard earlier tingled at the back of her head.

"I'll take that as a yes. But… if you're going to stay with me, I ought to know your name."

The hum deepened.

Ash closed her eyes and *listened.* She heard several faint whispers, but she couldn't make out what they said. She gripped the wood tighter.

Giving an object a true name was different from merely deciding what to call something. She couldn't say where true names came from, or why she heard them when others didn't. All she knew was that when a name was true, it slid like a button into a buttonhole and there it remained—fixing something to what she called it.

"*Kiki*?" she said, giving voice to one of the whispers she heard.

Immediately, the whispers stopped.

"Kiki it is then," said Ash. "Now, where should you sleep?"

She tried putting Kiki in the top drawer where all her other named objects usually stayed, but the stick was too long to fit. Still, Ash didn't want Kiki to feel left out. She knew how hurtful that could be.

After searching her room, she found the perfect place for Kiki between the headboard and the top edge of her mattress.

With Kiki settled, she went to the window to check on the boy in the cage. The sky had grown ominously dark. She could barely see the boy's huddled form through the metal bars. A soldier stood near the cage, keeping watch.

Earlier, Ash had tried to bring the boy a buttered biscuit, but the soldier wouldn't let her near the cage. He hadn't even smiled when she'd offered him half. He just told her to go away.

Wind swirled clouds of dust across the village square. It didn't seem right to leave the boy outside on a blustery night like this with only a moss cloak to protect him.

Ash was gathering a blanket to bring the boy when the sharp clang of a warning bell sounded. She looked toward the forest gate watchtower.

A second bell rang. Lanterns in several houses around the village square brightened as people stirred.

Then the third bell rang.

An illwen had been spotted! Two illwen attacks in two nights! She'd never heard of such a thing.

Below, the whole village snapped into action. Doors flew open and people poured into the square carrying lanterns and small children as they rushed toward the longhouse. The alarm quickly spread to the other towers.

Clang! Clang! Clang!

Clang! Clang! Clang!

There was no denying the warning signal.

Ash hurried to get ready before her dad yelled for her. She jammed her feet into her boots, pulled on her stormcoat, and hoisted Wayfarer onto her shoulders. She had trouble fitting her arms through the leather handles while wearing her coat, but she managed it.

She raced down the stairs to the store. The lantern hanging by the door had been lit, but no one was there.

"Mom? Dad?" she called.

No response. Maybe they couldn't hear her over the howling wind. Or maybe they were already outside, waiting for her.

Ash opened the front door and stood in the doorway. Wind pricked her skin and stung her eyes with dust. She tugged the stormcoat hood over her head and blinked to clear her vision.

The soldier Ash had seen earlier wasn't guarding the cage anymore. Ash squinted into the wind. "Mom? Dad!"

Still no answer.

She stepped back into the store and pushed the door shut. Her parents couldn't still be upstairs. They probably hadn't gone to bed yet when the warning bells sounded, so they would have been dressed and ready to go. Why weren't they here?

Through the storefront window, Ash watched people race toward the longhouse bordering the village square. One man carried a lantern. Three children followed him, holding hands so that no one got lost. Anyone who didn't get to the longhouse in time would be locked out.

By now, the lookouts in the watchtowers had stopped ringing the warning bells. After sounding the alarm, they'd climb down and run to the longhouse themselves. When an illwen attacked there was nothing to do but take shelter until it passed.

She cracked opened the front door again and searched the square. A wall soldier sprinted from the forest gate. The yellow glow of his lantern illuminated his terrified face.

"Mom? Dad!" she shouted into the gusting wind.

The stream of villagers rushing to the longhouse had lessened to a few stragglers.

Ash called several more times for her parents. A dog barked and a horse nickered. Animals weren't allowed in the longhouse during an illwen attack—not even small animals like chickens or goats. People said that illwen would possess them and cause them to run wild and destroy things.

The last of the stragglers vanished into the longhouse. Ash couldn't wait any longer. Her parents must have already crossed the square to the longhouse. They might be wondering why it was taking her so long to get there. She pulled Wayfarer tight against her shoulders and struggled out into the wind. Blowing dust stung her eyes.

When she was halfway across the square, light poured from somewhere behind her. Glancing back, Ash glimpsed her father silhouetted in the storefront entrance. He kept his arm wrapped tightly around Essa, Ash's mom. The white cloth of her finest dress billowed about her as she clutched the doorway. A lacy veil covered her face.

"Where were you?" called Ash.

"Get to the longhouse!" ordered her dad.

Ash couldn't stop staring at her mom. Not only was Essa wearing her finest dress, the veil that covered her face had a shimmering rectangular patch of cloth stitched into it over her eyes.

Crystal cloth, thought Ash. Her mom had sewn a piece of crystal cloth into her veil. But why? And why was she all dressed up?

Ash's dad tugged her shoulder. "Go!"

A sharp gust tossed pebbles and leaves against her as she followed her parents across the square. Ahead, her mom looked like a ghost with her white dress and veil billowing around her.

Garrett shepherded Essa down the stone steps to the longhouse door, then he ran back to help Ash. A soldier opened the door at the bottom of the steps for them. He frowned when he saw Wayfarer, probably thinking that's why they were delayed, but if he said anything, Ash couldn't hear it over the wind.

Once they were all inside, the soldier pulled the door shut behind them. Immediately, the roar of the wind lessened. Ash sucked in a breath. Even though the air in the longhouse was hot and stuffy, it felt good to fill her lungs. The dust outside had made it hard to breathe.

The soldier peered through the peephole in the heavy wooden door. "That's the last of them, sir."

"Lock it," ordered Mayor Tullridge.

It took two soldiers to slide the heavy post across the door.

3

A Knock in the Night

Ash's dad led her and Essa to their family's spot in the longhouse. Dozens of lanterns hung from the rafters, illuminating the large underground room. All told, nearly two hundred families huddled in the fortified chamber, plus the wall soldiers, webworm plantation workers, and the squatters who'd recently come to the village seeking land.

The constable kept the center aisle clear. Ash noticed several people holding tangled strands of webworm silk as she followed her dad through the longhouse. During last night's illwen attack, only a couple of superstitious plantation workers had held strands of webworm silk. Now, dozens of people clutched sticky white clumps of it. But that was nothing compared to what Ash saw when she came upon the Wombleys' area.

Two privacy screens had been placed around the Wombleys' area, forming almost a separate room within the larger public chamber. Ash craned her head to peer between the screens. A house servant poured water into glasses arranged on a folding table. Sitting nearby, Mr. and Mrs. Wombley looked like they were attending the governor's ball. Mrs. Wombley wore a yellow gown, tinted brown from the dust storm. A shimmering crystal cloth veil cascaded from the brim of her hat down to her chin as she rocked a baby in her arms.

Mr. Wombley had on a black coat, a tall black hat, and a scarf of fine white crystal cloth tied around his head, covering his eyes. The crystal cloth had been stretched tight over fancy spectacle frames so that he could see through it, while the tied ends draped behind him.

Ash's jaw dropped upon seeing all that crystal cloth. She'd heard people talking about the Wombleys' new Ocras Industries eye coverings, but she hadn't seen them the night before. Crystal cloth spectacles were reportedly the latest fashion for gentlemen, and the shimmering veil Mrs. Wombley wore made the small patch of crystal cloth her mother had sewn into her veil look like a pitiful, dirty scrap.

Crystal cloth was worth more than its weight in gold. Even though it was made from the webworm silk that plantation workers harvested in the fields beyond the wall, no plantation workers could afford such finely woven crystal cloth. All the silk they collected got sent to Lord Ocras's factories to be spun. Workers said it took several trees worth of silk just to make a hand-sized square of cloth, and the Wombleys were wearing enough to cover a dinner table. Even the baby Mrs. Wombley held had been swaddled in crystal cloth.

In addition to crystal cloth being the latest fashion, people claimed it protected the wearer from illwen. According to Ocras Industries, no one wearing Lord Ocras's patented Miracle Crystal Cloth had ever been harmed by an illwen.

That's why the Wombleys are wearing all that crystal cloth, thought Ash. *And that's why other people are clutching clumps of webworm silk—they saw the Wombleys wearing crystal cloth last night, and now they think that a few sticky strands of it will keep them safe!*

Ash searched for her mom, eager to share this observation with her. She spotted Essa near the back wall, arranging her own stitched lace and crystal cloth veil over her eyes. A thorn jabbed Ash's heart as she realized why her mom had dressed up. She was trying to look like the Wombleys—all proper and protected by crystal cloth.

Ash didn't want to believe it, but the evidence was right in front of her. Her mom had left her, scared and alone downstairs, while she put on fancy clothes and stitched crystal cloth into a veil for herself. The small square of cloth she'd used had been sent to the store as a sample two weeks ago. Instead of putting it out for customers to admire, her mom had taken it. She wasn't as bad as the Wombleys. She was worse. At least the Wombleys had enough sense to wrap their baby in crystal cloth, but her mom only thought of protecting herself.

The situation seemed terribly *amiss*, which was the best word Ash could think of for the horrid feeling she got when things weren't how she thought they should be.

"Keep moving. No dawdling in the aisle," said Constable Malthus.

Ash shuffled toward the blanket that her father had laid out at their family's spot along the back wall. Her mom sat at one end of the blanket, rubbing her forehead.

"Mom," said Ash. She wanted to ask her mom why she hadn't stitched crystal cloth into a veil for her daughter if it was so important. Ash knew they weren't rich like the Wombleys, but

Essa could have cut the sample square of crystal cloth into two pieces. Or three, since her dad needed protection as well. "Mom!" called Ash again, louder.

"Let her be. She's not feeling well," said her dad.

Ash frowned. Lately, her mom never seemed to be feeling well. She didn't have a sniffle or a belly ache, or anything a doctor could treat. She simply seemed tired all the time—so much so that some days she wouldn't leave the house. For the last week, she hadn't even tended the store, brushed Ash's hair, or cared to see what Ash ate for breakfast. She hardly acted like a mom at all anymore.

Ash wanted to sit someplace else, but there was no other place for her.

Outside, the wind skittered leaves across the roof and rattled the shutters. Each wall had one shuttered peek-hole built into it, just above ground. The holes were big enough for a soldier to lean his head and shoulders out to check when it was safe to leave.

No soldier would dare stick his head out now. The shutters would remain firmly closed and latched until the winds died down and all signs of an illwen attack passed.

Ash slung Wayfarer onto the blanket her dad had laid out. She set her back to her mom and opened the bag to check on her named objects. There was Holder, her doll. Near and Far, the two perfectly round, clear rocks she'd found. Nester, her soft yellow blanket. Telltale, the rope. Traveler, the pretty seed as big as her thumb that she'd discovered by the west wall. Aisling, the small blue bottle her mother had thrown out because the top was chipped. And Fledgling, the shimmery purple and green feather. Everything seemed to be there. Still, she couldn't shake the sense that she'd forgotten something important.

"Kiki!" she said, remembering the ironwood stick she'd left in her room. She felt terrible for leaving the stick behind.

A snap echoed through the longhouse. Probably a branch breaking in the wind. This was followed by more snaps and cracks. It sounded like a whole tree had fallen. Her dad gazed at the wooden rafters overhead.

"Close your eyes." He cupped his hand around Ash's shoulder. "Put your head down and rest. It'll pass soon enough."

Ash shook off his hand. "I forgot something."

"We can't go out until the storm has passed," said her dad.

"But—"

"Close your eyes and sleep."

Ash couldn't sleep. The nagging sense that she'd forgotten something important—something other than Kiki—kept tugging at her.

Another clatter shook the roof. Her mom rocked back and forth while muttering to herself. The clatter wasn't an illwen. Not yet. Illwen were louder.

She pictured Kiki alone in her room while the storm raged. Thinking of the ironwood stick reminded her of the dao fora boy. Where was he?

Ash stood and checked the area where the soldiers had gathered in the longhouse. She didn't see the boy with them, or anywhere else in the longhouse. Had they left him outside? Why hadn't she checked when she'd left the store?

"Sit down. It'll be fine," said her dad.

Ash shook her head. He didn't understand. "Dad, where—"

A loud thump reverberated through the longhouse. Three more thumps followed. *Thump! Thump! Thump!* Oddly, the thumps came from the main door.

People looked at each other, perplexed. A falling branch wouldn't make a noise like that, and illwen didn't knock. Several wall soldiers hurried to the door, but none dared unlatch the peek-hole shutter.

Another pair of thumps sounded, only this time they came from a peek-hole in the side wall.

"Let me in!" called a muffled voice.

"Someone's out there," said Constable Malthus.

People counted their loved ones.

"It's Mackay!" said a plantation worker with curly black hair. "He was working in the silk reeling room. He must not have heard the warning bells."

"What do we do?" asked the soldier guarding the door.

Mayor Tullridge talked with the wall officer. More branches clattered on the roof.

"Let him in!" shouted Ash's dad from the back of the long-house.

Mayor Tullridge fidgeted. Beyond him, soldiers waited for orders, but the mayor gave none. Ash's dad strode down the center aisle.

"Garrett, don't! It's not your affair," called Essa.

Garrett continued toward the door. "We can't leave him out there. Unbar the entrance."

Two of the wall soldiers moved to do as he said. As the owner of the only general store in the village, everyone knew Ash's dad. His words carried weight, especially among the plantation workers, squatters, and other poor folk who couldn't travel to Governor City to shop for goods.

"Are you blinking mad?" asked Mr. Wombley. The tied ends of his crystal cloth spectacles flowed around his shoulders as he stepped out from behind his privacy screens. “If you open that door, you’ll put everyone at risk.”

“The illwen isn’t here yet,” said Garrett.

“You don’t know that,” retorted Mr. Wombley. “Keep the door barred, Mr. Tullridge. You have a village to protect.”

Ash wanted to mention the boy they’d left outside, but if they wouldn’t let in one of their own, they certainly wouldn’t risk their lives for a dao fora boy.

A bitter taste coated her mouth. She pictured the boy trapped in the cage, left alone outside just like she’d been. Except he was still out there.

Friend of Strangers.

Too much seemed amiss.

Essa shuffled down the aisle after Garrett. Ash glared at her mom’s fancy white dress and dingy veil. Anger rose within her. You didn’t leave a child in danger, no matter how scared you felt. It was wrong.

More thumps rattled the door. The plantation worker who’d been locked out must have been using a rock or stick to make such a loud noise. “Please! Open the door!”

“If the illwen was near, he wouldn’t be calling like that,” said Ash’s dad.

Constable Malthus nodded. “He’s right. Unbar the door.”

One of the village deputies moved to do as the constable said, but the soldiers stood in his way. Wall soldiers worked for the governor, not the constable.

“Don’t be foolish,” snapped Mr. Wombley. “It could be a trick.”

The soldiers looked to their officer, and he looked to the mayor.

Mayor Tullridge fidgeted with his vest.

"Do it!" ordered Constable Malthus. He moved to lift part of the door timber himself. Ash's dad joined him, as did two deputies.

"Bah!" said Mr. Wombley. "Saving one man isn't worth putting everyone's lives at risk."

At a nod from the officer, the wall soldiers moved out of the way. One of them even helped the deputies lift the door timber. The moment they slid it clear of the iron brackets, the door swung inward.

Wind and dust howled into the longhouse, pushing over the Wombleys' privacy screens and blowing out several lanterns. People gasped as half the longhouse plunged into darkness. A figure stumbled through the gap, and the soldiers struggled to shove the door shut again. It took four of them to close it. Constable Malthus and Garrett quickly slid the heavy timber back into place.

The kerosene lanterns were relit. All the dust swirling about the room made the light appear dim and orange.

"Thank the gods," said Mackay, the plantation worker who'd been locked out. "I saw it climbing the wall. It looked bigger than a draft horse and meaner than a slapped snake."

People murmured anxiously. Almost no one who saw an illwen lived to tell the tale.

Mayor Tullridge made a statement about how everything had been taken care of and there was no need for concern. Soldiers clapped each other's backs and returned to their posts while Constable Malthus spoke with Garrett and Essa Narro, and Mr. Wombley's servants restored his privacy screens. Mr. Wombley stood in the aisle, glaring through his shimmering crystal cloth at the men who'd defied him.

With all the wind and commotion, no one took notice of the girl at the other end of the room as she unlatched the peek-hole shutter in the back wall, climbed up onto her carpetbag, and crawled out.

Into the Storm

Wind gusts tossed sand against Ash's cheeks. She tugged her hood tight and peered through the dust toward her parents' store. Despite the bright moonlight, she could barely see the cage. The boy appeared to still be locked in it.

To free him, she'd have to cross the square, enter the store, and find the key that her dad kept behind the counter. Then she could open the cage and return to the safety of the longhouse with the boy.

Ash lowered her head and set off into the wind to cross the square. Her hood flapped noisily, but it kept the blowing sand from stinging her skin. About halfway to the store, she heard tree branches crack and snap behind her. *Keep going,* she thought. *Don't look back.*

The dao fora boy sat cross-legged in the cage with his eyes closed and his moss cloak billowing around his shoulders. Ash blinked, not believing her eyes. He looked almost peaceful.

"Hey!" she called, shouting to be heard over the wind. "Are you alive?"

The boy opened one eye, then the other. "What are *you* doing here?"

Ash didn't know what to be more surprised by—the fact that he spoke her language, or that he acted like he belonged there and she didn't.

"There's an illwen coming. It's not safe out here," said the boy.

"I know. I came to get you."

"Why?"

She frowned. "Aren't you afraid?"

"I don't know. My heart's beating quickly and my face tingles. Does that mean I'm afraid?"

Ash wasn't sure how to respond. Most people would be terrified if they were trapped outside during an illwen attack, but this boy seemed more curious than scared. She wondered if what some of the villagers said was true—that the dao fora controlled the illwen and made them attack the village.

"Look," said the boy. "It's over there!"

She glanced in the direction the boy had indicated. What she saw made her stomach drop.

A massive, bristling creature crouched on the guardhouse roof on *this* side of the forest gate. A few of the sharpened wall posts had been snapped off. The illwen clenched another wall post in its jaws and tugged ferociously. A whole section of the wall rocked back and forth while its claws ripped shingles off the guardhouse roof.

The illwen looked like nothing Ash had ever seen—long and sinuous, with at least six legs. Its smoky body constantly changed shape, but the way it tugged on the wooden post reminded Ash of a dog trying to get a stick.

With a ferocious tug, it snapped off the sharpened post and thrashed its head in triumph. The broken post flew from its mouth and smashed the front of a house.

The illwen leapt off the guardhouse roof, chasing after the post. It hit the ground and rolled, or maybe tripped, over its eager legs. When it reached the house, it tore through the wooden porch railing to the front door. Then it sniffed the door handle.

Ash's mouth went dry and her heart raced, but she still didn't move. She couldn't stop watching the destructive forest spirit. It wasn't just a senseless monster—not like Ash thought it would be. Instead, it seemed to be searching for something.

The illwen climbed onto a roof and crouched. Feathers of black smoke curled off its back. It paused, gathering strength, then leapt and soared across the moonlit sky toward the longhouse.

In the air it appeared nearly weightless—little more than black smoke twisting in a breeze. But when it landed on the longhouse roof, it hit with a thump like a dozen gusts of wind smacking the roof at once.

Immediately the illwen scratched at the longhouse roof with its long, black claws. Ash squinted through the dust, amazed by its shifting form and clumsy, desperate behavior. Whatever it was searching for, it didn't seem to like roof tar. After giving the timbers a few scratches, it sniffed one of its paws and snarled.

Inside the longhouse, the sound of the illwen scratching and snarling on the roof must have been terrible. But outside its snarls sounded more anguished than fierce. *Wounded rage*, thought Ash, remembering the sounds Rosa had made after her dad had died.

The connection between the illwen and Rosa surprised her. Rosa's anger came from losing someone she loved. Could a monster love? Had the illwen lost someone or something it cared about?

"It's a big one," said the boy. "My hands are shaking. I think I am afraid."

"Me too."

"You should hide. They don't like villagers much."

"What about you?"

"I'll hide too." The boy grabbed the blowing ends of his moss cloak and pulled them over his head.

The illwen spun, as if it had heard them over the roaring wind. It stared at Ash.

"Better run," said the boy, peeking through a slit in his cloak.

Ash stumbled back. Wind gusted as the illwen leapt from the longhouse. Its dark gaze bored into her. Ash turned and raced toward her parents' store, not slowing until she made it through the doorway. Looking back, she saw the dark spirit pause near the cage.

The boy stayed deathly still with his cloak pulled over his head. He looked like a child who thought that if he couldn't see others, they wouldn't see him. The illwen sniffed hungrily. Its black-toothed mouth was large enough to crush the cage in one bite. She had to do something.

Ash leaned out and waved her arms. "Hey! Over here!"

The illwen whipped its head toward her and growled.

She yanked the door shut, set the lock, and darted behind the counter. Quickly, she searched the top drawer for the padlock key. "No, no, no!" she muttered, not finding any keys among the pencils, string, and other knickknacks.

A thunderous crash shook the storefront as the illwen slammed into the door. Huddled behind the counter, Ash wished she could shrink to the size of a mouse and scurry away. Then the scratching sounds from the porch stopped. She held her breath and listened. Maybe the illwen had lost interest and gone somewhere else.

Loud sniffs filled the silence.

She peeked over the counter and saw the illwen's long tail pass in front of the store window. It looked like a rope woven out of black smoke. Beneath the roaring wind outside and the terrified beating of her own heart, she sensed something else. Whispers.

Monsters have names, she thought, recalling something her mother had told her once when she'd woken from a nightmare.

Monsters have names, her mother had said. *They just don't know their names, so they're all shifty with their shapes. But if you can hear their names and call them properly, you can tell them what to be. Then they won't have to be monsters anymore.*

The illwen peered through the storefront window. Its eyes looked like two black pits among the swirling smoke of its head. It snarled as it spotted Ash.

CHISSS!

A paw smashed through the window. The illwen tore at the window frame, but it was too big to squeeze through the opening. It slammed into the door again. Shelves toppled and bottles shattered as the whole storefront shook. When the door didn't break, the illwen returned to the window and tore off hunks of wood with its teeth and claws, eager to get to her.

Ash bolted upstairs to her parents' bedroom. The sweet smell of her mother's perfume hung heavy in the air. She searched her father's dresser for the padlock key but couldn't find it.

Frustrated, she retreated to her room to get Kiki. "It's okay. It's going to be okay," she said, clutching the ironwood stick to her chest. Kiki's cool solidity comforted her.

Downstairs, the snapping and snarling stopped. Ash strained to hear what the illwen was doing. The walls of the house creaked while whispers murmured at the edge of her hearing.

She took a deep breath and tried again to *listen.*

Naming a living thing was harder than naming an object. Living things had more names, and those names could change as the creature changed. From the whispered names Ash heard, she sensed that the forest spirit hadn't always been an angry, destructive monster. It had been playful as a puppy once, until it lost what it cared about. Countless possibilities still existed within the creature, waiting to be called forth. But bringing those possibilities out wasn't just a matter of speaking the right name. She had to get the illwen to listen to her, too, and right now it seemed too full of wounded rage to listen to anyone.

Claws scraped the window. Ash scrambled back and nearly screamed. The illwen was climbing the side of her house.

Wood shrieked and cracked as the forest spirit tore through boards above her. Ash huddled in the corner of her bedroom. Her whole body shook. She glimpsed the moon overhead. Then the illwen's black, smoky snout jutted into the hole in the roof it had made. It sniffed for her like a dog sniffing for a treat.

That's it! realized Ash. *To get it to listen I have to give it something.*

She thought about what she could offer the illwen. She didn't know what exactly the creature was searching for, but from the whispers she sensed what it needed. With Kiki in hand, Ash raced down the stairs, out the back door, and across the yard to the barn.

The illwen kept clawing its way into her bedroom. Hopefully it wouldn't see where she'd gone. She lifted the latch on the barn door and pulled it open. One of the rusty hinges squeaked. Ash glanced back.

The illwen stopped clawing the roof and glared at her.

The Puppy of Doom

Chickens clucked and scampered around the barn, startled by her entrance, but they didn't make half the noise they usually did. They must have known something dangerous was coming. Even the friendly ones fluttered away, retreating to their coops.

Ash hurried to the hay pile where Brightstar, the lead hen, liked to roost. Brightstar watched her approach, scared yellow eyes round as buttons.

"Sorry, Brightstar." Ash shooed the hen away and lifted the hay-covered board the chicken had been nesting on. She reached into the space underneath for the box of secret objects she kept hidden there.

Thoomp! Sprinkles of dust fell from the beams above her. The illwen must have leapt onto the barn.

Ash yanked out the box and dug through its contents, feeling coins, marbles, and other valuable but unnamed items. It was too dark to see clearly so she had to rely on touch. At last, she found the silky ribbon and heart-shaped pendant.

She held the pendant up before her. It looked unlike any other pendant she'd ever seen—carved out of bone with two elegant loops forming a heart within a heart. It had arrived with a store shipment several months ago. They hadn't ordered it, but Essa adored the pendant and refused to send it back. She wore it every day, often rubbing it between her fingers. The bone loops had been worn smooth by Essa's touch, as if she'd pressed all her love and care into it. That's why Ash had taken it. Her mother held it so much that Ash wanted to hold it too.

At first, Ash only meant to borrow the pendant, but when Essa discovered it missing she got so upset that Ash feared admitting what she'd done. Instead of giving it back, Ash hid the pendant in the barn. It was a secret, painful thing she had to hide—a need for love that ran so deep it hurt.

Chunks of wood clattered down from the roof. The chickens flapped, but there was no place for them to go. Ash crouched by the door. If the illwen killed her chickens, she'd never forgive herself.

Suddenly, the scratching stopped. Through a crack in the door, Ash watched the illwen leap from rooftop to rooftop toward the boy in the cage.

"Ready, Kiki?" She squeezed the ironwood stick for courage, then slid open the door. "Hey! I have something for you."

The illwen turned and fixed its black eyes on her.

Ash closed her eyes to keep from running. She tried once again to find a true name for the illwen—a name that could speak both to what it was and what it could be.

A gust of wind blasted her face. When she opened her eyes the illwen had nearly reached her. Its black-toothed jaw widened to devour her.

Ash held up the heart-shaped pendant. "*LOST HEART PUPPY!*" she yelled, speaking aloud one of the whispered names she'd heard.

The illwen reared in front of her, claws raking the air as if it had encountered an invisible wall. It sniffed the heart-shaped pendant, seeming to recognize it as something precious—a heart for the heart it had lost.

"Lost Heart Puppy," repeated Ash.

The words sounded strange, but the words didn't matter as much as the meaning behind them. The illwen wasn't only a monster. It could still be the playful puppy that the whispers hinted at.

The illwen snapped at Ash. She didn't flinch or back away. To get the creature to take on the name, she had to believe that the name was true.

The forest spirit appeared perplexed by her strange behavior. Ash didn't know if it would devour her or become what she'd called it. Perhaps it didn't know, either.

"It's all right." She held the pendant out toward the angry forest spirit. "This is for you. Go on. Take it."

The illwen sniffed the pendant again. It bared its teeth, but it didn't snarl or snap this time. Instead, it delicately lifted the pendant between its front teeth.

Ash let go of the ribbon necklace. The heart-shaped pendant dangled from the creature's mouth. Slowly, she raised her hand to touch the illwen's muzzle.

"Lost Heart Puppy," she said. "That's who you are. You're not mean. You're just upset because you lost what you love, and so you've lost your way. I feel like that too sometimes—like I'm all alone and don't belong anywhere. But you're not alone. I'm with you now, so you don't need to be angry anymore. Isn't that right, Puppy?"

The illwen lowered its head and Ash scratched between its ears. It seemed to like that. The winds calmed and the spikes rising off its back softened as she murmured kind words to it.

"Get away from her!" shouted Garrett from across the square. He carried one of the soldier's muskets.

The illwen jerked its head up. Wounded rage flashed across its eyes and its hackles bristled.

"Wait!" cried Ash.

More villagers filed out of the longhouse behind Garrett. Ash's dad raised the musket to his shoulder. As if sensing his intent, the illwen growled, but it couldn't snap or bite without dropping the pendant.

"Dad, stop!" Ash stepped between her father and the illwen. "Don't hurt it!"

Quick as a breeze, the creature zipped between the longhouse and the barn, then disappeared down the road. The gusting wind left with it, leaving stunned silence in its wake.

Ash's dad lowered the musket. "It's gone."

Several wall soldiers, Constable Malthus, and a few other villagers gathered around.

"How'd you do that?" asked one of the wall soldiers.

"I didn't do a thing," said Ash's dad.

"It's not what *he* did you fopdoodles. It's what *she* did," said the widow McMurtry. She hobbled across the square and hooked a gnarled finger at Ash. "She's an *Ainm Dhilis*—a namer of spirits. Bless my soul, it's been decades since I've seen one, but she's one sure as a river is wet. Only a namer of spirits could dispel an illwen like that."

The soldiers and other villagers looked at each other, as if trying to determine whether the old woman was crazy. No one in the village had lived as long as the widow McMurtry, and no one had a memory that went back as far as hers.

Ash's dad didn't waste time arguing. He passed the musket to the soldiers and swept Ash into a hug. "You scared the life out of me, child."

Ash let him lift her off her feet. He hadn't hugged her like that in years. As nice as it felt, she couldn't help thinking about who wasn't hugging her. She peered over her dad's shoulder for her mom. Half the village had come out into the square, but not her mom.

Just then, Ash spotted something that chased her sad thoughts away.

A bundle of black-and-white fur tottered between the feet of the stunned villagers. It stumbled over its own paws, new to walking. Then it looked up at Ash, tail wagging enthusiastically. Ash squirmed out of her dad's arms and knelt to greet the little creature.

"Is that you, Puppy?" she asked, holding out her hand.

The little creature sniffed her fingers. It dropped the heart-shaped pendant into her palm. Then it looked at her expectantly, with one bright blue eye and one brown eye.

"It is you!" said Ash. "I'm glad you came back." She tied the ribbon with the pendant around Puppy's fluffy neck like a collar while the little creature licked her hands. He was so spirited, he seemed barely able to contain himself.

"Looks like you found a friend," said Ash's dad.

"Can we keep him?" asked Ash. "I wouldn't have survived without him."

Her dad sighed. After nearly losing his daughter, he couldn't say no.

"That pup… where'd you get him?" interrupted Mr. Rotterburg, a farmer who often came to the store.

"I think he's one of yours," said Ash's dad. "Didn't you have a litter of pups you were trying to find homes for?"

"I did." Mr. Rotterburg inspected the puppy, then drew back. His face turned paler than sour milk. "You can't have this one."

"Why not?" asked Garrett. "You told me you had more than you could take care of."

"That's true. The mother of the litter couldn't feed them all. The runt of the litter died."

"So what's the problem?"

Mr. Rotterburg pointed to the puppy. "*That's* the runt."

Garrett's brow knotted. "You must be mistaken. That pup doesn't look dead to me."

"No. That's the one," said Mr. Rotterburg. "I buried him this morning. He was the only one with mismatched eyes. I swear he was dead."

"I assure you he's very much alive, Mr. Rotterburg," said Ash. "I named him."

Mr. Rotterburg couldn't have looked more perplexed if a tree had spoken to him. "What did you name him?"

"Puppy," said Ash. She scratched Puppy behind the ears. He leaned into her hand so much he nearly fell over. "Lost Heart Puppy."

"For a namer she's not very creative," muttered one of the villagers.

Ash paid the villagers no mind. She winked at Puppy and Puppy winked back at her—an unspoken pact passing between them. No one needed to know what else Puppy could be.

"Come on, Puppy." She headed back to the longhouse to fetch Wayfarer and her other named things.

Lost Heart Puppy bounded after her, nipping at the laces of her boots.

Friend of Strangers

After the attack, most of the village gathered in the square. People were too upset to go home, despite the late hour. Two illwen attacks in two days seemed beyond bad luck. Someone had to be to blame. It didn't take long for the villagers' accusations to land on the dao fora boy.

"I told you dao fora were sending the illwen here," said the squatter who'd caught the boy. "They hate us."

Several villagers voiced their agreement. They thought the boy must have summoned the illwen, and they wanted to take their anger out on him right then and there.

"Hang him from the wall by his ankles!" said one. "That'll make the dao fora think twice before sending more monsters to attack us."

"Hang him by his hair," said another.

This was followed by suggestions to burn down the cloud forest where the dao fora lived.

"This is war," someone cried. "As long as dao fora are out there, we won't be safe."

Fear made them think dark, appalling thoughts. The angry voices in the crowd quickly drowned out those few who called for calm and peace.

Garrett told Ash to go back into the store, but there wasn't much of a store to go back to. The door had been clawed, the front window broken, and large chunks of the window frame were missing. Shattered glass and fallen shelves littered the store interior. The whole place smelled of vinegar from a jar of pickled eggs that had broken. Ash picked up Puppy so he wouldn't cut his paws on the shards of glass.

When Ash's mom saw the wreckage in the store, she didn't say a word. She just held her lace veil to her face and shuffled upstairs to her bedroom, as if the pitiful scrap of crystal cloth she looked through would filter out everything bad.

Once Essa left, Ash slipped back outside onto the storefront porch to watch the gathering from a distance. With Puppy in her arms, she crouched behind an empty rain barrel so her dad wouldn't see her. Things the villagers had said made her uneasy. Most of them were people she'd known her whole life, but they didn't sound like themselves anymore.

"What about the girl?" asked a farmer. "Maybe *she* knows something about these illwen attacks."

"Such as?" asked Ash's dad. "What are you implying?"

"Just that it's awfully odd, the way that illwen appeared to be listening to her. And I've never heard of someone trying to protect an illwen before. She's always been a strange one."

"My daughter was born here. This is her home. She'd never do anything to hurt the village," said Ash's dad.

"Then what was she doing out here?"

"And why was she talking to that doa fora boy?"

Garrett's brow twitched, but whatever angry retort he had in mind he kept to himself. "Mayor Tullridge, I think you should call a town meeting. Shouting at each other in the dark is no way to decide village matters."

The mayor cleared his throat and tried to look authoritative. "Right. Let's all stay calm and discuss this back at the longhouse. Before we do anything rash, we need to vote on it."

Gradually, the crowd of upset villagers and wall soldiers returned to the longhouse, the only structure big enough to hold everyone. Ash's dad glanced at the demolished store before following the mayor into the underground chamber. After they'd gone, Ash slipped out from behind the empty rain barrel.

Puppy squirmed in her arms like he wanted to run and play, but a yawn overtook him and he soon lay his head back down.

"I bet you're tired," said Ash. "You've had a busy day."

In response, Puppy nudged the crook of her arm. He seemed to like the feel of the cloth against his nose, and his puffs of breath warmed her skin. He grew still for a moment, then opened one eye to check that she was still there.

"It's all right, you can sleep. I won't leave you," she told him.

Puppy shook his head, as if trying to shake the sleep off him. Despite his efforts, his eyelids fluttered closed again.

"Bodies need sleep. You can't change that," said Ash.

Puppy finally stopped struggling to stay awake and tucked his head into her arm.

Cradling Puppy, Ash wandered to the rabbit cage where the boy sat. He watched her approach.

"You're not very good at hiding, are you?" he said. "Still, what you did was pretty amazing. I've never seen anyone tame an angry illwen like that. Is that him?"

"Shh!" Ash glanced around. Fortunately, no one else was nearby. "This is *Puppy*," she said.

The boy shrugged in a suit-yourself gesture. "I won't tell anyone what I saw. Besides, no one here would listen to me. Think they'll hang me by my ankles or by my hair?" He tugged on a clump of his long black hair, plucking out a single strand. "That didn't feel too bad, but that's just one. All of them at once might be a different matter. Or it might be a lot of the same." He grabbed a clump of his hair and tugged it. "Ow! It definitely feels different."

"No one's going to hang you," said Ash. "I'm going to get you out of here."

"But I just got here," replied the boy.

Ash studied him, perplexed that he didn't seem more concerned. "You're very strange."

"Am I?" The boy looked at his arms as if he didn't understand what about him might be strange.

"It's okay. People think I'm strange too."

"If you're strange then I don't mind being strange," decided the boy. "You're the only one here who's nice to me. Everyone else thinks I'm their enemy. Why don't you think I'm your enemy?"

Ash recalled the whisper she'd heard earlier. *Friend of Strangers.* Was it foolish to think he could be her friend? Everyone else seemed certain he was dangerous. "I haven't determined what you are yet."

"Because I'm strange?"

"Maybe. I don't know… Do you always ask so many questions?"

"What do you mean?"

"See? You're impossible!"

"Impossible *and* strange? I haven't been called either of those things before. Tavan has called me exhausting, ridiculous, and stubborn, but never impossible. Or strange."

"Who's Tavan? Is he here?" asked Ash.

"Oh no," said the boy. "Tavan wouldn't come here. He doesn't even know that I'm here. He'd be very upset if he found out I went to the village. *Never go anywhere near that wretched wall,* he told me."

"Then why did you come here? Were you trying to attack us?"

"Why would I attack you?"

"Because that's what the dao fora do. Isn't it?" added Ash, uncertain. "The men who caught you said you were sneaking around, looking for a way to attack."

"I wasn't sneaking around. If I was sneaking, they never would have seen me. I was trying to get caught."

"Why on earth would you do that?"

"So they'd take me into the village," he said, as if this should be obvious. "I wanted to see what was on the other side of the wall. Getting caught seemed the easiest way to do it. And it worked!"

Ash's head spun as she tried to follow the boy's logic. She liked to keep everything in its proper place. If you were dao fora, you stayed in the forest. If you were a villager, you stayed in the village. Becoming a prisoner just to see what was on the other side of a wall made no sense to her. "Aren't you worried about what might happen to you?"

"I don't know. Should I be?"

Ash sighed. She was beginning to see why Tavan, whoever he was, had called the boy exhausting. She'd never met anyone so peculiar. He didn't seem to understand the most basic things. "Did you make the illwen attack us?"

"Me?" The boy's eyes widened. "I couldn't do that even if I wanted to. And I don't. But something's causing them to come here. That's why I wanted to see what's on the other side of the wall—so I could find out why the illwen are interested in this place."

Ash watched the boy's face to see if he was lying. He didn't behave at all like the dao fora warriors she'd heard about. And the way he spoke, with his endless questions and Governor City accent, wasn't what she'd expected either. "You're very confusing."

"Because I'm strange?"

"No. Because you're… friendly. *Friend of Strangers*—that's who you are." The name slid into place, taking on a satisfying weight, the way names did when they were true.

"Friend of Strangers," repeated the boy. "I like it. But it's a lot to say, especially if you need to say it quickly. Tavan calls me Fen. You can too."

They continued talking. Fen had plenty of questions. Among other things, he wanted to know her name. When she told him, he had even more questions.

"I get to be Fen, Friend of Strangers, and you're just… *Ash*?"

She nodded.

"Why?"

"Beats me. My mother named me. I didn't get to name myself."

"Why not?"

"Because that's not the way it's done here."

"But why?"

And so it kept going for nearly an hour, with Fen asking about who lived here, and what was wrong with everyone's feet that made them cover them up all the time, and why did everyone live in houses made of dead trees? For every question Ash answered, Fen asked five more. Finally, Ash's dad shouted her name from across the square.

Ash startled, causing Puppy to stir in her lap.

"I thought I told you to go inside," snapped Garrett. His voice sounded tight as an overwound watch spring. He strode across the square toward her while villagers shuffled out of the longhouse. Several villagers regarded her and the dao fora boy with wary looks. They clearly didn't approve of her talking to the boy.

"Go to bed," ordered her dad.

She looked at Fen. The dao fora boy had covered himself with his moss cloak again. He was like a tree clam that had closed for the night. At least he'd finally stopped asking questions.

Ash stood. Her feet prickled with pins and needles from sitting for so long. Puppy yawned and licked his nose.

"What are they going to do to him?" she asked, nodding to where Fen huddled under his cloak.

"Nothing tonight," answered her dad.

"What about tomorrow?"

Her dad didn't answer. He walked to the demolished store porch, picked up one of the chairs that hadn't been destroyed, and set it near the cage.

"I have first watch." He slumped into the chair and sighed. "Now go to bed."

Dread Eggs

Puppy squirmed out of Ash's arms and tottered around her room, sniffing and chewing random things. He hadn't slept for long, but now he seemed wide awake and full of rambunctious puppy energy. Kiki and Wayfarer leaned against each other in the corner.

Puppy gave the ironwood stick an eager chomp before Ash could warn him not to.

He immediately dropped the stick and inspected the wood. After giving Kiki a respectful lick, he continued his exploration of the room.

Ash stacked splintered pieces of her ceiling in the corner. Despite how exhausted she felt, she couldn't sleep. Too much had happened, and too much still seemed amiss.

It wasn't only the damage from the illwen attack that bothered her. It was the way people had reacted after the attack, becoming angry and talking about Fen like he wasn't human.

Some villagers had even looked at *her* that way. And her own mother hadn't stood up for her.

"People didn't used to act like this," said Ash to herself. "No one's behaving the way they should. Everything's amiss."

Puppy cocked his head, as if trying to decipher what she meant. She lifted him onto her bed to pet the soft fur behind his ears. After a few seconds, he rolled onto his back and let her pet his belly while he tugged on her blanket. Ash welcomed the distraction.

Puppy stopped squirming and lay belly up with his front paws by his chin. *I agree,* he said. *Something's amiss. I don't know what, but something's definitely missing.*

After everything that had happened, hearing Lost Heart Puppy speak barely surprised Ash. In fact, if she was surprised by anything, it was how ordinary his voice sounded. He didn't move his doggie mouth and say words aloud. Instead, she heard him the same way she'd heard whispered names in the past—a faint voice that arose in her mind, like a thought that didn't come from her.

"If you're talking about the large hole in the roof, I think you know who did that," said Ash.

Puppy glanced at the hole in the ceiling. He didn't look the least bit guilty. His tail thumped the dust-covered blanket while he squirmed on his back. Ash wondered how much he remembered of his life before becoming Lost Heart Puppy.

No. I like seeing the stars, he said, gazing at the hole in the roof. *Something else is missing.*

"From what?"

From me. He circled and chased his tail until he stumbled on a bit of blanket. Then he curled up and sniffed himself, as if trying to smell what wasn't there. *I'm... belly empty.*

"You're probably hungry."

Puppy sat up and cocked his head. His black ear fell over his bright blue eye while his white-tipped ear pricked up. *Hungry?*

"You need to eat food," she explained.

He sniffed the air. *I smell chickens. Are chickens food?*

"No. Well, yes," said Ash. "But they're not food right now."

Will they get to be food soon?

"You're not eating my chickens," said Ash.

Puppy slumped. *But I'm hungry. How do I make the hungry go away?*

"You eat something. Then it will go away for a little while."

Puppy jumped off the bed and looked around. He darted under the bed and dragged out an old boot. *What about this? Can I eat this?*

"No. That's a boot."

It smells nice, said Puppy. He gave the leather a bite.

Ash let him have the boot since it didn't fit her anymore. "Go ahead, if it makes you happy."

Puppy closed his eyes and gnawed on the leather. *Mmmm... salty.*

While Puppy chewed the boot, Ash's thoughts drifted back to how things had changed in her village. Illwen attacks used to only happen rarely. Years would pass without one occurring. But over the past few months they'd had several. And now two in a row. Was that why everyone seemed to think it was okay to keep a kid in a cage? It made no sense to Ash. When things became difficult, you needed to work together, not turn against each other.

It was like a spell had been cast over the village. That seemed as good an explanation as any for why people kept acting so fearful and mean.

Ash considered what Fen had said about something causing the illwen to attack her village. Maybe, if she could figure out what was making the illwen attack, she could get them to stop—just like she'd gotten Puppy to stop. Then the fearful spell that had changed her village would lift and things could go back to how they'd been before.

"Puppy?" she asked.

Hmmm? he replied, still chewing on the boot leather. He'd managed to bite off and swallow a few pieces.

"Did something cause you to come here?"

You did, he said, as if this should be obvious. *You called me Lost Heart Puppy, and then I was here.*

"I mean before that. Was there a reason why you came to this village?"

Before that I wasn't Lost Heart Puppy.

"Do you remember what you were then?"

Puppy stopped chewing the boot. His brow wrinkled as he considered her question. Suddenly, his eyes rolled back and he slumped onto his side. He whimpered like he was having a bad dream and his paws began to twitch. Wisps of black smoke rose off his back.

"Puppy? Are you okay?" asked Ash, frightened by the change that had come over him. She stroked the soft fur behind his ears.

Puppy's eyes fluttered open. *Puppy?* he echoed.

"Yes. You're Lost Heart Puppy."

I am?

"Of course you are. I named you."

And I belong here? With you?

"Yes. You're my Puppy."

The black smoke sucked back into his small body and his paws stopped twitching.

Ash bit her lip, relieved that he seemed to be returning to himself. She decided not to ask him again what he remembered of his life before becoming Lost Heart Puppy. If she wanted him to stay Puppy, it seemed best to treat him as if he'd always been Puppy. Granted, he was a puppy who could talk, but there were stranger things.

He nuzzled her hand. *And you'll take care of me?*

"Of course I'll take care of you."

And you'll feed me? He lay his head on his forepaws and batted his big puppy eyes at her.

Ash grinned. How could she refuse a hungry puppy? "Stay here," she told him. "I'll find you something."

Downstairs, Ash tiptoed among the toppled shelves in the store, looking for something to feed Puppy.

Among the broken jars on the floor lay several pickled eggs. She grabbed three and took them to the washbasin to rinse off any glass shards. Ash didn't think her dad would mind that she took the eggs. They couldn't sell them now. She even rinsed off a fourth egg for herself. Pickled eggs were an acquired taste, and one that she'd recently developed.

She was about to sneak back upstairs when she heard voices coming from the front porch. Ash crept closer to the cracked door and peeked out. Mr. Rotterburg was talking with her dad while he sat in the chair, keeping watch over the dao fora boy.

"I checked the grave, Garrett," said Mr. Rotterburg.

"What grave?"

"Where I buried that pup. It wasn't there."

"Maybe an animal dug the body up and took it," replied Ash's dad. "Plenty of creatures are going hungry now. It's not only people who are suffering from the drought."

"No," said Mr. Rotterburg. He sounded nervous, but Ash couldn't see his face very clearly. There was only one lantern lit on the porch, and Mr. Rotterburg stood just beyond the edge of its glow. "There was no trace of the pup's body or any animal digging it up. It's like it just got up and walked away."

"Are you sure it was dead?"

"'Course I'm sure," grumbled Mr. Rotterburg. "I'm telling you, Garrett, something strange is going on. First that dao fora gets captured, then an illwen attacks, and now a dead pup comes back to life."

"What's your point, Mr. Rotterburg?"

"My point is, if we're going to keep this village safe, we need to get rid of that savage." Mr. Rotterburg gestured toward where Fen huddled in the cage.

"The town voted," said Ash's dad. "The boy will go on trial tomorrow."

"You know as well as I do what the results of that trial will be. Let's save ourselves the trouble and take care of this tonight before he gets another blasted illwen to attack us."

Ash's dad removed his spectacles and rubbed the bridge of his nose. He looked tired and small in the chair, but his voice was firm. "Go home, Mr. Rotterburg. We're not doing anything with the boy tonight."

Mr. Rotterburg scuffed his boots in the dirt. "I came here as a courtesy, Garrett. You treated me and my family kindly when we first arrived. I haven't forgotten—that's why I'm telling you this. There are others who feel the same way I do, and we're not gonna wait until some podsnapper trial tomorrow. We're gonna do whatever it takes to stop these attacks tonight. No one's sleeping until that boy is gone—and I mean gone for good. We're getting rid of that pup too. We got to set things right. Either you can help us deal with these evil willers, or you can step inside and look the other way when we come for the prisoner and that pup. But when I come back I won't be alone, and you best not stand in our way."

Ash's skin went cold as Mr. Rotterburg's words sank in. He sounded calm, but his words were all teeth and knives.

"Go home, Mr. Rotterburg," repeated Ash's dad.

Mr. Rotterburg shook his head. "We'll be back before sunrise. You've been warned. Don't be so dodgast stubborn that you get hurt."

Ash stayed still until she was certain that Mr. Rotterburg had gone. After a few minutes, her dad got up. Ash scrambled to the stairs at the back of the store so he wouldn't catch her spying on him.

She knew she should go to her room, but something held her back. Was her dad going inside and abandoning the boy like Mr. Rotterburg had told him to do?

Garrett shuffled behind the store counter. Ash heard his keys jangle as he opened a lock. Then his footsteps crunched broken glass as he went back out. When Ash peeked from behind the shelves, he was sitting in the chair on the porch again, only now he had a blanket wrapped around his shoulders and something long and black lay across his lap. It took a moment for Ash to recognize what it was.

His flintlock rifle.

An ache took hold of Ash, similar to the belly emptiness Puppy had described, but it wasn't hunger. It was more like her stomach had dropped out of her, leaving a hole in her center.

Dread, she thought, naming the emotion.

She'd never felt dread like this before, but she knew that's what it had to be. The people she'd spent her entire life with were turning against her and her family. They were coming for Fen and Puppy, even if they had to hurt her dad to get them.

Out of the corner of her eyes, Ash saw Puppy standing at the top of the stairs. His tail thumped against the boards. *Eggs?*

Ash remembered the pickled eggs she'd collected.

She crept back upstairs and gave all four eggs to Puppy. The dread had stolen her appetite.

Lock and Keys

For a long while, Ash lay in bed and tried to convince herself that she must have misheard things. Fen didn't seem worried, so why should she worry about him? And her dad wouldn't let Mr. Rotterburg take Fen and Puppy. Things couldn't be that bad. It wouldn't be the first time she'd imagined scary things at night only to have everything be fine in the morning.

She slept some but kept waking. The dread she'd felt earlier didn't go away. It churned in her, prodding her to recall what she'd seen and heard. Her dad almost never got his rifle out—not even when illwen attacked. The only time Ash had seen him use it was when Mr. Ibenez's horse broke its leg and the doctor said the poor animal needed to be put out of its misery. The fact that her dad thought he needed his rifle now made her insides twist.

What was he afraid of? This was their home. These were their neighbors. Everyone liked her dad. Mr. Rotterburg must have been lying about people coming to take Fen and Puppy by force. It was bad enough that people seemed okay with keeping a kid in a cage. But to come in the middle of the night and… and what? Kill him? And Puppy? It couldn't be true.

Then why the rifle?

Every second that passed, the village seemed less and less like the one she'd grown up in. As much as she didn't want to believe that people in her village would hurt Fen and Puppy, it seemed all too possible now. She decided that she couldn't just hide out in her room and sleep. She had to free Fen before anyone hurt him. And she had to get Puppy away from here too, at least until things calmed down and returned to normal.

Ash lit a candle and checked Wayfarer to make sure all her named objects were still there. Given everything that had happened, she didn't want to leave anything behind. Named objects were special. She might need them, and bringing them with her gave her courage.

She slung Wayfarer's straps onto her shoulders, then picked up Kiki and faced the door. "Ready, Puppy?"

With his belly full, Puppy seemed content to sleep all night. He struggled to his paws and waddled over to join her.

Carry me? He batted his mismatched eyes.

"I can't." Ash tugged one of Wayfarer's straps and raised Kiki to show that her hands were full. "You'll have to walk."

Puppy groaned. *No more eggs.*

"I told you eating all of them wasn't a good idea. You'll feel better soon. Now hush. We don't want to wake anyone."

You woke me, muttered Puppy.

Ash slipped into the hall and tiptoed down the stairs. Once she made it to the store, she peered through the broken window at the rabbit cage where Fen slept. Darkness filled the square. The moon had gone down behind the trees and the porch lamp had run out of kerosene. The only light came from the stars. A few birds chirped, which meant sunrise wasn't far off. It was later than she'd thought. She clenched Kiki tight. Any minute now, Mr. Rotterburg and the others might come for Fen and Puppy.

She headed out the back door where they took deliveries. Once outside she turned her attention to the next problem: how to free Fen from the cage.

Ash considered asking her dad to release Fen, but then Mr. Rotterburg and all the other villagers would get angry at him. They'd call him a traitor and Constable Malthus would arrest him. They might even hang *him* off the wall.

No… she couldn't ask her dad to break the law. She had to free Fen without her dad knowing. Ash looked to Puppy to see what he thought, only he wasn't with her.

"Puppy?" she whispered.

No response.

She was about to call for him again when she spotted his two white paws, white ear, and wagging, white-tipped tail—those were the only things that stood out in the darkness. He trotted back from around the side of the store.

He's asleep, he said.

"Who?"

The man in the chair holding that stinky metal stick.

"It's a rifle," said Ash. "Don't go near it."

Why would I? It smells worse than onion juice.

Ash wondered when Puppy had smelled onion juice, but she couldn't get distracted. This was her chance to free Fen without her dad knowing.

She snuck around the side of the store. A lantern flickered further down the main road, near where Mr. Rotterburg lived. Not long after a rooster crowed. Time was running out.

Ash hurried to the edge of the porch and studied the slumped form of her dad in the chair. Every now and then his nose twitched and his head bobbed. If he was asleep, it wasn't a very deep sleep.

She checked the main road leading to the square. Yellow rays of lantern light swept across the side of a barn in the distance. Someone was coming!

Ash bolted to the rabbit cage. "Fen, wake up," she whispered.

The mossy mound in the cage stirred.

"There you are," muttered Fen. "I wondered when you'd return."

"We need to get you out of here."

Fen rubbed his eyes. "What's that for?" He pointed at Wayfarer.

"Shh…" said Ash. This was no time for Fen's endless questions. "We have to get you out of here now."

Another rooster crowed.

Ash glanced at her dad in the chair. He stirred, but he didn't open his eyes. In his hand, a keyring with several brass skeleton keys gleamed in the moonlight. That's why she hadn't been able to find the padlock key in the drawer. Her dad had kept it with him.

The keyring had been clipped to his belt. To get the key, she'd have to lift his hand, unhook the clip, and pull away the ring—all without waking him. It didn't seem possible.

Puppy raced back from the far side of the square. *They're almost here! Six smelly men with pointy metal sticks.*

Fen didn't appear to hear Puppy's words. Like the whispered names of things, only she seemed to hear Puppy's voice. Even so, Fen must have noticed the lights and heard the approaching villagers because for once he stayed quiet.

Ash jammed Kiki between two metal bars of the cage. The ironwood hummed in her hands, eager to be of use. It was stronger than most metals. She'd seen squatters bring dented axe heads to the store, misshapen from trying to chop down an ironwood tree.

After shoving and pulling on Kiki, she managed to bend two of the cage bars apart—but the gap wasn't big enough for Fen to slip through.

She glanced back at the approaching lantern lights. There had to be a way to get Fen out of the cage.

Kiki! The whisper repeated in her head, as if the stick loved the sound of its own name. *Kiki. Kiki. Kiki.*

"Hush!" she said, unable to figure out what to do with so many distractions.

Kiki. Kiki!

"Kiki…" grumbled Ash, annoyed.

"Do keys come when you call for them?" asked Fen.

Key key!

Ash studied the two twigs that branched off the end of the ironwood stick. Both had little bumps on the tips, like the tips of the brass skeleton keys on her dad's keyring. They were about the same size as skeleton keys too. No wonder the stick had whispered its name to her.

She slid the tip of one twig into the padlock keyhole.

"That's an odd looking key," said Fen.

There was no time to explain. The first twig didn't fit, but the second slid into the lock. An ordinary twig would have snapped right off, but ironwood was different. With a careful twist, the lock clicked open.

Ash swung the cage door wide and Fen crawled out. Light from the lanterns had nearly reached them. They ran to a clump of mulberries on the far side of the store.

Huddling behind the bushes, they tried to catch their breaths. Several seconds passed without a sound. Ash wondered if the men were just farmers going about their morning business, and no one was coming for Fen or Puppy after all.

Then the shouting started.

The Mistcat

"Ring the warning bells! Wake the wall soldiers!" yelled Mr. Rotterburg. "The dao fora are attacking!"

Two warning bells sounded from the forest gate watchtower. The signal quickly spread to all the other watchtowers. Soldiers stumbled from the barracks and ran to their posts, preparing their muskets for a dao fora attack.

From her hiding spot in the bushes, Ash watched the commotion spread until the whole village awoke. The yellow lights of lanterns shone along the walls of homes and stores. A few stars could still be seen overhead, but the sky near the horizon had lightened. Sunrise wasn't far off.

Ash searched the sky for poison arrows. She pictured hordes of dao fora warriors storming the gates. Most of the people pouring out of their homes looked terrified. But no arrows came over the walls. No muskets boomed. Things beyond the walls seemed relatively quiet.

After a couple minutes, the watchtower soldiers called to each other in confusion. Instead of shining their lanterns outward at the forests and plantation fields, they directed them inward at the village houses and barns. That's when Ash realized the warning bells were because of her and Fen. *He* was the attacking dao fora they feared.

Gruff voices echoed from the square. A wall officer organized a group of soldiers to find the escaped prisoner. Constable Malthus argued with him about who should be in charge. Things looked chaotic, but it wouldn't take them long to organize and search the village.

"You have to leave," said Ash.

Fen stepped toward the forest gate.

"Not that way!" She grabbed his hand and tugged him back.

"Isn't the gate that way?"

"It'll be guarded," said Ash. "They'll catch you. I know another way out." She led Fen deeper into the village.

Puppy bolted in front of her and sniffed the air. *There's a man carrying fire ahead.*

Ash hid behind a tree with Fen and waited for the man to pass. Then she led Fen along a small path that wound between houses and yards, while Puppy trotted ahead to scout things out. He warned her of people he smelled or heard long before Ash saw them.

By the time they reached the part of the wall that Ash had been searching for, the sky had lightened from black to dark blue with a rosy glow near the east. Soon the sun would peek through the trees and the wall lookouts would easily spot them. They had to hurry.

She darted into a cluster of bushes that grew near the wall. Raffi, Rosa's brother, had taken her and Rosa here two months ago. The bushes hid a small gap at the base of the wall. On a dare, Ash had squeezed through it.

Rows upon rows of jujube trees grew in the plantation fields on the other side. Ash had wanted to pick a few jujube fruits to taste, but as soon as she saw the webworm silk covering the branches, and the writhing clumps of webworms in their silken tents, she lost her appetite. After a quick glance around the field, she crawled back through the gap, sickened by what she'd seen.

Now, though, she felt glad that Raffi had shown her the gap in the wall. It was the best chance Fen and Puppy had to escape. She pulled back the slab of bark they'd propped against the wall to hide the gap.

The opening looked too small for an adult to squeeze through. When Raffi had shown it to her and Rosa, he said he couldn't even squeeze through it. Ash knelt by the wall posts, hoping Fen would be able to fit. He was just as skinny as her, if not skinnier, and Puppy wouldn't have any trouble getting through the gap. He could walk through it with his head held high if he wanted to. Then, once things calmed down, she could sneak Puppy back into the village to live with her.

She wiped her hands on her shirt to get rid of a few threads of webworm silk that tickled her fingers. Some webworms had migrated onto the bushes and plants on this side of the wall. Although webworms would infest almost any plant, their favorite food was jujube trees.

"Fen! Over here," said Ash. "You can get out this way."

"You want me to crawl through *that*?"

"You need to leave. It's not safe here."

"I won't do it."

"What's the big deal? If I can fit, you can fit." She kept wiping her hands on her shirt to get off the sticky webworm silk.

Fen pointed to the bushes around the gap. "I'm not going near *that*."

He wasn't worried about the gap. He was worried about the webworms on the bushes around it. What was it with this boy? An angry mob didn't scare him, but a couple of caterpillars did? She thought webworms were gross, too, but she wouldn't let them stop her.

"They're just webworms," she said, rubbing her fingers on her shirt. Several threads still clung to her. "You need to go. Now!"

Fen edged away from the wall. "I don't like webworms. They make people act strange."

"You're being ridiculous."

Puppy sniffed a webworm tent. He immediately jumped back and rolled on the grass, rubbing his paws against his muzzle as if fire ants were stinging him.

Ugh! He's right. They smell terrible.

"Don't be silly. Plantation workers collect webworm silk every day. It's what Lord Ocras makes crystal cloth out of, and everyone wants crystal cloth." Ash kept wiping her hands on her shirt.

"What's crystal cloth? And who's Lord Ocras?" asked Fen.

"Soldiers are coming," said Ash. "If they catch you, they'll kill you. This is the quickest way out."

Fen turned back toward the forest gate.

"You can't go that way! You'll be caught."

Fen kept walking.

Ash groaned. Why was he being so difficult? "You're impossible!"

"And strange, exhausting, ridiculous, and stubborn," replied Fen.

The sky had lightened enough that people could see without lanterns. There was no way Fen would be able to sneak out the forest gate, or any of the other gates. If he didn't leave through the gap in the wall, she'd have to hide him somewhere in the village until night fell. But where? Soldiers would keep searching for him.

Fen ducked behind an old stone well. "There! That's what we need."

Ash crouched next to him and followed his gaze. A large fig tree shaded a clearing ahead. Some of its broad branches arched out so far from the trunk that they brushed the ground. The tree had been there long before the village had. Miraculously, no one had cut it down. On a hot day it was the best shady spot in the village. Goats, chickens, and people liked to gather beneath it. All Ash saw under its sprawling limbs now was a blanket of morning mist rising off the grass. "It's just a tree."

"And mist!" said Fen.

"So?"

"So… mistcats!"

Ash had heard wall soldiers tell stories of dao fora warriors riding into battle on the backs of giant mistcats, but she'd never seen such creatures. She wasn't even sure they existed. It seemed more like a tall tale soldiers told kids to scare them. She certainly didn't see any mistcats under the tree. "There's nothing there."

"And you think *I'm* strange? How do your people get around?" Fen tugged her toward the tree.

Ash worried that they'd be spotted, but no soldiers shouted. The mist must have been thick enough to keep them hidden.

Fen knelt at the base of the tree and put his hand on one of the wide roots snaking above ground. He closed his eyes in silence.

"Are you praying?" asked Ash.

"I'm calling them."

Ash didn't hear him calling anyone, but she decided not to mention this.

She stared into the mist. Soon it would burn off and people would see them. Already, parts of the mist began to swirl and lift, as if stirred by a breeze. Only there wasn't a breeze. Regardless, the mist moved, becoming thicker in places and thinner in others.

A broad head with high, triangular ears and a jaguar-like body took shape only ten steps away. It looked wispy and insubstantial, the way the illwen had, except it was the silvery-white color of mist.

Puppy growled.

"You see it too?" whispered Ash.

I see a large, arrogant cat, grumbled Puppy.

The mistcat stepped toward them, silent as a cloud. Its paws left dew on the grass, and its shape rippled as it moved. It looked beautiful and dangerous. There was no mistaking the dagger-long teeth, or the quiet, intent way it prowled toward them—a predator stalking prey.

"That's a big one," said Fen. "I have a knack for calling them. You better name it before it kills us."

"Name it?" replied Ash. She'd never named something on command before. Names came to her when *they* wanted to be known, not when she wanted to know them. "You don't just name something willy-nilly. It doesn't work that way. Why don't you name it?"

"Oh, I don't know how to name mistcats. I only know how to call them," said Fen.

The mistcat prowled closer, staring at her. "What if I can't name it?"

"Then we should run. I wonder if we could outrun a mistcat? Probably not."

Ash tried to calm her racing heart and *listen.* She couldn't hear any names. No whispers came to her at all.

She closed her eyes to concentrate. Still nothing. When she opened her eyes, the prowling cat was just a few steps away. It looked nearly as big as a horse, but lower to the ground and with thicker legs. Its gaze flicked from her to Fen, as if deciding which one to devour first.

"I don't hear anything," said Ash. "I can't do it."

"Why not? I saw what you did with the illwen. Compared to that, this should be easy. Many dao fora hunters can do it."

"How?"

"Good question." Fen cocked his head. "Tavan hasn't told me how yet. He said I'm not old enough to learn."

"What if *I'm* not old enough?"

"That would be bad. Mistcats have no sense of humor. The last time I called one it was less than half this size and it still almost ate me. That's why you should never call a mistcat unless you know its name. Didn't you know that?"

Ash would have glared at Fen, but she couldn't take her eyes off the deadly creature in front of her.

Puppy stayed next to her, growling. The mistcat paid him no mind. Its predatory eyes remained on Ash, returning her stare. At least they seemed to be eyes, but they were also shifting, becoming something else. Ash peered into them until all she saw was mist.

Logically, she knew that she was still standing under a tree next to Fen and Puppy, but she didn't see them anymore. Instead, she saw images in the mist—deer munching on the leaves of young trees in the forest. One of the deer was about to eat the last leaf on a sapling when a mistcat leapt from a branch onto its back.

The deer struggled, but with a swift bite to its neck, its struggles stopped.

Death Bringer, thought Ash.

She didn't dare speak this name aloud. If she called the approaching mistcat Death Bringer, it might end *her* life with a swift bite to her neck.

The images in the mist shifted again, like changing shapes in a cloud. As soon as she recognized one thing, something new materialized. She saw a burnt forest, full of fallen trees. Then a woman, dressed like Fen, with a moss cloak and deerskin pants, planted seeds in the bare ground. Years passed in seconds as the seeds grew into saplings. Some were eaten by deer. Others became massive trees. When the forest returned, so did the mist.

The dao fora woman—the one who'd planted the seeds—looked older now. She placed her hands on the roots of a tree she'd planted and a mistcat stepped out of the forest ahead of her. The woman knelt and the mistcat lowered its head in greeting.

Ash pieced together a story from the images. The trees created the mist that gave life to the mistcats. In return, the mistcats protected the trees. But they couldn't protect trees from fire. When areas burned, the mistcats vanished until the dao fora planted seeds and brought the forest back. That's why the mistcats let the dao fora ride them—they worked together to protect the forest.

Forest Protector, thought Ash.

Before she could say this name aloud, the images in the mist shifted once again.

This time, Ash saw people dressed like villagers carrying torches into the forest. They set bushes and trees on fire. It was what squatters did to clear land, but the flames grew out of control. A massive firestorm tore through the forest. Ash saw the dao fora woman who'd planted the seeds try to stop the fire from reaching an ancient tree. Flames surrounded her. The mistcat moved to help her, but it faded in the heat. Then the woman nodded to it and walked into the smoke.

The visions stopped, leaving only the mistcat crouching before Ash. It appeared to be the same mistcat that she'd seen in her vision—the one whose rider had vanished in the fire set by squatters.

The mistcat's lips curled back in a threatening posture. Ash swallowed. From the look of it, it seemed eager to kill her.

She had to name it. But what? Forest Protector? People from her village had cut down thousands of trees in the forest. They might have even set the fire that had killed its rider. She doubted that a mistcat named Forest Protector would look kindly on a villager like her.

There had to be another name. A hidden name.

Ash thought again of the first vision she'd seen of the mistcat pouncing on the deer. It didn't kill the deer because it hated deer. It killed it because the deer were eating all the saplings in the forest. But the forest needed some deer. Trees that grew too close together crowded each other out. It was all a matter of balance.

"*Balance Keeper*," said Ash. She spoke the words clearly while staring at the mistcat, willing the name to fit.

The mist beneath the tree began to rush into the ghostly jaguar form of the mistcat, as if giving the creature a name gave it irresistible gravity. More and more mist from the surrounding area flowed into it. The tiny water drops joined into larger drops, until the mistcat became a solid figure made of water.

The creature looked clear as glass yet moved with liquid grace. Now that Balance Keeper was solid, her growls could be heard.

Ash knelt, like the dao fora woman in her vision had done. "It's okay," she said, stretching out her hand. "I'm your friend."

The mistcat's eyes narrowed and her ears pricked back. Clearly the mistcat didn't see her as a friend. She saw her as part of the problem—no different from villagers who cut down trees and destroyed the balance of the forest.

Ash gritted her teeth, fearing that she'd picked the wrong name.

Never trust a cat, grumbled Puppy.

"Huh… That's not good," said Fen.

Ash glanced at him, but he wasn't looking at the mistcat. Instead, his gaze seemed focused on something beyond the mistcat, near the center of the village. She saw houses, streets, and barns in the early morning light. She saw a group of soldiers too, followed by farmers carrying machetes and other weapons. The mist that had kept them hidden only moments before had flowed into the mistcat, leaving them completely visible to anyone who glanced their way.

"Think they'll see us?" asked Fen.

"Let's hope not," whispered Ash.

"Halt!" shouted one of the soldiers. "There! By the tree. Surround them!"

Arrows in the Wall

The soldiers fanned out, taking up positions around Ash, Fen, and Puppy.

"They've summoned a demon!" bellowed Mr. Rotterburg. He stood among a crowd of frightened villagers, pointing at the mistcat.

Ash recognized several people in the crowd—Rosa and Raffi, Mayor Tullridge, Mr. Wombley, and Ms. Silva, the schoolteacher. Ash looked for her dad but didn't see him.

The officer gave an order and soldiers approached. Ash backed up until her heels bumped the base of the tree. If the mistcat didn't get them, the soldiers certainly would. Everyone was against them. How could so much have gone amiss?

"Ready muskets!" commanded the officer.

Two of the soldiers carried long, heavy muskets. At the officer's command, they knelt and loaded the barrels. Other soldiers drew sabers and stood guard.

The mistcat suddenly turned and snarled at the soldiers. Spikes of water pricked from her shoulders, glistening in the first rays of sunlight.

Balance Keeper, thought Ash. That's why the mistcat had turned on the soldiers. If most of the village was against them, then Balance Keeper would protect them. Maybe it wasn't the wrong name after all.

Balance Keeper crouched and glanced at Ash and Fen, as if inviting them to climb on.

Fen leapt onto the mistcat's glassy back. "Aren't you coming?"

Ash hesitated. This was her home. She pulled the straps of Wayfarer tight across her chest and searched the faces in the crowd. People she'd known her whole life glared at her with crazed, hostile expressions.

"Take aim!" ordered the officer.

The soldiers leveled their muskets at Balance Keeper. At *her*.

"Steady!" commanded the officer. "On my mark."

Ash wanted to tell them to stop. She'd done nothing wrong. All she'd tried to do was help a friend. She hadn't hurt anyone. But people didn't see her anymore. They saw an enemy of the village.

She took Fen's hand and swung her leg over the mistcat's back, sitting in front of the dao fora boy. "Puppy, come on!" She held out her arms to catch him.

Puppy crinkled his muzzle. *I'm not riding a cat. I'll do fine on my own four paws, thank you very much.*

Ash pressed her heels into the mistcat's sides, like she'd seen riders on horses do. "Go!" she urged.

Balance Keeper stayed still, glaring at the soldiers.

"Why isn't she moving?"

"You named her. I think you have to tell her where to go," said Fen.

"I don't know where to go. I've never been anywhere else."

"Then tell her to go over the wall."

"Go over the wall!" said Ash.

Nothing happened.

Ash glanced at the soldiers crouching with their muskets. Her mom moved through the crowd beyond them. Essa still wore her fancy dress, dirty from the night before. The veil drawn over her eyes hid her face. She pushed through the crowd, then froze.

She'll protect me, thought Ash. *She'll tell the soldiers they've made a terrible mistake, then everything will be okay.*

Essa didn't say a word. She stood, frightened and mute, as if she didn't recognize her own daughter.

Ash's chest tightened. Each second her mother remained silent jabbed another thorn into her heart. Why didn't she tell the soldiers to put down their muskets? How could she do nothing?

The hurt Ash felt flared into anger. She closed her eyes and pictured herself escaping the soldiers, the crowd, and the silent form that had been her mother. Then she'd soar over the wall into the cloud forest beyond it.

As soon as this vision took shape in her mind, the mistcat surged into motion.

The sudden movement nearly sent Ash tumbling off of Balance Keeper's back. Luckily, Fen caught her and helped her stay on.

They were already halfway to the soldiers. Wind swept her hair back from her face. The two musketmen aimed straight at them.

"Look out!" yelled Ash as Balance Keeper bounded toward the soldiers.

"Fire!" shouted the officer.

In the same instant, a black-and-white bundle of fur darted across their path.

Puppy!

Before the musketmen could squeeze their triggers, Puppy snatched one of the muskets in his teeth like he was fetching a stick. His momentum carried him into the other musket and he knocked both guns aside. One went off with a deafening *BOOM!* and a puff of black smoke. The other musket spun across the dirt road, leaving the soldiers in disarray.

Balance Keeper leapt over the wide-eyed soldiers and landed gracefully beyond them.

Farmers and villagers scrambled to get out of the mistcat's way. Ash glimpsed their shocked expressions as they streaked past. At least some looked shocked. Others appeared terrified.

Puppy raced by her side. An ordinary dog would have been left far behind, but Puppy seemed to have no trouble keeping up with the mistcat. His tongue lolled from his mouth as he ran, giving him a slightly ridiculous expression.

They passed her parents' store at the corner of the square. Once Balance Keeper reached the open square, she picked up speed, bounding toward the forest gate.

"Guard the gate!" shouted soldiers on the wall. They raised their sabers. Others frantically loaded shot into their musket barrels.

The closer Ash got to the gate, the larger and more daunting it looked. She had no idea how they'd make it over the high gate posts, but Balance Keeper didn't slow.

The mistcat's back arched and bunched, throwing Ash forward. Then Balance Keeper's hind legs pushed off the ground and she stretched into the air—propelled by a powerful leap toward the top of the gate.

Time slowed to a crawl. Ash looked down at the soldiers crouched below. She saw Puppy jump onto the shoulder of one soldier, and from there to the gatehouse roof. She saw her dad in his white storekeeper shirt, standing among the wall soldiers. He'd probably been asking them if they'd seen her anywhere when she'd charged the gate. The moment passed too quickly for him to speak, or for her to wave goodbye.

Balance Keeper's claws dug into the top of the gate, hoisting them up and over. They landed on the far side, coming down as fluid and graceful as before, while Puppy tumbled through the tall grass beside them.

Time sped once they reached the ground. The mistcat bolted down the dirt road between rows of jujube trees to the cloud forest, quick as water seeping into cracks in a dry field.

Ash glanced back before the trees blocked her view.

All she could see was the village wall—a long spiked barrier made of hundreds of round logs, sharpened at the tops. The wall sliced across the land, cutting her off from the only home she'd ever known.

Part 2

Stumps in the Forest

Balance Keeper paused at the edge of the cloud forest. Ash had been clutching the mistcat's neck, watching the ground blur by at a gallop. Now that they'd stopped, she could finally look up.

What she saw took her breath away. The trees at the edge of the forest stretched higher than the tallest watchtowers in her village. Other trees further in looked even taller. Their distant tops brushed the clouds.

"Go on." Ash urged Balance Keeper forward. She wanted to see such enormous trees up close, but once again she couldn't get the mistcat to move.

Before, Balance Keeper had responded when she'd envisioned soaring over the wall. Perhaps the way to tell a mistcat where to go was by picturing things. Ash tested her theory by imagining the forest. Still, the mistcat didn't move.

Frustrated, she glared at a plant with red flowers. Ash pictured herself leaning over it to smell the flowers. As soon as the image took shape in her mind, Balance Keeper bolted toward the plant.

Ash spotted other things. A vine that looked as thick as her leg. A tree full of white, hanging berries. It wasn't easy, but each time she formed a clear image in her mind of being near the thing she saw, Balance Keeper set off toward it, gracefully leaping roots, bushes, and anything else that stood in the way.

"Do you have any idea where you're going?" asked Fen after they'd galloped back and forth for a while.

"Not really." Ash wanted to go home, but she couldn't—not until she broke the fearful spell that had changed her village and proved that she wasn't a traitor.

Her chest ached as she recalled how people she'd known her whole life had turned against her. She wished she could explain that she'd only been trying to make things better, but who would listen to her? Everyone in her village thought she was helping their enemy. Her own mother hadn't even stood up for her. Remembering her mother's silence made the thorns in her heart twist deeper.

Things were more amiss than they'd ever been. Someone had to be to blame.

"Fen, will you answer one question for me?" she asked while Puppy chased a squirrel.

"Sure. I love questions."

Ash turned so she could see him sitting behind her. "Why are the dao fora causing illwen to attack my village?"

"What makes you think they are?"

"You said yourself that something was causing the illwen to come to the village. It has to be the dao fora. They hate villagers."

"Really?" He leaned back. "How many dao fora do you know?"

"I'm not talking about you," said Ash. "You're different. But other dao fora attack squatters and plantation workers outside the wall. My friend's dad was killed by them."

"If you want to know why dao fora attack squatters, go that way." He pointed toward a distant ridge.

"Why? What's there?"

"You'll see. It's not far," said Fen.

Ash directed Balance Keeper over the ridge and down a valley, to a place where the trees stopped. Sunlight streamed through a gap in the green canopy above. Below, a triangular-shaped clearing of blackened earth absorbed the mid-day heat.

Only a few spindly seedlings, planted in rows, grew out of the dry, cracked ground. The clearing looked like a graveyard with burnt tree stumps giving grim reminders of the forest that had once grown there. A few of the stumps looked big enough to build a house on.

"Careful. If they see you, they might shoot you," whispered Fen.

"Who will shoot me?"

Fen pointed toward a pile of logs at the far end of the clearing.

Ash slid off Balance Keeper and cupped her hands over her eyes to block out the sunlight. A small, rickety shack slumped next to the log pile. The area around the shack looked like a garden, with rows of wilted potato plants and skinny corn.

This place smells bad, said Puppy.

Balance Keeper didn't seem to like the place much either. A low, liquid growl rumbled in her throat.

Ash stayed behind several ferns at the edge of the clearing. She noticed a woman sitting on a stump near the shack, scraping corn off a cob into a bucket. A man carrying a musket stepped out of the forest beyond her.

"There's at least a dozen more clearings like this around here," whispered Fen. "Some are bigger. The only reason dao fora attack villagers is because villagers keep destroying the cloud forest where they live."

"They're not destroying it," countered Ash. But even as she said this, she saw that Fen was right. The trees the squatters had cut down must have been hundreds, even thousands, of years old. There was no way to replace trees like that.

Thinking of the lost trees saddened her. She knew why squatters cleared sections of the forest like this, and she couldn't blame them for doing it. She'd met dozens of squatter families who'd come to her parents' store. Most of them were nice. They spent all their money to travel to frontier villages like Last Hope because they were told there'd be land to farm. But when they arrived, there wasn't any land left.

That's why squatter families cleared sections of the cloud forest to farm. Once they cut down the big trees, they burned the rest to make the soil more fertile. Since slashing and burning the cloud forest was illegal, squatters who were caught were fined and forced to work on webworm plantations to pay off their debts. Even so, many of them risked it. *Burn or starve*—that's what squatters said.

"They're hungry," said Ash. "They just need a little land to farm so they can feed their families."

Fen laughed.

"What's so funny?" asked Ash.

"If it's food they want, they're going about it all wrong."

"What do you mean?"

"You should see the Sky Tree where the dao fora elders live."

"Why?"

"That's something you'd have to see to understand. Too bad villagers like you can't go there."

Ash studied the ugly burnt scar in the forest. She tried to imagine dozens of burned areas like this scattered throughout the forest from all the squatters who'd traveled through Last Hope. To the dao fora, it must have seemed like villagers were attacking their home instead of the other way around. No wonder dao fora hated villagers and sent illwen to attack them.

"There has to be a way to fix this," she said, more to herself than Fen.

"I'm not very good at fixing things," said Fen, "but Tavan is. He used to be part of the Sky Tree council. If dao fora have a problem, they talk with the council. Then the council decides what to do."

"Tavan? That's your friend, right? Would he help me?"

"He might," said Fen. "Or he might shoot poison arrows at you. It's always hard to tell with Tavan."

Fen told Ash which way to go to find Tavan's camp. She picked out landmarks in the distance and carefully envisioned being near them. It took a great deal of focus, but she was getting better at it. She got better at holding on when Balance Keeper jumped, too, so Fen didn't have to keep her from falling off.

After a while, Balance Keeper slowed. Instead of leaping from branch to branch, the mistcat loped along the forest floor, panting. Ash and Fen slid off the mistcat's back. Balance Keeper looked thinner than she had before.

"What's wrong with her?" asked Ash.

"It's the heat," said Fen. "Mist evaporates in the heat of the day. You should dismiss her before she fades."

Ash put her hand on Balance Keeper's cool, liquid neck and envisioned the mistcat returning to the upper branches of the trees.

In a blink, Balance Keeper leapt onto a low tree limb, then to another limb and another, fading into mist as she went.

"We'll have to walk the rest of the way," said Fen.

Some of us walked the whole way, quipped Puppy.

Fen led them to a stream that they followed until it joined a river. "There's Tavan." He pointed to a man sitting on a log near a distant bend in the river.

Tavan's head was shaved and he had a curiously hairless face. He wasn't wearing a shirt, but a necklace of white feathers covered his chest. The dirt-stained pants he wore looked like the same thick cloth pants that most plantation workers wore.

Fen crouched behind a clump of ferns, staying out of sight. "Think I should talk with him, or do you want to surprise him?"

Ash noticed the bow leaning against the log next to the man and the quiver of arrows slung across his back.

"It's probably best if you talk with him first," she said.

"Right. But he might be angry that I left."

I hope he has food. I'm belly empty again, said Puppy.

"Me too," replied Ash. She hadn't eaten since the night before. After riding and walking so far, she felt faint with hunger.

Fen gave her a perplexed look.

"I'm… just agreeing with you," said Ash, deciding not to explain that Puppy could talk. "Still, even if Tavan's angry that you left him, won't he be relieved to see you?"

"Maybe. Only one way to find out." Fen left the ferns and headed toward the river bank. "Tavan!"

The dao fora man grabbed the bow and notched an arrow to the string. "Who's there?"

"Me," replied Fen.

"Fen? Great skies, where've you been?" Tavan relaxed the bow. "I searched everywhere for you."

"I went to the village."

"The village? I told you to stay away from there!" Tavan spoke the common tongue with the same Governor City accent that Fen did.

Puppy trotted out from behind the ferns, sniffing the air. *He does have food,* he said. *It's not eggs, but it smells nice.*

"Puppy, no!" Ash moved to pull him back, only it was too late. Tavan spotted them.

He drew his bow, aiming an arrow at her chest. "Who are you? What are you doing here?"

"She's my friend," said Fen. "I brought her here."

Tavan kept the arrow trained on Ash. "This is no place for her. She needs to leave. Go on! Go home!" he added, like he was shooing away a stray dog.

"I can't go home," said Ash.

Puppy continued through the ferns. No one paid him any mind.

Here's the food! He jumped, tugging something out of Tavan's back pocket.

Tavan spun and shot at Puppy. Or rather, he shot at where Puppy had been a moment before. The arrow thumped into the mud while Puppy darted back with a strip of dried meat in his mouth.

It's salty! And delicious! said Puppy.

Tavan notched another arrow to his bow.

"Wouldn't it be rude to shoot them? She did save my life," said Fen.

The dao fora man glared at Ash and Puppy. After several tense seconds, he lowered his bow. "Forgive me. I'm not used to visitors," he said. "Thank you for saving my son."

Tavan made a fire and set three fish he'd caught over the coals. While he cooked, Fen told him about how he'd gotten captured outside Ash's village and been held captive there. When Fen got to the part where Ash tamed the raging illwen, Tavan's eyes narrowed.

"She did what?" He gave Ash a wary look.

Fen continued his story, repeating parts, but Ash left to sit by the river. She took off her boots and dipped her feet in the water, only catching bits and pieces of what Fen said.

Puppy trotted over, carrying the arrow Tavan had shot at him in his mouth. He set it down near Ash.

Throw it? he asked.

Ash picked up the arrow and studied it. It was cleverly made, with three black feathers on one end and a sharp point of chipped onyx bound to the other end. Ash wondered if the tip was poisoned. An arrow like this had killed Rosa's dad.

She shoved the tip between two river stones and snapped it off. Then she tossed the rest of the arrow along the riverbank. Puppy bolted after it, leapt, and snatched it out of the air. He trotted back and set it on the ground in front of her.

Again? That was fun! Why is this fun?

Ash played fetch with Puppy while listening to what she could hear of Fen and Tavan's conversation. When Fen finished his story, he told Ash that he was going to bathe, and disappeared around the bend in the river.

Tavan strode to where Ash sat. He frowned at the broken arrow. Puppy snapped it in half again and tore the feathers off the shaft.

"Those are difficult to make," said Tavan.

"Then don't make them," replied Ash.

Tavan grunted. It was a strangely ambiguous sound. Ash couldn't tell if he was angry or agreeing with her.

Once Puppy had thoroughly destroyed the arrow, he trotted off to explore more of Tavan's camp.

This smells good. Puppy tugged on a deer hide stretched over sticks near the fire pit. *Can I roll in it?*

"No," said Ash.

But I want to!

Tavan watched Ash and Puppy carefully. "Your dog. What is he?"

"Puppy? He's…"

Puppy stopped tugging on the deer hide and cocked his head. *Super? Brilliant? Fantastic?*

"He's a mutt," said Ash.

A mutt? huffed Puppy.

"He's the illwen Fen was talking about, isn't he?" Tavan kept his voice pitched low so only Ash could hear.

Ash didn't want to talk about what Puppy had been before becoming Puppy.

"Hmm…" grunted Tavan. "You're right not to answer me. No good will come from talking about what he used to be. Especially around Fen. Understand?"

"Sure," said Ash, although she didn't see what Fen had to do with it.

Tavan nodded and returned to the fire.

When Fen came back, he sat on the log next to Ash. Tavan gave them each a whole fish to eat. Puppy devoured his in a few bites, then watched Ash eat hers.

Are you going to finish that? His tail thumped the dirt.

Ash couldn't resist Puppy's big, sad eyes. She took a few more bites, then gave him the rest.

"You helped return Fen to me. For that I'm grateful," said Tavan once she finished eating. "I'll take you back to your village now. Your people must miss you."

"No," said Ash.

Tavan raised an eyebrow—at least he raised what might have been an eyebrow. He barely had any hair on his face, so the gesture simply made his forehead resemble wavy lines in brown river sand.

"I can't go back to my village. They think I'm a traitor," explained Ash.

"Then I'll take you to another village. Do you have relatives elsewhere?"

Ash shook her head. Her father's parents were both dead, and her mother's relatives lived across the ocean. She'd never met any of them.

"Then I'll take you to Governor City. That's as far as I can go," grumbled Tavan. "I spent time there years ago. You can tell the governor you were taken captive by a dao fora warrior and forced to help him escape. No one will call you a traitor if you were taken captive."

"But that's not what happened," said Fen.

Tavan shrugged. "It's the only way to get her people to take her back."

"No," said Ash.

"You can't stay here, child. This is no place for you. I need to take you somewhere tonight."

"Will you take me anywhere I wish to go?" asked Ash.

"Anywhere within reason. I suppose I owe you that."

Ash recalled what Fen had said earlier about the dao fora taking their problems to the Sky Tree council. If she could talk with the council, they might help her with her problem. She might even be able to convince them to stop attacking villagers.

"Take me to the Sky Tree," she said.

Tavan's whole forehead wrinkled into wavy lines. He laughed—a low, rumbling belly laugh. "Crazy child. The dao fora will shoot you if you go anywhere near the Sky Tree. They hate intruders like you."

"I know," replied Ash. "That's why I need to speak with them."

12

Forest Smells

Tavan tried several times to persuade Ash to let him take her back to her village, but she refused. As long as people thought she was a traitor, she couldn't go back. She had to change things first. If she could get the attacks on her village to stop, the fearful spell might lift and people would see that she'd only meant to help. She might even be seen as a hero for stopping the attacks and saving her village. Ash pictured her mother opening up like a flower and welcoming her home with wide arms.

She knew it wouldn't be easy to convince the Sky Tree council to make peace with her village. Even so, it couldn't be harder than taming an illwen. Or convincing a mistcat to let her ride it. She tried to explain all this to Tavan, but he laughed at her reasoning.

"Child, if you want the dao fora to stop attacking villagers, get your people to stop destroying the cloud forest."

Ash thought of the squatter's camp she'd seen earlier. She didn't like what the squatters did to the forest, but the cloud forest was plenty big and the squatters just needed a little land to farm. Maybe, if the dao fora understood that the squatters meant them no harm, they'd be able to find a way to get along. Her dad had told her stories of how dao fora used to come to the village to trade. If they'd gotten along before, couldn't they get along again?

"You said you'd take me anywhere I wanted to go."

"I won't take you to your death. That's no way to repay a debt," replied Tavan. "And even if I wanted to, I couldn't take you to the Sky Tree council."

"Why not? Fen said you used to be part of the Sky Tree council."

"That was a long time ago. The council and I had a disagreement. Fen and I live on our own now."

Ash sensed he was telling the truth, but he seemed to be lying too. *There's a name for what he's doing*. She stilled her breathing and listened. The name came to her like an echo splashing up from a deep well.

Evading.

"Get some rest," said Tavan. "It's a long journey to Governor City. We leave tonight, when the moon is overhead and the mist is rising."

"Ash. Wake up!"

Ash pressed her face into Nester the blanket and tried to go back to sleep, but it was no use. Whoever had called her kept shaking her shoulder.

"Let's go," whispered Fen.

"Go where?" she muttered. She refused to go to Governor City.

"Didn't you want to talk with the Sky Tree council? We have to hurry. Tavan won't be gone long. He's off checking his fish traps."

Ash sat up. "You'll take me to the Sky Tree?"

"You helped me. Why wouldn't I help you?"

"What about Tavan?"

"He's just upset because he doesn't get along with the Sky Tree council anymore, so he doesn't want to see them," said Fen. "I bet I can find them, though. That is, if you still want to talk to them."

Ash hastily wrapped Nester the blanket around Holder, her doll, and packed them both into Wayfarer. Then she looped Wayfarer's straps over her shoulders and grabbed Kiki for courage. Puppy was already stumbling about, sniffing trees. "All right. I'm ready."

Fen set off into the cloud forest. Ash hurried after him, making sure that Puppy stayed with her. She could barely see the white tip on of his tail and his two white paws in the darkness. Moonlight trickled through the leaves, giving the trees a faint silvery glow.

Once her eyes adjusted, Ash noticed other lights in the forest. Mushrooms growing on fallen logs gave off a greenish glow, and the eyes of animals and insects glinted in the trees and bushes around her. The forest wasn't asleep at all. Everywhere she looked shadows moved while creatures chirped, trilled, buzzed, and skittered. The sounds of the forest were even more layered and complex at night than during the day.

She had trouble keeping track of Fen—his moss cloak blended in perfectly with the trees, and his footsteps barely made a sound. He paused a few times to look back at her when she stepped on a leaf or snapped a twig. Hopefully, the burble of the stream would keep Tavan from hearing her. Ash considered taking off her boots and walking barefoot like Fen, but she didn't think her feet would last long on the rough ground.

Puppy bounded back and forth to sniff things. The night seemed full of good smells to him. *Squirrel pee!* he exclaimed. *It's sour!* Then he scampered to another tree. *Moles! Mouse droppings! Wet worms! Rotting leaves! Owl pellets!*

For him, every smell was a new and wonderous discovery.

Ash sniffed the air, but she didn't smell any squirrel pee. Just the rich, loamy scent of damp wood and leaves. Every now and then, she smelled something so sweet she could almost taste it. *Moonflowers.*

The tangy-sweet scent reminded Ash of her mother, and how her mother used to talk about wanting a garden full of moonflowers. That was before the drought made growing flowers a luxury almost no one could afford.

Ash slowed. She scanned the dark forest but didn't see or hear Fen anywhere.

"Where is he, Puppy?"

Lost Heart Puppy paused by her side and sniffed several times. *Upwind. Someone else is there too. They smell like black cherries and fig vines.*

Puppy bounded ahead to investigate. Ash did her best to tiptoe through the underbrush after him.

She nearly tripped over Fen. He lay curled up between the roots of a tree, his cloak only partially covering his chest as he took deep belly breaths. Of all the places to fall asleep, why here?

"Fen?" She shook his shoulder, but he didn't wake.

Something stung her neck.

She reached back and pulled a twig from her neck. One end had been carved to a point and the other had a puff of feathers, like a miniature arrow. The sharpened end gleamed wetly in the moonlight.

Warmth spread from the sting at her neck, bringing with it a heavy sleepiness. Ash slumped forward and nearly fell onto Fen. She managed to catch herself, but the sleepiness made her so heavy she couldn't sit up anymore. She couldn't even keep her eyes open.

"*Puppy?*" she whispered as darkness claimed her.

Dao Fora

Some tiny creature—an ant or a spider—crawled across Ash's face. She pictured it making its way from her chin to her brow. To the ant, her face must have been a mountain, and her eyebrows were like two stands of trees. Each footstep tickled as the ant made its long journey. She was the land, and the land felt the ant.

Ash sucked in a breath and startled awake. Her face still itched so she raised her arm to brush the insect from her brow.

The moment she moved, people spoke in fast, sharp words. She didn't understand what they said. Ash tried to get her eyes to focus on the figures standing around her, but her vision blurred. The sudden movement made her dizzy. Puppy growled, protecting her.

Ash felt her neck where the poison dart had struck her. Only a small bump, the size of a mosquito bite, remained. She blinked and tried again to get her eyes to focus. It was no longer night, but it didn't seem to be day, either. The sun must have just risen. Mist swirled along the ground beneath the trees like a living thing.

At last the dizziness passed enough for her to discern five dao fora and two mistcats surrounding her. A few of the dao fora held bows with arrows aimed at her and Puppy. Another held a long blowgun to her mouth, the end of it pointed at Ash.

All of the dao fora were dressed similar to Fen, with leather leggings and moss cloaks. What Ash could see of their bare skin had been painted with swirls, stripes, and other designs. They were taller than Fen, and muscular. Seeing them, Ash wondered how anyone could have ever thought Fen was a warrior. These dao fora looked far more threatening.

"You awake?" asked Fen. He sat beside her, smiling broadly. "I found a dao fora hunting group. If we can get them to take us prisoner, they might take us to the Sky Tree council."

"*That's* how you planned on getting us there?"

"It's how I got to see your village," replied Fen. "As long as they don't kill us, it should work."

Ash groaned. Half the time Fen did things just to see what happened.

The hunters continued talking to each other in their quick, sharp language. Ash couldn't understand a word of it, but from their gestures she gathered that they were arguing over what to do with her and Fen.

"Do you understand them?" she asked Fen.

"Only a little. Tavan refused to teach me the dao fora language. He said it wasn't good for me to know, but I did learn a few words—especially curse words, and the big one is using lots of them. Including some I've never heard before."

Ash looked at the guy Fen had indicated. He was the tallest and the angriest in the group, gesturing at them with a bone-handled knife. At first Ash thought he must be the leader. Then she noticed that he kept looking to the two dao fora in the middle.

They appeared to be twins. Both were young—sixteen or seventeen. They were the exact same height, with high cheek bones, acorn-shaped faces, and striking gray eyes. Their straight black hair was cut and arranged in the same way—shaved, except for a patch of long hair on top that had been bound in a ponytail. One appeared to be male and the other female.

"Can you ask them to take us to the Sky Tree council?"

"I'll try," said Fen. He cleared his throat and spoke loudly. "*Clay sono ta vie. Uki ay na?*"

The dao fora immediately stopped talking.

Then the tall one became even more upset. He waved his knife in front of him, glaring at Fen then Ash, as if uncertain who was the greater threat.

At last, the female twin holding the blowgun spoke to the big guy. The feathers she wore around her neck were all blue-black, and she had black stripes painted on her face and arms. Her colors were in stark contrast to her brother's. He wore mostly speckled white feathers and had red swirls painted on his face and arms. Instead of carrying a blowgun or a bow, he held hunting bolas—three leather cords with rocks tied to the ends. Ash recalled seeing a bush hunter practice with a similar weapon once. When thrown, the weighted ends made the leather cords wrap around whatever they hit.

"What did she say?" asked Ash.

"She spoke very fast," replied Fen. "Something about the tall one being a puddle of goat spit and needing to eat more fish eyes… I had trouble getting it all."

"Tell them I came here to talk with the council."

"*Asa yi nay, tuva ta vie—*" started Fen, but the female twin cut him off.

"*Mabh falsa*!" She pointed to Fen but looked at Ash. "We cannot speak to him. It's not allowed."

Ash looked to Fen. "Do they know you?"

"I don't think so."

"Then why did she call you *mabh falsa*?"

"I'm not sure. I think it means something about… death."

Ash didn't like the sound of that. "My name is Ash," she said, addressing the twin who'd spoken to her. "This is Fen and Puppy. They're my friends. We came a long way to find the Sky Tree so that I could speak with your leaders."

The dao fora spoke with each other in their language, looking and gesturing to them as if they weren't even there. Ash started to get angry. It didn't help that she was hungry too.

"It's rude to talk about us in front of us," she said. "I know you understand what I'm saying. You spoke my language perfectly."

The twin with the white feathers and red swirls looked amused by this. "Not perfectly, but enough to be rude." His voice was softer than his sister's. "Villagers like you are blind. We cannot take you to the Sky Tree."

"I'm not blind. I see fine," said Ash.

Both twins chuckled.

"Did I say something funny?"

"Not blind here," explained the male twin, pointing to his eyes. "Many who cannot see with their eyes are far from blind. Villagers are the opposite. They do not see, even when their eyes show them what is true. Because you're a child, we'll let you leave the forest. But if you return, we'll dip our arrows in the poison no one wakes from. Sava and Timo will lead you out."

The two dao fora hunters with bows gestured for Ash and Fen to get up. They kept their arrows pointed at them. The shorter one prodded Ash with his foot, urging her to walk.

Ash's cheeks burned. This wasn't how things were supposed to go. She didn't come all this way to be kicked out of the forest by a group of dao fora who were barely older than her. And she didn't like having poison arrows aimed at her, either. Every time she glanced back, Sava and Timo shook their bows menacingly.

"Puppy, want to play fetch?" she whispered.

Yes! I love fetch. All this talk is getting very boring.

"Think you can fetch the arrows they're holding?"

The pointy sticks? Can I break them? I like the way they snap!

"Sure," said Ash. "Snap them in half."

Puppy darted into the brush. The dao fora hunters paid no attention to the little dog. They probably thought he was wandering off to sniff and pee. Puppy got a running start and came at them from the side, snatching both arrows from the bows in one mighty leap.

He landed and bit down, snapping the arrows in half. Once they were broken, he held the feathered ends between his paws and eagerly ripped the feathers off. Then he looked up at the dao fora and wagged his tail.

Sava and Timo appeared stunned. Puppy had moved so fast, he'd been a blur. One of the dao fora tried to notch another arrow to the bowstring, but his hand shook so badly he couldn't.

Again? asked Puppy.

"Go for it," said Ash.

Puppy jumped and snatched the arrow from Sava's hand. He snapped it in half and sat, tail thumping.

"*Mabh falsa!*" said Timo. He scrambled back through the woods toward where the twins and the tall hunter stood.

The terrified dao fora gestured and sputtered about what had happened. The female twin finally spoke a few sharp words to him, and he grew silent.

Then the male twin approached Ash. "Who are you?"

"I told you, my name is Ash. I'm from the village of Last Hope. I came to speak with the Sky Tree council. These are my friends, Fen and Puppy."

The twins conferred with each other in harsh voices. Ash began to wonder if getting Puppy to break the arrows might have been a mistake.

Finally, the twins came to a decision.

"We'll take you where you need to go…" said the male twin.

"…if you can give us something of great value to prove that you're not completely blind," finished the female twin.

14

The First Test

"I don't have anything valuable to give them," Ash told Fen.

Fen looked at the carpetbag she carried. "There must be something in there."

"Everything in here's important to me."

"Tavan says that people are more alike than different. If something's important to you, it's probably important to others."

"Not these things. I can't give away any of these things," said Ash.

Fen cocked his head. "I think it's a test. And tests are supposed to be hard, aren't they?"

Ash sighed and slid Wayfarer off her back. She undid the buckle that held the carpetbag closed.

The dao fora edged closer to peek inside. Ash tilted the bag toward herself. Everything in Wayfarer was named, and named things were precious to her. They'd whispered their names to her for a reason.

"Hold on." She dug into her pockets. Among the lint and dirt she found two coins—a ten-piece and a fiver. It wasn't much money, but maybe the dao fora wouldn't know that. "What about this?"

Fen crinkled his nose at the coins. "How are those valuable?"

Ash wanted to explain that you could buy things with them, but they probably couldn't buy anything with them here. And they couldn't go to the village to spend the coins. She slid the coins back into her pocket and reached into Wayfarer, hoping a better answer would come to her.

Her fingers brushed Holder, her doll, and the soft yellow weave of Nester, her blanket. How many nights had those two comforted her and kept her safe? Then there was Telltale, the rope. Traveler, the pretty seed she'd found. Far and Near, the two smooth, round stones who'd sung to her when she'd first touched them. Fledgling, the feather. And Aisling, the small blue bottle her mother had thrown away. These things, along with Kiki, were all she had left to remind her of home. She couldn't give any of them away. Besides, why would the dao fora consider a rock, an old blanket, or a chipped bottle to be of great value?

There had to be something she could give the dao fora. Her boots, maybe? She'd have to walk barefoot through the forest, but she'd sooner go barefoot than give up one of her named objects. She doubted the dao fora would consider her dirty old boots to be of great value, though. They didn't even wear shoes.

The tall dao fora warrior tapped the flat side of his knife against his palm, growing impatient. The twins seemed to be running out of patience as well.

Ash sifted through the contents of Wayfarer again and *listened.* All of her objects were silent, except one. Traveler, the large seed she'd found by the west wall, whispered its name when she touched it.

"Hush," replied Ash. But the seed didn't hush.

She cupped her hand around the seed to calm it. It felt warm and smooth in her palm. When she'd found it in the grass by the wall, she'd marveled at where it had come from since all the trees in the area had been cut down. It must have traveled a long way to get where it was—that's why she'd named it Traveler. Then again, the seed might have whispered the name to her because it wanted to travel here.

Here, echoed a whisper in her head.

"Enough," said the female twin. "Your people always cling to worthless things. The blindness has you."

Ash held out her hand. "Here," she said, speaking the whisper she'd heard.

The dao fora frowned as she opened her fingers, revealing the seed in her palm. It seemed such a plain, ordinary thing. She felt foolish, offering it to them. After all, they were in a forest. Seeds were everywhere. This couldn't be the right answer.

The tall dao fora warrior plucked Traveler from her palm and studied it. Ash feared he'd toss it away. Instead, he passed the seed to the twins. They both treated it with reverence.

"Most of your people offer coins, beads, or other worthless trinkets, but this," said the male twin, "this is the seed of a *tra vae* tree—a tree of rare strength and long life. You call it ironwood. To us, seeds like this have very great value."

The twin took the seed and tucked it into a pouch tied to his waist. Ash recalled Tavan wearing a similar pouch, just like merchants kept coin pouches on them. Did dao fora use seeds as money?

The twin knelt by a patch of sunlight on the forest floor and began to dig a hole. His sister and the tall dao fora warrior helped. Once the hole was ready, they placed Traveler in it and carefully pushed dirt back over it. Ash watched, perplexed. If the seed was valuable, why bury it?

"A kept seed doesn't grow," said the twin, noticing her confusion. "It must be planted to become a tree. Truly valuable things only have value when they're given away. Come. We'll show you where you need to go if you want to see the council."

The sun blazed overhead, burning off the morning mist. The dao fora twins had dismissed their mistcats. Still, Ash had trouble keeping up with them.

Instead of walking single file through the forest, the dao fora spread out. The two with bows stayed off to the sides, barely visible, and Ipé, the female twin, jogged ahead. Every now and then Ash spotted her crouching on a rock or ledge, scowling at Ash for being so slow.

Jerrah, the male twin, seemed more patient. He stayed closer to Ash so she didn't lose sight of them. It was from listening to Caihay—the tall dao fora who kept calling out the twins' names like a nervous mother until Ipé sent him ahead—that Ash learned who they were.

I hope they have food at the Sky Tree, said Puppy. *I could eat ten eggs. Or a chicken. Do chickens taste like eggs?*

Ash paused to pet Puppy behind his ears. "I'm hungry too." She hadn't eaten anything since the night before when Tavan had given them the smoked fish. "If they're polite, they'll feed us."

Jerrah looked at her strangely.

Ash stopped talking. The dao fora already seemed suspicious of Puppy. It probably wasn't smart to talk with Puppy in front of them.

They traveled over a series of hills. Ash tried not to fall behind, but she struggled with carrying Wayfarer. The straps rubbed her shoulders raw, and her back ached.

Jerrah stopped halfway up one steep hill to wait for her. He hadn't even broken a sweat. "You carry too much," he said. "It weighs you down."

Ash scrambled up the rest of the hill to prove that she could handle it. When she reached the top, she knelt to catch her breath. Ipé was already most of the way up the next hill, and Caihay was nowhere in sight.

Jerrah kept walking. Ash sucked in a breath and hurried after him, down and up another hill. Then another.

Eventually, they entered a gully between two ridges. The trees on both sides blocked most of the sunlight, and the air in the gully hung heavy with moisture. Moss grew on all the tree trunks and much of the ground. Long swaths of gray-green moss dangled from tree branches, giving the place a gloomy appearance.

Fen stumbled on a slick rock. He stayed down, staring at the ground in front of him.

Ash hurried to his side. "Fen? You okay?"

He nodded but didn't get up. "I don't feel good. I need to rest for a bit."

"You're probably hungry."

Fen shook his head. "This place… I don't like it."

He's right. It smells sad here, said Puppy.

Ash sniffed the heavy air of the gully. All she smelled were wet leaves, rocks, and moss.

Ipé walked back to where they'd stopped. "They can stay here." She gestured to Fen and Puppy. "If you want to continue, you must come alone. Unless you're too frightened?"

Was this another test? Jerrah had been kinder to her since she'd given them the *tra vae* seed, but Ipé still didn't seem to think much of her. "I'm not frightened."

"That's because you don't know what's ahead," replied Ipé.

Timo and Sava, the two hunters with bows, stayed behind to keep watch over Fen and Puppy while Ash continued down the gully with Jerrah and Ipé.

"There." Ipé pointed to a dark vine-covered area at the base of a mossy rock wall ahead. "That's where you must go."

It took Ash a moment to realize that the dark area Ipé had indicated was the mouth of a cave. The sight of the vine-draped opening in the rocky wall made her neck prickle.

Ash hoisted Wayfarer onto her shoulders and stepped toward the cave. The opening was larger than she expected. If it was a mouth, it would be a mouth big enough to swallow a horse and cart whole.

"What is this place?"

"In your language it's called the Cave of Sorrows," said Jerrah. "But it was not always known as such."

Ash studied the mouth of the cave again. The name fit. Water trickled down the stones surrounding the cave like tears rolling down a giant's cheeks, and a low moaning sound came from deep within. It might have only been a breeze blowing across the cave opening, but it sounded sorrowful.

"We can't go in with you," said Jerrah. "If you enter, you must do so on your own."

"What's in there? Is the Sky Tree council this way?" asked Ash.

Ipé and Jerrah exchanged a look—the sort of look that passed between two people when they didn't want to answer a question. Finally, Ipé spoke.

"What you seek is in there. Know this—if you take anything from the cave, you'll never leave."

"You don't have to go in," added Jerrah. "It's not too late to turn back. Return to your dead tree walls. Go home, villager."

Home. Ash pictured her mother, sitting on the edge of her bed, telling her stories by candlelight. It was a memory of Essa from long ago, before she'd grown sick with fear. Her mother used to tell her the most wonderful stories about sorcerers, talking animals, and brave heroes on golden horses, while brushing and braiding Ash's hair. That was home.

But this memory was soon trampled by others—soldiers pointing their muskets at her, farmers calling her a traitor, and her mother cowering behind a dingy crystal cloth veil, saying nothing.

She had to stop the attacks on her village. Until she did, she couldn't go back, no matter how scared or lonely she got, because she had no home to go back to.

Ash pushed aside the vines and stepped into the cave.

The Cave of Sorrows

The cool cave air smelled of wet stones and something vaguely metallic. A faint breeze came from ahead, where all Ash could see was darkness.

She gripped Kiki and pulled Wayfarer's straps tight against her shoulders. Then she moved further into the cave, shuffling her feet across the dirt floor.

The sounds of her footsteps echoed back to her along with a hissing sound. Maybe the wind? Or her own breathing? Ash held her breath. The hissing sound didn't go away.

As her eyes adjusted to the darkness, Ash noticed long scratches in the grime that covered the cave walls and ceiling. It looked like someone had dragged sharp stones along the rocks as they walked. A few smaller passages branched off the tunnel Ash followed, but she didn't dare go down these. If she got lost in the dark, she might never find her way out.

At last, Ash noticed a pinprick of light ahead. She continued toward it. The further into the tunnel she went, the louder the hissing became. She paused.

Ssstolen... Ssstolen... Ssstolen...

"Is someone there?" she asked.

Ssstolen...

A shadow moved at the edge of her vision. Ash turned and more shadows scattered, slithering like snakes along the cave floor and walls.

Ssstolen...

Something brushed Ash's leg. She wanted to run out of the cave, but she refused to turn back.

It's just another test, she told herself. *I can't let fear control me. It's only fear. Put it in a jar on a shelf.*

"Hello?" she called. "Who are you?"

The hissing stopped. The slithering snake-like shadows stopped moving as well. Perhaps she'd only imagined things.

Ash slid her feet across the rocky floor in case there really were snakes on the ground. As long as she didn't hurt them, they wouldn't hurt her. Each sliding footstep filled the cave with a shuffling sound.

But when Ash stopped, the shuffling continued. The bit of light coming from the mouth of the cave behind her suddenly dimmed.

Ash glanced back. Something large and spikey blocked her view of the cave opening. Fear surged through Ash as she recalled the scratches on the ceiling. This was no imagined shadow.

She hurried toward the distant pinprick of light at the end of the tunnel, moving at a swift walk, then a jog, then a reckless run. The scraping and shuffling behind her kept getting closer.

Ash ran with her hands outstretched, swinging Kiki like a cane to warn her of obstacles. Even so, she tripped twice over rocks and scraped her knees.

The scraping sound grew louder—*Creesh! Creesh! Creesh!*—like a giant dragging a sack of bones through the cave.

At last, the tunnel opened into a large cavern. Sunlight poured through a hole in the domed ceiling. Ash blinked, struck by the sudden brightness. Tree roots and vines dangled through the opening above. Water dripped from some of the vines, plunking into a bright-blue pool in the center of the cavern. Light reflected off the pool and dappled the stone walls. After the slimy darkness of the tunnel, the beauty of this place stunned Ash.

She hurried around the pool, searching for a way out in case whatever had chased her through the tunnel entered the cavern. Stone pillars connected with stalactites hanging from the cavern ceiling. How many thousands of years had it taken the stones to form like this? The cavern seemed as old, or maybe even older, than the forest itself.

In the outer wall of the cavern, Ash found several alcoves with what appeared to be shrines to various figures that had been carved into the stone. Necklaces, feathers, sea shells, and other offerings decorated stone altars beneath the carvings. Ash picked up a squirrel skull from one altar and blew the dust off it. The skull hummed beneath her touch, but it didn't whisper any names to her.

She continued searching the cavern for an exit. The only passage she saw was the one she'd entered through.

Creesh! Creesh! Creesh!

The scraping sounds grew louder, causing the pool in the center of the cavern to ripple.

"You've upset the Sorrows."

Ash turned to find a woman sitting near the pool. She'd been so still that Ash hadn't noticed her before. Her woven moss cloak matched the gray stones around her, and her hood hid much of her face.

"You shouldn't have taken that." The woman nodded to the squirrel skull in Ash's hand.

"I wasn't taking it. I was only looking at it." She set the skull back on the stone altar beneath the squirrel carving.

The scraping sounds continued, filling the cavern.

"It's angry," said the woman. "I hope you brought something to feed it. If not, it will certainly eat us both."

To Feed the Sorrows

"Feed it what?" asked Ash.

All she saw in the cavern were rocks, water, and a few patches of moss, but she doubted an angry cave beast would settle for a handful of moss.

"Have you brought nothing to offer it?" asked the woman.

There wasn't any food in Wayfarer—that was one thing Ash hadn't packed. She hurried along the outer wall to check some of the shrines. Perhaps someone had left food as an offering.

One shrine had a large moth carved into the stone, but the altar beneath it was empty. Beyond this, Ash found a shrine that depicted two wolves fighting. Then one that showed a hawk, and one with a carving of a hummingbird flying above a flower. Bundles of flowers had been left beneath this carving, but the petals were old and dry, their colors long faded.

She found a shrine with a stone tortoise that had holes for eyes. And another with a carving of a monkey, its head tilted in a curious expression that reminded her of Fen.

Nowhere did she see any food. The dusty shrines looked like they hadn't been tended to in years.

"Be still! It's close," snapped the woman. She pulled the hood down over her face and huddled motionless near the edge of the pool. "Do not run."

The creature that emerged from the dark tunnel looked like a dragon made of stone. Its long, serpentine body scraped against the tunnel floor and ceiling as six stumpy legs dragged it into the cavern. Every inch of the dragon appeared to be covered in stones, but in the cracks between the stones Ash glimpsed the smoky essence of an illwen.

Stolen! hissed the dragon illwen. The whisper sounded in Ash's head, the way Puppy's voice did, only harsher and shriller. The creature paused for a moment as it searched the cavern. Its hard gaze settled on Ash.

Stolen by you!

Ash backed further into the cavern. She tried to keep pillars of rock between her and the dragon illwen.

"I didn't steal anything," she said.

I know what you are, hissed the illwen. *I've seen your kind before. You take and take and never give back.*

Ash looked to the woman for help, but the woman stayed completely still, blending into the rocks around her. The illwen paid her no mind. It prowled closer, focusing only on Ash while its long, stony tail blocked the tunnel behind it.

Ash thought of the way she'd named Puppy—how she'd changed a raging illwen into something playful and kind. Perhaps she could change this illwen as well.

She took a deep breath and *listened.* The only whispers she heard were "stolen," "take," and "gone."

"Gone Dragon," said Ash, hoping the name might make the creature leave.

The dragon struck and Ash jumped back, barely avoiding the snap of its stone teeth.

You cannot name me! snarled the illwen. It reared to strike again. *I am the Sorrows. I won't be bound by you.*

Ash backed against the cavern wall as the illwen struck again. Instinctively, she raised Kiki for protection. One end of the ironwood stick braced against the wall and the other end jabbed the dragon illwen in the snout, stopping the creature's attack.

The dragon reared and roared. A gust of wind tore through the cavern. Feathers from the nearby hawk shrine swirled into the air.

Ash scurried behind a pile of rocks and slid Wayfarer off her back. Other than the tunnel she'd entered through, which the dragon blocked, the only way out appeared to be the hole in the high cavern ceiling. Several vines and tree roots dangled through the hole. If she climbed the rock pile, she might be able to reach them and climb out.

Ash slid Kiki into Wayfarer so both her hands would be free. Fledgling, the feather, had settled on top of her other belongings in the bag. Before closing Wayfarer, she pulled the feather out and tucked it behind her ear for luck. To reach the vines overhead, she'd need all the luck she could get.

With Wayfarer on her shoulders, Ash scrambled up the rock pile. The illwen spotted her and prepared to strike. There was no time to waste. She jumped, reaching for a bundle of tree roots hanging down. It was a crazy, desperate leap from the top of the rock pile. The stone jaws of the illwen snapped closed where her feet had been, and her fingers grasped the ends of the roots.

For a moment Ash hung in the air, but the straps of Wayfarer weighed her down and the roots slipped through her fingers.

Her heart skipped as she crashed onto the cave floor, landing so hard her breath whooshed out.

The illwen moved to devour her, but something caught its attention. Fledgling, the feather, see-sawed through the air and landed on the creature's snout. The illwen's eyes crossed as it tried to look at the feather. If Ash hadn't just fallen several feet onto hard ground, she might have laughed at how ridiculous the creature looked.

Slowly, the illwen turned its head toward the shrine beneath the hawk carving. It tilted its snout so that Fledgling slid off. When the feather settled on the stone altar, the illwen made a deep, contented purr.

The Sorrows wasn't hungry for food. It was hungry for offerings to the shrines.

Ash checked the tunnel, but the illwen's tail still blocked her escape.

Not enough, grumbled the Sorrows. *Too much is gone. Too much lost. Stolen...*

What else could she give the illwen?

She reached into Wayfarer and felt Near and Far. The round stones snuggled into her palm. She'd found them on the bank of a stream months ago. They were the only clear stones among the gray river rocks. She often held them up to her eyes, as if they could show her things the way a magnifying glass or a telescope could—that's why she'd named them Near and Far.

It suddenly occurred to her where the stones might fit.

Ash hurried to the carving of the tortoise and pressed Near and Far into the empty eye holes. They trembled beneath her fingertips as she set them in place. The stones weren't a perfect fit, but they seemed to want to be there and they made the tortoise carving appear more complete.

The Sorrows lumbered closer, its stone belly scraping the floor. Ash shuffled back to keep her distance from the illwen as it studied the tortoise carving.

The dragon's expression became surprisingly tender. Then the memory of whatever it had lost consumed it with sadness again.

Still gone, mourned the illwen. *Still lost... They stole the Heart of the Forest, and then they stole my children, leaving only sorrows. I am the Sorrows.*

Ash couldn't help feeling sorry for the illwen. She knew how painful losing something you cared about could be, but to lose your children? Such a loss seemed too much to bear. "Maybe I can help you find what you lost," offered Ash.

Liar! hissed the illwen. *Namers do not help others. Namers only want control. I let a namer help me once, and now everything is gone. Lost. Stolen!*

The illwen snapped at her. Ash scrambled back and reached into Wayfarer for something else to give the illwen.

What she grabbed made her throat clench and heart stutter, but the object didn't protest. Like Fledgling, Near, and Far, it seemed to want to be here. Only this time, Ash couldn't imagine letting it go.

The Sorrows coiled, preparing to strike.

Ash pulled out what she'd grabbed. "Would you like to hold her?" she asked. "That's what I do when I'm sad."

Her hands trembled as she lifted the doll. “Her name’s Holder because sometimes she holds me, and sometimes I hold her.” The doll was the first thing she’d ever named. She didn’t care if people thought she was too old for a doll, or that people teased her for talking to Holder. Holder was what she’d always turned to when she felt most alone. She’d spent so much time with the doll that it seemed part of her now.

The Sorrows stretched its dragon snout to sniff Holder. This time Ash didn’t back away. If Holder wasn’t afraid, she wouldn’t be either.

A stone scale fell from the dragon’s snout. Then another and another stone fell, until a cascade of rocks dropped from the illwen’s smoky form. So many rocks fell at once, they filled the cavern with a thunderous rumble. The illwen’s dark, swirling essence transformed before Ash’s eyes into the wispy shape of a woman.

Ash’s breath caught. The woman was a giant—more than twice the size of her own mother—but she looked kind. She reached for Holder with open arms.

Ash told herself it would only be for a minute. Biting her lip, she let the illwen take the doll.

The Sorrows cradled Holder, looking down at her the way mothers were supposed to look at their babies. The way Ash’s mother had looked at her once. A powerful ache welled up in Ash. She wished she were back in her village with her mother and father.

The Sorrows carried Holder to a shrine at the far end of the cavern.

Ash followed.

This was the largest shrine in the cavern. A carving of a dragon holding its spiked tail in its mouth encircled the stone altar. It was the image of a fierce protector guarding something precious, but the altar in the center stood empty. Whatever the dragon had once guarded was gone.

The illwen gently set Holder on the shrine. The stone altar wasn't flat like the others. Instead, it curved like a bowl or a bassinet. For several seconds the illwen stared at Holder, humming softly. Caring for the doll seemed to remind the Sorrows of what it had once had, and what it had once been.

Love. That was the other side of sorrow.

The illwen gazed lovingly at the doll lying on the stone altar. Gradually, its smoky gray body faded back into the shadows of the cavern.

Once the illwen had gone, Ash edged closer to the shrine. She reached for Holder. The loneliness that was always there, tucked deep inside her, seemed larger and more painful now. She desperately wanted to hold the doll and pretend that she was home.

"If you touch her, the Sorrows will return."

Ash startled.

The woman in the moss cloak stood a few feet behind her. Her hood was pushed back, revealing the shaved head and ponytail hairstyle of the dao fora. Except where Ipé and Jerrah each had one ponytail, this woman had four, arranged in a row from her forehead to the back of her neck. Wrinkles radiated from her eyes and lined her forehead, giving her a weathered look.

"The Sorrows will watch over her. Have no fear of that. But you must leave her behind."

Ash gazed longingly at the doll. How could she leave Holder? Her hand stretched toward the shrine. She heard no whispers from Holder now. The doll seemed content where it lay. Still, Ash's chest ached.

She missed her parents and her home. She missed her room and her bed, and the barn with her chickens. She missed sweeping the store porch and seeing the familiar faces of people she knew crossing the village square. She missed how things used to be.

Ash stepped back from the shrine.

"Hurry," said the woman. "The Sorrows won't be appeased for long."

The woman took two steps toward the center of the cavern and faltered, her legs giving out beneath her. She slumped against a stone pillar.

"Are you all right?" asked Ash.

"I'm thirsty," said the woman. "I've been waiting a long time. Will you bring me water?"

Ash hurried to the pool. She wondered why the woman hadn't taken a drink when she'd been sitting by the pool, but perhaps she couldn't with the Sorrows around.

She slid Wayfarer off her shoulders and dug through the now almost empty bag for Aisling, her small glass bottle. Usually, she kept Aisling wrapped in Nester for protection. Now that the bag was nearly empty, the bottle had jumbled loose. Other than Nester, the blanket, and Aisling, the bottle, the only named object she had left in the bag was Telltale, the rope.

Aisling's blue glass shimmered in a shaft of sunlight when Ash took it out. Her mother loved pretty bottles. Aisling had been part of Essa's collection until one day it fell and got chipped, so her mother threw it away. Ash rescued Aisling from the garbage when her mother wasn't looking. The name meant "dream" in the language her mother had grown up with. It was one of the few words from her mother's homeland that Ash knew.

She dipped the bottle into the clear water of the pool, filled it, and pressed the cork into the chipped top. The bottle wasn't large, so she didn't want to risk spilling the little it held on her way back to the woman.

Ash handed the bottle to her. "Here. Drink."

The woman examined Aisling in the light. Then, with startling speed, she tucked the bottle into a pouch at her waist and climbed the stone pile. When she reached the top, she leapt and grabbed a bundle of roots dangling from the hole in the cavern ceiling.

"Hey! That's mine!" yelled Ash. After everything she'd lost, she couldn't lose Aisling too.

The woman kept climbing. She didn't seem old or weary now.

Ash hurried up the stone pile after her. She crouched and jumped, reaching for the same tree roots she'd tried to climb before. Maybe it was because Wayfarer was lighter now, or maybe it was her desperation to get Aisling back, but this time she managed to hold on.

She climbed like the woman had done, grabbing more roots and vines. Ash searched the gap in the cavern ceiling above, but the woman had already clambered over the top edge.

Stolen! hissed an all-too-familiar whisper.

A breeze stirred the cavern, sending shivers up Ash's spine.

17

A Sip of Memory

Wind filled the cavern with a mournful howl. It was the same sound Ash had heard when she'd first entered the cave. She continued climbing, desperate to make it out before the Sorrows caught her.

At last, she reached the top and hoisted herself onto the ground above. The dao fora woman who'd taken Aisling sat beneath an enormous tree, calmly watching her.

"You stole my bottle," said Ash.

"And you should thank me for that." The woman held up Aisling. "The Sorrows would have never let you leave with this."

Ash glanced back at the hole to the cave, worried that the illwen might follow her out. All seemed peaceful in the forest around her. She couldn't even hear the moan of the wind anymore.

"Here, villager." The woman handed the bottle to her.

"I thought you were thirsty."

"I am, but that's water from the Pool of Memory. It's for a very different kind of thirst. If you want to know why illwen keep attacking your village, take one sip and you'll remember what caused all this. Take two sips, and you'll forget."

Ash studied the woman. "Who are you? How did you know I came here to stop the illwen attacks?"

"My daughter told me you were coming. She sent a messenger to find me."

"Your daughter?"

"I believe you've met her, and my son. They're twins—similar in appearance, yet as different as fire from water."

"Ipé and Jerrah," said Ash.

The woman nodded.

Ash recalled how Ipé had sent Caihay, the tall dao fora warrior, ahead. He must have been the messenger the woman referred to.

"I've been waiting a long time for one like you to arrive," said the woman.

"One like me?"

"An *Ainm Dhilis*—a namer of spirits. Few have such an ability. Years ago, when I drank from the Pool of Memory, I remembered that a namer would come here again, but I did not remember you being so young."

Ash furrowed her brow. "That makes no sense. If you saw it years ago it would be the future. How could you *remember* the future?"

"The same way you remember the past. There's little difference. Drink and you'll see."

Ash uncorked Aisling. The liquid in the little blue bottle looked ordinary enough. It smelled like ordinary water too. She tipped the bottle against her lips and took a sip.

The water tasted crisp and clean as it trickled down her throat. She leaned back, but instead of coming to rest against the tree, Ash fell through the leaf-covered earth down toward the clear pool below.

She found herself in the cavern again, only it looked different than before. Fewer stones cluttered the floor. Less of the domed ceiling had crumbled, and less sunlight filtered in. Even so, the cavern appeared bright and colorful. Yellow, blue, red, and purple light flickered across the stone walls.

The light came from several swift figures. They were hard to see because they kept swooping around the cavern like playful breezes given form. Their shapes constantly shifted, resembling a hawk, coati, or fox one moment, and colorful wisps of smoke the next.

Illwen! These were illwen before they became angry and dark!

Ash knew this the way she knew things in a dream—without words or explanations. Before it became the Cave of Sorrows, it was the Cave of Illwen.

The shrines all looked different, too. Each one overflowed with offerings. Flowers on the stone altars appeared fresh and bright, and woven bracelets, necklaces, gems, crystals, bones, carvings, and other offerings crowded the shrines, honoring the illwen.

Every now and then, one of the swift wisps of color would pass through an offering. When they did, the object would sparkle and hum like a finely made bell. Even after the illwen continued on, a faint glow lingered in the object, fading but not disappearing. Illwen left behind traces of their energy in everything they touched. Sometimes dao fora entered the cavern and left new offerings to show their respect for the spirits of the forest. Then the illwen would dart about excitedly.

One object in the cavern stood out to Ash—a shiny silver sphere sitting on the altar surrounded by the dragon carving. Illwen passed through the sphere, filling it with their energy until it glowed with all of their colors.

The Heart of the Forest, thought Ash, recalling what the Sorrows had said was stolen. It was the most beautiful object she'd ever seen.

For a long time, Ash watched the illwen swoop and dart about the cavern. One was quick and playful. Another slow and graceful. One seemed a trickster, chasing its siblings. Another drifted like a cloud. To see them all together in the cavern was like seeing a living rainbow.

Then the vision changed. Several men entered the cavern, carrying lanterns. They weren't dressed like dao fora. Instead, they appeared to be villagers. The illwen hid from these newcomers. Orange lantern light flickered across the cavern walls as the men took necklaces, gems, crystals, carvings, and other offerings from the shrines and stuffed them into burlap sacks.

At first, the illwen simply watched, confused, but the more the thieves took, the more agitated the illwen became. A few illwen took on fierce forms, becoming snakes and wolves. They tried to scare the thieves away. Some of the men cowered, but others threw rocks at the illwen.

In the chaos, the thieves stole the Heart of the Forest.

A howl filled the cavern when the illwen noticed the empty shrine, and an enormous red dragon appeared. Its tail thrashed the walls, causing parts of the cavern to crumble. One thief, struck by falling rocks, dropped his lantern. Kerosene spilled across the cavern floor and whooshed into flames. The illwen retreated from the fire, and the thieves made their escape.

Ash wondered if the theft of the silver Heart of the Forest was what had upset the Sorrows, but the vision didn't stop there. She saw the cave again, sometime later, except now she saw it from outside, near the base of the ridge where Ipé had told her to enter.

A man approached. He didn't look like any of the thieves. He was tall, almost regal, with a white shirt and a tall black hat of the style wealthy gentlemen from Governor City wore. On his back he carried a large leather pack.

A giant woman blocked the entrance into the cave. She stood nearly twice as tall as the man and glowed with reddish light. Ash recognized her as the Sorrows, yet she wasn't known as the Sorrows then. She was the cave's Guardian.

"I've come to return what was stolen," said the man.

The Guardian crossed her arms, refusing to let him pass.

"It's all here." The man turned, showing the Guardian the pack he carried. He shook it to jangle the contents. "Everything the thieves took, including the Heart of the Forest."

The Guardian looked surprised, then skeptical. She reached toward the pack. Through the gap in the top, she must have glimpsed some of the stolen items, because her expression softened. She led the man into the cave.

He followed her through the darkness into the cavern with the pool. Once there, he slung the leather pack onto the ground and undid the straps that held it shut.

Several illwen came out of their hiding places to see what he'd brought. Their light filled the cavern once again, but their shapes were wispy and uncertain. Two of the bravest took on the forms of giant wolves. They edged closer and sniffed the bag as the man reached in and fumbled around.

The man pulled out two sacred objects—a crystal and a carved bone. The wolves edged closer, eager to see what else he had.

Next, the man withdrew a length of silver chain. It was the same shiny silver color that The Heart of the Forest had been.

One of the wolves sniffed the chain. The man quickly looped the end around the wolf's neck and snapped the links closed with a silver lock.

Panic filled the illwen's eyes. It tried to change shape and slip free of the chain, but it couldn't. The chain collar kept it bound in the form of a wolf.

The other wolf-shaped illwen attempted to bite the chain off its brother. While it tugged at the links, the man locked a second length of silver chain around this illwen's neck.

Both illwen clawed at their chain collars, but they wouldn't come off.

"The chain is named Unbreakable," said the man. "It was forged from the Heart of the Forest that my thieves took from here. I melted it down and made four lengths of this chain from it. Because it contains your power, it cannot be broken by you—not by any of you."

The man reached into his bag and pulled out another length of silver chain. The remaining illwen backed away, terrified. All retreated except one.

The woman who'd blocked the man's entrance into the cave began to shift, becoming an enormous red dragon again, larger even than the stone-scaled dragon Ash had faced.

"Go!" commanded the dragon to the remaining illwen. "Do not return here. Do not let him catch you."

Some of the illwen burst through the hole in the ceiling, breaking off rocks and dirt as they fled. Others fled through the cave entrance. The two wolves that the man had bound stayed on the ground, clawing at their chain collars.

Once her children had gone, the dragon drew in a mighty breath and unleashed a stream of fire at the man.

But the man was ready. He held out a length of the silver chain before him like a shield. Instead of melting, the links absorbed the dragon fire until they glowed red and hummed with energy, just as the Heart of the Forest had done when illwen passed through it.

Gradually, the red-hot glow spread to the links the man held. His skin sizzled and his face contorted in pain.

Seeing this, the dragon blew more fire at the man. She raged and blew until her breath ran out, but the man didn't let go of the chain.

"At last," he snarled as the dragon gasped for breath. "Now I have everything I need to command those I've bound."

The man wrapped the glowing chain around his head. His hair and skin burned from the red-hot links, but he didn't let go. He held the ends together on his brow. "*Srianadh!*" he said.

Instantly, the chain became a cool, silver crown around the man's head.

A grin twisted his mouth. "I name you *Anobaith*," he said to the first wolf he'd bound. His words resonated with fiery power.

The illwen stopped clawing its chain collar and came to his side.

The man turned to the other wolf. "You are now *Eagla*."

The giant wolves stood on each side of the man, hackles raised and teeth bared as they growled. But they weren't growling at him anymore. They growled at the dragon.

The Guardian retreated, stunned that her own children would turn against her.

While the dragon illwen was forced back by the wolves, the man pulled one more length of silver chain from his bag. Only one untouched illwen remained in the cavern. Shaped like a giant cocoon, it rested on a stone altar with a moth carved above it.

A peculiar white glow came from something within the cocoon, while the outer silk glistened and shimmered like crystal cloth. Although the cocoon appeared to be alive, it didn't change shape or leave as the other illwen had done. Perhaps it couldn't. It seemed caught in a state of transformation—not yet one thing or another.

The man's burnt hands trembled as he locked the last length of chain around the cocoon.

"You are the most important one," he said to the cocoon. Then he lifted it up and whispered a name to it that Ash couldn't hear. In his arms, the cocoon looked like a baby swaddled in crystal cloth, with no head or face.

The man placed the chained cocoon in his pack and called the wolves to him. They came instantly, following his every command.

The dragon cowered in the back of the cavern. Her reddish glow had completely gone out. She was a shadowy, mournful creature now.

The Sorrows, thought Ash, realizing that this must be what had caused the Sorrows to become so sad—her own children had been chained and forced to fight against her.

With that thought, Ash's vision shifted once more. She shot over the forest like an arrow toward her village, only her village appeared different. Several buildings around the square had been destroyed by fire. The ground, trees, and bushes looked burned, too.

Ash wondered if she was seeing the remains of some fire from long ago, but parts of the wall around the village stood. The wall had been built in her lifetime, so it couldn't be the past, could it?

Fire blackened most of the wall. In other places, whole sections had burned down. The forest and webworm plantations around her village appeared burnt as well. Not a single green leaf remained on a tree. Not a blade of grass stood unscorched. Ash saw a woman, covered in soot, kneeling on the front porch of her parents' store.

It was her mother, crying into her hands.

Ash wanted to reach out to her, but the view of her village became hazy and distant. She snapped back into her body and awoke.

The leaves on the tree branches overhead glowed green—a thousand shades of green, illuminated by the sun beyond them. Her eyes watered at the sight of the lush, living leaves. She thought of the blackened branches she'd seen in her vision and wept.

Sky Vines

"Do you remember now?" asked the dao fora woman.

Ash blinked to clear her eyes. The sip of water she'd taken from the Pool of Memory had filled her with an awareness that went beyond words. The more she recalled what she'd seen, the more questions she had.

"The man who chained the illwen, who was he?"

"He was a namer, like you. My people call him the Shadow Namer because he brings out the darkness in things. He's the one causing the illwen to attack your village. If you want to stop the illwen attacks, you must find him and free the illwen he enslaved."

"Where is he?"

"That's something I was hoping you would know."

Ash stared at her. "Me? I'm just a kid. I don't know anything about this."

"I believe you know a great deal about this," replied the woman. "After all, you have a great deal in common with him."

Ash drew back, horrified that the dao fora woman thought she was at all like the man in her vision.

"Years ago, the cloud forest changed," continued the woman. "The rains came later and left sooner. As the season of drought grew longer, trees died and mistcats died with them. The land became sick. I went to the Cave of Illwen to drink from the Pool of Memory so that I might discover how to make the forest well again. But when I reached the cave, the Guardian had grown angry. She tried to stop me from entering. I had to be brave and clever like you. Even so, I didn't get away unharmed." The woman pushed back her moss cloak, revealing long, jagged scars on her arm that stretched from her shoulder down to her wrist. It looked as if her arm had been torn open by the dragon's teeth. "One must give up a great deal to drink from the Pool of Memory."

She replaced her cloak and sat back against the tree. "I escaped with a small gourd of water, and I took one sip beneath this tree—just as you've done. In my vision, I saw what the Shadow Namer had done and I knew why the forest had become sick. You see, he not only stole the Heart of the Forest and used it to bind three illwen—three elemental spirits of the land. He also turned the illwen he bound against the forest. Since then, all the illwen have become lost, angry spirits, and the forest has withered."

The dao fora woman gestured to several brown treetops in the distance. "As long as any illwen are enslaved, the drought will get worse and the forest will die. Because a namer bound the illwen, only another namer can free them and restore balance to the land."

"And you think that other namer is me?" asked Ash, incredulous. The idea of facing the Shadow Namer she'd seen in her vision—with his chain crown and two giant wolves at his command—seemed absurd to her. She wasn't a hero from a fairytale. How could she face someone so powerful?

The woman gave Ash a long look. She seemed to be thinking the same thing—there was no way this child could save them. Then she shrugged. "Perhaps you're the *va-tay*."

"Va-tay?" asked Ash.

"It means last hope. That's the name of your village, isn't it? Last Hope. It seems fitting that you're from there since that is what you might be for us."

"I didn't come here to face the Shadow Namer and free the illwen," said Ash. "I came to help my village. In my vision I saw it… everything had burned."

"Not all visions are of the past. Some are of things to come. The destruction you saw might still be prevented."

"Then I have to warn them." Ash stood. She couldn't remember seeing her father in her vision. Was he okay? Was that why her mother was crying on the porch?

"And what will you tell them?" asked the dao fora woman.

"I'll tell them what I saw. With the drought making everything so dry, one of the squatter's fires might get out of control and destroy the village. I'll tell them to stop burning the cloud forest before it's too late."

"Will they listen to you?"

Burn or starve, thought Ash. Squatters wouldn't stop cutting and burning the forest just because some girl told them about a vision she'd had. Everyone in the village would think she was crazy as well as a traitor. No one would listen to her. They'd probably arrest her the moment they saw her.

"I want them to stop burning the forest too," said the woman. "But if your people haven't stopped before, why would they stop now? The Shadow Namer has blinded your people. They don't see that burning the forest also harms them. They don't see that without trees the rain won't come, and without rain nothing will grow. Soon the streams will stop flowing. Then where will they be? Even a child can see how foolish burning the cloud forest is, but the Shadow Namer keeps your people blind to what they do. Only when his control over the land is broken will they see how destroying the forest destroys them as well. That's why you must find him and free the illwen he took."

Ash clenched her jaw. This wasn't her plan. All she wanted was to be able to go home. "Aren't there other namers? Ones who actually know what they're doing? Can't you get one of them to free the illwen?"

"I've tried, but namers are rare. You're the first one to come here since I drank from the Pool of Memory." The dao fora woman sighed. "Perhaps being so young is an advantage. One can have many names. I believe you don't know all your names yet. Far from it. You may be more than you think."

Ash looked down. If the dao fora woman knew how people in her village saw her, she wouldn't think so highly of her.

"You must be tired," said the woman. "Come with me and I'll give you food and a place to rest. Then my hunters will take you wherever you decide to go."

"Your hunters?" It occurred to Ash who she must be talking to. "Are you the leader of the dao fora?"

"Sometimes I am. Sometimes I'm not. A leader is only such when others choose to follow her. You may call me Suma." The woman stood and nodded for Ash to follow her. "This way. The Sky Tree isn't far from here."

There was still a sip or two from the Pool of Memory left in Aisling. It seemed wrong to dump it out, so Ash pressed the cork back into the bottle and tucked it into Wayfarer.

Suma led her down the far side of the ridge into a cool, shady part of the forest. Barely any sunlight filtered through the branches overhead. When Ash looked up, all she saw were tree limbs draped in moss, interlacing like fingers holding up swaths of green. Few plants grew on the forest floor. There were just fallen leaves, mud, and the occasional fern. It made walking easier, since they didn't have to avoid bushes or brambles, but Ash found the darkness depressing. When a breeze rustled the branches above, sprinkles of water rained down. Why would anyone live in such a dark, muddy place?

Ipé, Jerrah, and Caihay joined them as they traveled through the dark forest. Ash wondered about Fen and Puppy. She asked Jerrah where they were.

"Timo and Sava are watching over them. They'll not be harmed," he replied. Then he pointed to a large tree near the top of the hill. "We're here."

Ash looked around. All she saw was a broad tree trunk with silvery bark. "*This* is where your people live?"

Jerrah grinned and led Ash to the other side of the tree where Suma stood, holding a thick vine rope. She pulled the rope to test it.

"It's easiest to get there by mistcat," said Suma. "Unfortunately, there's not enough mist for them to form right now, so we must go another way." She handed Ash the vine rope.

"Am I supposed to climb this?" asked Ash. The rope appeared to be slung over a high tree branch. It would be a long climb, and Ash couldn't see anything other than branches and leaves above.

"Hold tight," said Suma.

Ash gripped the rope and Suma made a high-pitched, trilling call.

The rope shot upward, pulling Ash with it. Her stomach dropped as she soared into the air. Three large gourds, full of water, were attached to the other end of the rope. As they fell, they hoisted her up. Soon Ash dangled forty feet in the air.

A dao fora woman reached for her with a hooked stick and helped her onto the nearby tree limb. Ash hugged the tree trunk to steady herself while the woman gave her an amused look. After a few minutes, the gourds reappeared, only now they were empty. Someone below must have dumped the water out and pulled the other end of the rope to send the gourds back up.

The dao fora woman filled the gourds with water from a hollow vine. When Suma called to her from below, she pushed the gourds, now heavy with water, off the tree limb.

In a matter of seconds, Jerrah was hoisted onto the limb beside Ash. He grinned at her astonished expression.

"Is this where you live?" asked Ash again. She didn't see any other dao fora around, besides the gourd woman.

"Not exactly." Jerrah grabbed another vine rope and passed it to Ash. "Don't let go."

He made a different trilling call and the rope Ash held shot upward.

Her breath caught as she was pulled even higher into the tree. Once again, three gourds full of water raced past her, going the opposite direction. This time, the gourds must have been too heavy because when the rope stopped, she was tossed into the air.

Hands caught her and helped her onto a tree limb.

Ash's body trembled. She couldn't even see the ground below. She gripped the tree to keep from falling.

"Are you still breathing?" asked Jerrah, arriving a couple minutes later. "Look out, not down. Only birds look down."

Ash kept her chin raised so she couldn't look down. What she saw when she looked out took her breath away for entirely different reasons.

Ghostly, half-formed mistcats lounged in the branches around her like tufts of jaguar-shaped clouds resting in the trees. Beyond them swayed woven hammocks and leaf-covered shelters. Purple and white flowers dappled the moss on the top side of the tree limbs, and hummingbirds fluttered around the flowers, collecting nectar. The more Ash looked, the more life she spotted—lizards, frogs, birds, squirrels, monkeys—all living up here like a whole other forest growing on top of the forest she knew.

"This is where you live?"

"This is where we sleep," replied Jerrah. "Where we live is up there." He pointed to the highest branches above them.

Ash swallowed. She couldn't imagine going higher. Jerrah passed her another vine rope, but she refused to let go of the tree trunk. "Isn't this far enough?"

"Not if you want to see the Sky Tree," replied Jerrah. He made a trilling call, and the rope pulled him upward.

The vine and gourd pully system lifted Ipé, Caihay, and Suma to the limb that Ash clung to. Ipé rolled her eyes at Ash and continued on, but Ash still couldn't get herself to let go of the tree trunk. She was already so high up, she could feel the tree sway.

"You're almost there," said Suma. "You can do this."

It was her soothing voice that finally convinced Ash to let go of the tree trunk and grab the vine rope with both hands.

19

The Sky Tree

Sunlight stung her eyes and warmed her cheeks. Ash had to blink several times to see. Fortunately, she didn't let go of the rope.

"*Ya'teh*," said a man. "*Ya'teh. Ya'teh*!"

"He wants you to step off," explained Jerrah.

Ash looked at the ground Jerrah stood on. It appeared green and spongy, like a patch of newly sprouted grass. How could there be grass high up in a tree?

"*Ya'teh*." The man tried to help her.

Ash tentatively stepped onto the green ground. It seemed solid enough, until she noticed gaps that she could see through. Her legs shook. What she stood on wasn't solid at all. She had to find a branch, or tree trunk, or something to hold onto.

She crawled to a nearby branch, her fingers sinking into the green mat. It wasn't grass, floating in the air. It was moss—similar to the moss the dao fora wove into cloaks.

Swaths of moss stretched from tree to tree in layers. Everywhere Ash looked, people were standing, sitting, and walking across it. There was even a group of dao fora children playing a ball game on two strips of moss stretched between neighboring trees.

"*This* is where we live," said Jerrah.

Suma and Caihay arrived a moment later, but Ash could barely take her eyes off the incredible sights around her.

Clouds drifted through some of the treetops, leaving behind glistening sprinkles of moisture in the moss mats. When a breeze rippled the moss, water drops rained down on the land below. In other areas, broad leaves had been arranged to funnel water drops into gourds for storage. The whole system seemed designed, both naturally and by the dao fora, to collect water from the sky.

"The food is almost ready," said Suma. She led Ash toward the edge of the moss mat they stood on. The dao fora climbed deftly up the moss, but when Ash tried to follow, her boots couldn't grip the wet moss. After sliding back several times, she took off her boots and put them in Wayfarer. Bare feet worked better for climbing moss mats.

When she reached the edge, she stood on the branch next to Ipé and Jerrah, pleased to have made it this far.

Suma handed Ash the end of a vine. She took it, but she wasn't sure what she was supposed to do with it. There didn't seem to be any levels above this one.

Ipé sighed, impatient, and snatched the vine from Ash. "Do this."

She jumped off the edge, swung over the gap between trees, and let go at the high point of her swing. Ipé landed gracefully on a moss mat in the neighboring tree. She looked back at Ash and smirked.

Suma caught the vine and handed it to Ash.

Ash made sure that Wayfarer and Kiki were secure on her back before taking the vine. She refused to let Ipé think that she was too scared to follow. Swallowing her fear, she gripped the vine and stepped off the edge.

In her mind, Ash pictured herself letting go and soaring through the air as Ipé had done, but she let go at the wrong time. Instead of landing where Ipé had, she plummeted into the gap between trees.

She yelled and reached for something to hold onto, but her fingers found only air. Her stomach lodged in her throat, taking her breath away as she fell. Ash closed her eyes, certain she'd plummet to her death.

Something soft and springy caught her.

Opening her eyes, she discovered that she'd landed on a moss net stretched between branches several feet beneath the one she'd left.

Suma swung down beside her. "We call that a sky birth. When you fall and a tree catches you, it's because the forest wants you here." She offered Ash her hand. "Now you can eat with us."

Ash took a shaky breath. It felt like her soul had left her body and was only now creeping back.

They crossed another gap to a large central tree. Ipé brought Ash a steaming bowl of green soup. It took her several minutes to calm down enough to even think of eating. When she did, she was surprised by how delicious the soup tasted. Meaty slices of orange mushrooms flavored the green broth.

"This is… good," said Ash.

"Anything tastes good when you're hungry," replied Suma.

"But this is really good."

Suma chuckled. "That's *tun'ka.* We usually dip this in it." Suma gave her a piece of brown bread with several black figs in it that tasted sweet and nutty. When Ash dipped the bread in the *tun'ka*, the sweet and salty flavors complemented each other.

Ash wondered how they cooked things like bread and soup in a tree. She didn't see stoves or cook fires anywhere. Still, the soup was steaming hot.

On a moss mat a few branches over Ash spotted a short, elderly man stirring a clay pot. There weren't any flames beneath the pot. Instead, sticks held what looked like a clear disc over the top of the pot. Sunlight poured through the crystal disk, heating up the soup. A few other sun disks heated rolls wrapped in leaves, and nuts arranged on a stone.

"These are my favorite." Suma handed Ash a leaf bowl with several red fruits in it.

"Ruby fruits," said Ash, recognizing the heart-shaped delicacies.

"We call them *isna.* You eat them?"

"Not usually," said Ash. Ruby fruits were rare and expensive. Her father had gotten a dozen delivered to the store once, but Mrs. Wombley bought them all. Luckily, her dad had kept one fruit that had gotten bruised on the delivery wagon. After dinner that night, he cut it into pieces so they could each try a little. It was the most tangy, delicious thing she'd ever tasted.

Ash selected one of the red fruits and took a tiny bite. The tangy-sweet fruit tasted even better than she remembered. She wanted to grab another one but didn't want to seem greedy. She passed the bowl back to Suma.

"Don't you like them?" asked Suma.

"They're amazing."

"Then eat. Those are for you."

Ash's eyes widened. There were more ruby fruits in the bowl than her dad had sold to Mrs. Wombley for the price of a pig.

Suma gave her other foods after that. Tender green spirals that she called tree stars, a yellow, spongy fruit that tasted like cheesecake, small red bananas that were better than any bananas she'd had before, and dark, chewy berries that were so sour they made her squint.

"Where'd you get all this?" asked Ash. She didn't know where her dad had gotten the ruby fruits, but she knew they were hard to get, as were the black figs in the bread. And she'd never seen most of the other fruits, nuts, and vegetables before.

Suma looked confused by her question.

"Do you trade for them?" asked Ash.

Ipé, who was sitting close enough to overhear, started to laugh.

"*A'ta!*" Suma scolded Ipé. Then she turned back to Ash. "It's all here." She pulled down a branch, showing Ash little green heart-shaped fruits. Some of the more ripened ruby fruits had a rosy hue to them.

"*Tun'ka,*" said Jerrah, touching a clump of hanging moss.

"Tree star," said Ipé, plucking off the small, unfurled tip of a fern that had been growing on the topside of a tree limb.

Jerrah pointed to other trees and plants. "Black vine figs. Sun fruit. Bee flower. Red bananas. Sour berries."

Everything they'd eaten grew in the trees around them. Ash couldn't believe she hadn't noticed. Maybe villagers really were blind.

Jerrah and Ipé kept pointing out edible leaves, nuts, flowers, and mushrooms. As they named things, Ash's understanding of the cloud forest changed. It wasn't simply a bunch of trees. It was a farm, and the dao fora were farmers. Only, their farms existed on many levels in the trees.

This must be what Fen was talking about when he said I needed to see the Sky Tree, thought Ash. If she hadn't seen it herself, she wouldn't have believed it. More food grew in one tree than squatters grew in fields several times this size.

Eventually, Jerrah and Ipé led Ash to a moss hammock on the middle level where she could rest. She felt guilty for sleeping when so many things were still amiss, but after all that she'd done and all that she'd eaten, she couldn't keep her eyes open.

As she drifted off, an idea took root in her mind. It was a spindly, wandering idea at first, like a bean sprout with wispy tendrils searching for sunlight, but the more her idea grew, the more hopeful she became. Even if she couldn't stop the illwen attacks, there might be another way to help her village and prove that she wasn't a traitor.

Seeds

The next morning, after eating a delicious breakfast of black fig bread and ruby fruits, Ash shared her idea with Suma. "You want people to stop burning the cloud forest, right?"

"That's something all my people want," said Suma.

"And if the villagers stopped burning the forest, would the dao fora stop attacking them?"

"We're only defending the trees that bring us life," said Suma. "If your people keep destroying the cloud forest, all will perish."

"I know," said Ash. "But the reason they're cutting down and burning the forest is to farm."

"The reason makes no difference. Without the forest, there'll be no water. Nothing will grow. All will perish."

Ash took a deep breath, eager to get Suma to see the idea that had blossomed in her head. "Suma, what if they farmed food like this?" She held up a ruby fruit.

"*Isna* needs shade and mist to grow. It only grows in the cloud forest with its brothers and sisters. It can't be planted in a burnt field like your people do."

"Exactly!" said Ash. "If the villagers knew how to grow food in the trees like you do, then they wouldn't need to cut down the cloud forest. They'd want the forest to be here."

Suma sat back on her heals. "It's a nice vision, but it won't work. The Shadow Namer has blinded your people. They don't see what's important anymore. They only know fear and greed. That's why they build walls and raise fields of webworms while people starve."

"But they'd like this." Ash gestured to the ruby fruit. "They'd like *tun'ka*, black figs, tree stars, and other things you grow, too. You could teach them how to grow all of this."

"Why would they listen to one of the dao fora? They see us as their enemy."

"We could work out a peace treaty," said Ash. "People want the fighting to stop. This is how we could make that happen. If you give them seeds and teach them to grow food like this, they'll stop cutting down the cloud forest and everyone will be happy."

Suma sighed. "You need to face the Shadow Namer and free the illwen he enslaved. That's your task—not teaching farmers how to grow food."

"I saw my village burning," said Ash. Images of the charred and smoking buildings from her vision haunted her. Several times in the night she'd woken from bad dreams, itching to go home and warn people, but she knew she couldn't, not without a way to get them to listen. Now she had a plan. "Wouldn't you do anything to save your home? I have to save mine."

Suma pursed her lips. She appeared to be considering Ash's plan. "Wait here," she said. Then she stood and swung to the tallest tree in the middle.

Ash watched Suma climb beyond her sight. Ipé sat on a nearby limb fletching an arrow, while Jerrah braided vines together into a rope. Neither of the twins said anything to Ash, but after a few minutes, Jerrah passed her some vines to braid. For almost an hour, Ash wove strands of vine together. She tried to match Jerrah's pattern, but the rope she made was sloppy and rough compared to his. Perhaps it was childish to think that she could ever get the fighting to stop.

"Yi!" called Suma when she returned. "Get up, before the mist burns away." She passed leather pouches to Jerrah and Ipé and gave them instructions in the dao fora language.

Suma gave Ash a third pouch. It had black fig bread and sun fruit in it, along with several ruby fruits. "Go swiftly," she said. "Speak with your elders. At high sun on the third day, I'll meet you and your leaders outside your village to discuss terms for peace. If your people agree to stop destroying the cloud forest, we'll give them seeds and teach them to grow food in the trees near the village. Is this as you want it?"

"Thank you! I won't let you down," said Ash.

"*You* might not, but can you say the same for your people?" Suma looked troubled. "I'm doing this because I believe you are someone who could free the illwen from the Shadow Namer. That is what needs to be done. I only hope you'll realize this before it's too late."

Wisps of morning mist still swirled around the tree trunks when they reached the forest floor. Ipé and Jerrah went to different trees to summon their mistcats. Out of the corner of her eye, Ash noticed that someone else had followed them down.

"Caihay?"

The tall dao fora warrior stepped out from behind a tree.

"What are you doing here?"

"Please." He held out his hand, offering her a woven bracelet with blue and green stones set into it. "To keep you safe."

Ash took the gift. "Thank you. It's beautiful."

Caihay smiled and turned to go.

"Wait." It felt wrong not to give Caihay something in return. Ash slid Wayfarer off her shoulders and reached into her mostly empty bag. Her fingers touched Nester, the soft yellow blanket that reminded her of home. After sleeping in the forest, she didn't need the blanket as much anymore—not the way she'd needed it before. She thought Caihay might need Nester's softness more.

"This is for you, if you'd like it," said Ash.

Caihay brushed a corner of the blanket against his cheek. "I'll wear it always."

Ash was about to tell him it wasn't for wearing, but Caihay had already wrapped Nester around his waist like a skirt. He deftly tied the corners together and swished his hips back and forth, showing off the yellow blanket. Maybe Nester wanted to be a skirt.

"You have good… *sinach*," said Caihay, switching back to the dao fora language. "It means coo-rage."

"Courage?" asked Ash.

"Yes." He placed his hand on his heart. "Keep *sinach* here."

"I will," said Ash.

Jerrah approached, sitting astride a muscular mistcat. "You can ride with me." He offered her his hand.

Ipé had already mounted her mistcat. She didn't offer Ash a ride.

Ash stepped past them to a tree with silver bark and broad, sinuous roots. It looked similar to the fig tree in her village that Fen had used to call Balance Keeper. She pressed her hands against the base of the tree and closed her eyes. In her mind, she pictured how the tree's roots spread through the earth beneath her, touching other trees and sharing water and nutrients. A whole network of tree roots extended throughout the forest.

"Balance Keeper," she whispered.

Nothing happened. Ash repeated the name, only this time she coupled the words with envisioned images of the mistcat—sending the words and the images out into the network of tree roots.

Something cool brushed her neck. Ash startled and opened her eyes. Balance Keeper nuzzled her. She stroked the mistcat's glassy ears and the creature purred. It was nearly twice the size of the other mistcats.

Jerrah and Ipé gaped at her.

"Thank you for the offer, but I'll ride my own mistcat," said Ash. She hoisted herself onto Balance Keeper's back.

"You're full of surprises, villager," said Jerrah.

Ipé scowled and set off into the forest.

Ash envisioned following the dao fora. Balance Keeper surged into motion, carrying her toward where they'd left Fen and Puppy.

Ash! Is it you? You smell like you! Where did you go? How could you leave me? I missed you! Puppy licked her face enthusiastically while his butt wiggled. *You're back! You're back! You're back! What did you eat for breakfast?*

"I missed you too," said Ash. She rubbed Puppy's soft belly fur and scratched behind his ears in the place he liked best.

Puppy finally calmed down enough to sniff the leather pouch Suma had given her. *Did you bring me food? You wouldn't believe how hungry I am.*

She pulled out a ruby fruit. "You want this? It's delicious."

Puppy sniffed the red fruit and wrinkled his nose. *Not that. I want real food.*

Ash dug around in the pouch. There was black fig bread and sun fruit, but she didn't think Puppy would like either of those. Finally, she found some strips of dried deer meat wrapped in a leaf at the bottom of the bag.

"You mean this?" She held one of the deer strips out to him.

Yes, yes, yes! That smells amazing!

Puppy took the deer strip and trotted happily beside her, carrying it to a stand of trees near a stream. The two dao fora hunters who'd been told to look after Fen and Puppy stood nearby. They no longer had their bows or arrows. Ash noticed a pile of broken arrows strewn across the ground. She grinned as she imagined Puppy tearing the arrows apart. Then she saw Fen near the stream, fishing with a pole fashioned out of one of the dao fora warrior's bows.

"Is that you, Ash?" He cocked his head when she approached. "Or is it someone who looks like you?"

"It's me," said Ash.

"Does that mean I'm me, too?"

"Yes. Of course you're you."

"Oh, good. I was beginning to lose track of myself."

Fen sounded peculiar. Ash thought he might be angry at her for leaving, but he didn't seem angry. Just confused.

"It's good to see you again, Friend of Strangers." She gave him a hug.

"It's good to be seen again," he replied.

Ipé spoke with Timo and Sava in the dao fora language. They nodded to her, then jogged into the forest, heading toward the Sky Tree.

"Why didn't they call mistcats?" Ash asked as they disappeared.

"Not all dao fora have learned the name of a mistcat," said Jerrah. "It is a great honor to ride one. Ipé likes to brag that she's the youngest in our tribe to ride a mistcat on her own, but that's not true. I am."

Ipé glared at her twin. "I rode mine before you."

"Yes, but you were born first. You're older. So, when I rode mine, I was younger than you."

Ipé rolled her eyes. "I was born on the same day as you."

"Still older," said Jerrah.

"How old were you when you first rode a mistcat?" asked Ash.

"Younger than you," replied Jerrah. "But I've never seen a villager ride a mistcat before, so maybe you're the youngest in your tribe to do it. Like me."

Ipé scoffed and swung onto the back of her mistcat. "Let's go, baby brother. The sun's getting bright. We won't be able to ride much longer."

"See? She tires quickly in her old age."

Ipé narrowed her eyes and commanded her mistcat to leap over her brother. The liquid jaguar cleared him in a graceful arc.

"Careful! You don't want to fall. Old bones break easily!" teased Jerrah.

Ash helped Fen onto Balance Keeper's back, then urged her mistcat to catch up with Ipé and Jerrah.

"You're going the wrong way," she said once she reached the twins.

"I know this forest better than you," snapped Ipé. "Your village is this way."

"We're not going to my village. Not yet. I need to speak with the leader of my people first."

"Isn't your leader at your village?"

Ash thought of Mayor Tullridge. As much as she wanted to go home, she doubted Mayor Tullridge would listen to her. And even if she could get him to listen, he wouldn't be able to persuade the plantation owners and squatters to stop clearing the cloud forest and farm in the trees instead. She needed to speak with someone they'd all listen to. Someone who didn't see her as a traitor.

"Our leader lives in another city. A big city, beyond the walls of my village," said Ash.

Jerrah and Ipé shared a look.

"There's a man who'll take me there," she added. "We just need to find him."

Before Ipé could disagree, Ash urged Balance Keeper to return to Tavan's camp.

They traveled for most of the morning, until Ipé told them to stop. The mistcats were panting, and the two Ipé and Jerrah rode looked skinnier. Balance Keeper wasn't as big anymore, either.

"There's too much sunlight for the mistcats," said Ipé.

Ash slid off Balance Keeper's back and studied the trees overhead. Ipé was right—more light filtered down in this area, burning off the morning mist. The trees weren't as thick or as tall as they'd been, and less moss grew between the upper branches.

When she'd first entered the cloud forest, she'd thought it was all the same—just trees, moss, and ferns. Now she saw that the plants growing here were different from the ones in more shaded parts of the forest. And the trees, though still large, were smaller than the ones the dao fora lived in. Because the trees held less moss, they collected less moisture from the clouds, and less water rained down. Some of the trees had turned brown and were losing leaves.

The forest here seemed sick. Ash hadn't realized it before because she'd never seen what a healthy forest looked like. Now that she knew how big and lush the trees deeper in the forest could be, she could see how much the trees here suffered from the drought.

She turned back to Balance Keeper. The mistcat had moved into a patch of shade. Jerrah and Ipé had already dismissed their mistcats.

Ash put her hand on Balance Keeper's forehead. She pictured the trees around her becoming lush and healthy again, like the trees deeper in the forest.

The mistcat lowered her head, seeming to understand her vision. Then she crouched, and leapt into a nearby tree, fading as she returned to the depths of the forest.

"We'll have to walk the rest of the way," said Jerrah.

Puppy was already running ahead, sniffing leaves and chasing after squirrels. *I smell fish! This way!*

Ash situated Wayfarer firmly on her shoulders and hurried after Puppy. They walked down a ravine and followed the stream back to the riverbank.

Puppy spotted Tavan first. He ran up to him, tail wagging. Obviously, he'd decided that Tavan was okay.

"Fen!" Tavan dropped the hide he'd been stitching and ran to his son. "Thank the stars, you're alive!" He scooped Fen up and hugged him tightly.

For several seconds Fen dangled like a rag doll. Gradually, he lifted his arms and hugged Tavan back.

"I thought I'd lost you," said Tavan.

Ash marveled at all the emotions that crossed Tavan's face. There was anger that Fen had gone away, and joy that he'd come back, coupled with a fierce protectiveness. But most of all, there was love. She'd never seen so much love, plainly expressed. He alternated between hugging his son, kissing his head, and scolding him for running off. The more Tavan hugged his son, the more Fen appeared to become himself again.

21

Governor City

Tavan agreed to take Ash to Governor City, but he refused to take Ipé and Jerrah. The twins seemed fine with this. They wouldn't even look at Tavan when Ash introduced them, and they refused to talk to him.

"It's forbidden to speak to exiles," Jerrah told Ash later.

"Do you know him?" asked Ash.

"Knew him," corrected Jerrah. "He's dead to us now."

"Is that why you won't talk to Fen, either? Because he's an exile?"

Jerrah glanced at Fen, then quickly looked away. "He's… dead to us as well."

Ash wanted to ask if this was why Ipé had called Fen a *mabh falsa*, but Jerrah walked off, making it clear that he didn't want to talk about it.

Since they couldn't call their mistcats during the heat of the day, they stuck around Tavan's camp and rested. Ash played games with Puppy and Fen in the river. The water wasn't deep enough to swim in, but Puppy enjoyed splashing after sticks in the current. By the time the sun went down, all three of them were exhausted. Ash fell asleep shortly after dinner.

Tavan woke her later that night. "Time to go. The mist is thickening," he said.

A silver sheen of moonlight illuminated the outlines of trees around them. Swirls of mist drifted along the cool, damp ground.

"You awake, Puppy?" Ash petted the bundle of fur next to her.

Lost Heart Puppy tucked his muzzle under a paw, ignoring her. She had to scoop him up and carry him to where Tavan waited at the edge of camp.

Tavan had already called his mistcat. Gone were the streaks of reddish-brown paint on his face, and the woven moss cloak and necklace of feathers. He wore his plain brown pants and a button-down shirt now. Except for his hairless head and bare feet, he looked like a plantation worker.

After gathering her things, Ash found a tree that she could use to call Balance Keeper. Jerrah and Ipé called their mistcats as well.

"We'll meet you in two days outside your village," said Jerrah. Then he set off into the forest with Ipé, heading back toward the Sky Tree.

For the first couple of hours, Ash carried Puppy in her lap. He didn't seem to mind riding on an arrogant cat now, although he stirred and complained about being jostled. *It's sleep time*, he grumbled.

"Tell me about it," replied Ash. She wished she could sleep more, too, but they had far to go, and they'd only be able to ride their mistcats until it got hot.

Two days. That's all the time she had to find the governor and convince him to meet with Suma outside her village. Doubt gnawed at her, but she couldn't turn back now. Suma was counting on her, and she had to do something to fix what was amiss so she could go home.

She stroked the soft fur behind Puppy's ears. *Talking to the governor can't be any more difficult than taming an angry illwen*, she told herself.

Nevertheless, the closer they got to Governor City, the more nervous she became.

The forest eventually gave way to an open expanse of burnt ground and cut stumps. Tavan slid off his mistcat and touched the dry, blackened ground.

"I was here less than a year ago," he said. "This was still covered in trees then." His gaze took on a distant, haunted look. "We better hurry. We won't be able to ride much longer."

The mistcats raced across the burnt ground until they encountered fields of jujube trees planted in rows. The small, stunted trees looked eerie in the morning light, with their branches shrouded in white webworm tents.

Puppy refused to go through the webworm infested rows, so they had to change course and travel around the jujube plantations. A few workers, collecting bushels of webworm silk before the heat of the day, spotted them bounding across a burnt field and pointed.

Ash tried to imagine how strange they must have looked to the workers—a barefoot man with a shaved head, a skinny boy in a moss cloak, and a girl with a carpetbag on her back, riding giant liquid jaguars. Not to mention the black-and-white blur of Puppy, running through the grass and leaping up to snap at crows. The workers must have thought they were still dreaming. By the time one plantation worker realized he was awake and called out to others to look at the strange sight, Ash, Tavan, and Fen were just specks on the horizon.

At last, they reached a road that Tavan said would take them to the city. Traveling across hard, open ground under the rising sun had taken its toll on the mistcats. Tavan quickly dismissed his and Ash did the same. Balance Keeper loped back toward the shade of a distant stand of trees.

They traveled by foot after that. At one point, they passed a walled-off village. Ash thought it looked like the village she'd grown up in, except bigger. She counted at least six watchtowers jutting above the village wall. A couple of the towers appeared twisted and splintered, as if they'd recently been damaged in an illwen attack.

"Is that Governor City?" she asked.

"No," said Tavan. "That's a frontier village like the one you come from."

Horse carts pulling bundles of cut logs and bushels of web-worm silk rumbled past. Fen's eyes grew wide at the sight of the horses. He ran to pet one, which earned him a curse from the driver and nearly got him a lash from the driver's whip. Tavan tugged Fen out of the way.

But Fen's curiosity was relentless. Every time a horse cart passed, he edged into the road, reaching to pet the horse while calling out questions to the driver. "What does he eat? Does he talk? Does he like pulling the cart? How fast can he go?"

Finally, one driver brought his cart to a stop.

"Where you heading?" he asked.

"Governor City," said Tavan.

"That's a long walk for a hot day."

"Can I pet him?" asked Fen, already patting the horse's flank.

"Here." The driver handed Fen a carrot. "Give this to Trip and he'll be your friend for life."

Fen's face lit up as he fed the horse. "It tickles!"

"Now you've done it," replied the driver. "Old Trip won't want to go anywhere without you. You best hop on."

There was only space for one more person on the bench where the driver sat, and Fen quickly clambered up onto it. The driver squinted down at Ash and Tavan. He wore a wide-brimmed hat that shaded most of his face. What Ash could see of his expression seemed friendly. "Looks like you'll have to ride in the back," he said. "It's not much, but it beats walking."

Tavan thanked the man and helped Ash up into the back of the cart. It was full of cut logs. They weren't very comfortable to sit on, but Ash was glad to get off her feet. Even Puppy seemed sick of walking. He curled up in Ash's lap to rest.

It's good to have a lap to curl up in, he said. Then he opened one eye and cocked his head at her. *You need a lap to curl up in.*

Ash nodded. She felt the same way.

Tavan settled across from her and started to weave several palm fronds he'd collected into a sunhat. While he worked, he kept an eye on Fen, who was busy talking the driver's ear off. The driver appeared to enjoy the company, laughing as he answered Fen's endless questions.

"How old is Fen?" asked Ash.

Tavan's eyes flicked to his son again, but Fen gave no indication that he heard them. They were far enough back that even if Fen stopped talking, the rumble of the cart wheels would drown out their voices. "You ever ask him that question?"

"No."

"Good. Don't."

"Why not?"

"Fen's not like other children," said Tavan. "When he was young, he caught a fever. For the first couple days, he kept shivering. Then the shivering stopped and his breathing became so shallow, I had to press my ear to his chest to make sure he was still alive. But he held on. Some part of him held on. He's stubborn that way and stronger than he looks. Even so, he never fully recovered. Since the fever, he's been… different."

"I like that he's different," said Ash.

Tavan grunted. "You're wise. Most folks fear what's different. They disapprove of those who don't behave the way they expect them to, and Fen rarely behaves the way folks expect. He's too curious. Trouble is, Fen doesn't want to be seen as different. He wants to belong. That's why I have to look out for him." Tavan set the circle of palm fronds he'd woven on his head to check the fit, then continued weaving more leaves together. "Anyhow, if you ask him how old he is, it'll just remind him that he's small for his age—because of the fever. I'd appreciate it if you don't upset him with such questions."

"Sure. He's my friend," said Ash.

"Good. Then don't make him run off again." He glanced up from his weaving and gave Ash a stern look. "That was more dangerous for him than you know."

"I didn't mean to put him in danger."

"The whole world can change without anyone meaning it to. It doesn't matter what you mean. It matters what you do."

Ash sat back against Wayfarer. The landscape on both sides of the road had changed from the lush green trees of the cloud forest to dusty brown plantation fields that stretched for as far as she could see. She considered what Tavan had said. People might have meant to cut down a few trees for wood, or clear a field to grow food, but did they mean to cut down all the trees? Could the whole forest disappear without people meaning it to?

Tavan took a sip from his water gourd and passed it to her.

Ash limited herself to two small sips. This was the only water they had left, and she didn't think they'd be able to get more anytime soon. All the streams they'd passed were either dry or so muddy they didn't look drinkable.

Tavan nodded at her restraint. He took the water gourd back, clambered onto the logs, and offered the rest to Fen and the driver.

Around midday, they approached a village with several stone towers rising above the outer wall. Ash even saw a church steeple in the distance, like one pictured in a book she'd read.

"Governor City is more beautiful than I expected," she said.

"That's not Governor City," replied Tavan. "That's another frontier village."

"But the forest isn't anywhere near here."

"It was a few years ago."

They passed more towns and the road they traveled became busier. Still, every time Ash asked if the town was Governor City, Tavan shook his head. "Not yet. You'll know when we get there."

The rumbling movement of the wagon eventually lulled Ash to sleep.

She woke awhile later when the wagon lurched to a stop. Ash sat up blearily.

"Better get off here," said the driver. He nudged Fen, who'd fallen asleep on the man's arm. "If I pull into the lumberyard with passengers, my boss will make you work for the ride."

Tavan thanked the man and hopped off the back of the cart. He was wearing the palm hat he'd made. With his shaved head covered and his hairless face shaded, he looked even more like a plantation worker. Fen yawned, stretched, and said farewell to the driver and to Trip, the horse. The driver tipped his hat and merged back into the busy traffic.

More awake now, Ash looked around in awe. Dozens of horse-drawn carriages clopped back and forth along streets lined with two- and three-story brick buildings. Puppy bounded about, sniffing and tasting things while Ash tried to make sense of all the new sights, sounds, and smells. Everything blended into a dizzying hubbub. Manure, rotting fruit, and the acrid smell of burning coal filled her head, while the shouts of newsboys and fruit sellers clamored for attention. A haze in the air made her eyes water. Even so, Ash couldn't stop looking.

The road wasn't dirt but stone—thousands of stones set into the ground, like if the village square went on and on. Beside the road stretched a boardwalk bustling with people. Some of the passing men wore black suits and tall hats with crystal cloth spectacles. The women wore dresses of every color with feathered hats and shimmering crystal cloth veils that hid their faces. Most of the veils were so long the women resembled iridescent ghosts drifting by.

Meanwhile, people covered in dirty rags huddled in doorways and slumped beside the road. The fancy men and women stepped right over the rag people like they weren't there. It boggled her mind that people so rich could pass ones so poor and not even look at them.

"What is this place?" asked Ash.

Tavan straightened his palm hat. "Welcome to Governor City."

Seeing how big and bustling the city was made Ash's doubts about talking with the governor come roaring back. She clutched Kiki for reassurance. "There are so many buildings… How will we find where the governor lives?"

"That's the easy part." Tavan pointed to a building on a distant hilltop. Dozens of flags flapped atop the columned white structure. Above it hovered what looked like a giant silver treenut with a train car strapped to its belly and whirligigs on each side.

An airship!

"The governor had the Capitol built on the highest point in the city," said Tavan. "If that weren't enough to show people where he lives, he had the Capitol buildings built in the shape of his initials—I.C. for Ivo Castol—although I'm told the letters are only visible from above. The hard part isn't finding him. It's getting in to see him."

They headed up the main street toward the hill where the Capitol stood. The closer they got, the higher the brick buildings on each side of the street became. Along the way, Tavan explained that when he was younger, he'd been curious like Fen. He wanted to see how villagers lived, so he worked as a bush meat hunter and sold meat in Governor City.

One of the butchers he sold meat to was a kind elderly man who offered Tavan a job working at his store. Tavan agreed, and the man taught Tavan how to read and speak like a gentleman. When the man died a few years later, Tavan left the city. He still returned every now and then to trade and get supplies. This was the first time he'd come with Fen, though.

Fen had questions about everything he saw. While Tavan tried to answer them, Puppy chattered to Ash.

Rotten milk! Goat pee! Dead rats! I don't even know what this is, but I want to roll in it!

Ash worried that Puppy might get lost. She told him to stay with her, but he noticed a cat and chased it down an alley.

"Leash your dog!" shouted a cart driver.

Ash ran across the street to grab Puppy. She found him barking at the cat and wagging his tail. The cat crouched on a barrel, hissing at Puppy.

Why won't she come down and play?

"She doesn't seem very friendly," said Ash.

Most of the people didn't seem very friendly, either. The fear that had plagued her village, making people distrust each other, seemed worse here. Ash could see it in people's faces as they hurried past, scowling and glaring at her. They were all a little like the hissing cat. She scooped Puppy up in her arms. He squirmed, but she didn't let him go. Either she carried him or she put a leash on him, and she didn't think he'd like that.

On her way back to Tavan and Fen, she spotted a general store. It was the first familiar thing she'd seen in the city. The store had a wooden porch and windows on each side of the door showing the latest goods—just like her parents' store, except this store had four windows while her family's had only one.

Among the posters and advertisements tacked on the board next to the entrance, Ash saw a picture of a face she recognized.

Her own.

The drawing on the poster was done with dark ink that had smudged some. It made her eyes look too big and her mouth too small, but even if she hadn't recognized herself, she would have recognized her name.

WANTED!

Ash Narro

Short stature. Brown hair. Brown eyes. Dangerous.
Wanted for aiding enemies of the people
and helping known criminals escape.

REWARD IF CAPTURED!

Contact Provincial Authorities to Collect.

Dangerous? thought Ash. That wasn't something she'd ever been called before. She felt surprisingly pleased by the description.

Ash tore the poster off the wall and hurried back to where Tavan and Fen stood.

"What's that?" asked Fen.

"It's how we're going to see the governor." She handed Tavan the poster before Puppy chewed it. "You're going to collect a reward."

Bound

Two guards, dressed the same as wall soldiers, stood outside the Capitol gates. Ash's nose itched as she approached them, but she couldn't scratch it. Her hands were tied in front of her with Telltale, the rope.

Tavan held the other end of the rope. He led Ash toward the Capitol gates while Fen walked behind and shoved her every now and then.

"Sorry," said Fen. "You sure you want me to push you?"

"It has to look real," muttered Ash. "Pretend you hate me. And don't smile."

"Why not? Don't mean people smile?"

"Shh… You're not supposed to talk to me."

"Don't mean people talk?"

Ash gritted her teeth and studied the Capitol buildings beyond the wrought iron fence. Several had missing shingles and broken balconies from recent illwen attacks. Ash had seen a few signs of illwen attacks in some of the frontier villages they'd passed on the way here, but this looked worse.

"I've come to collect my reward," declared Tavan. He held the poster up for the gate soldiers to see.

"Why's she tied up?" asked one soldier. "She's just a little girl."

"That's exactly what she wants you to think. It took six men to catch her, and I'm the only one still standing," said Tavan.

Ash narrowed her eyes, doing her best to appear *dangerous*.

The soldier laughed. "Go tell your stories to the other beggars."

"Believe me, I wish it were a dratted story," replied Tavan, sounding just like a plantation worker. "This *little girl* went batty-fang on a company of soldiers and helped a dao fora warrior escape. She's a traitor and a witch. That's why there's a reward for her."

"You're mad as hops. Now shove off," ordered the older soldier.

"Wait… I heard about that," said the younger soldier. He seemed quieter than the other, but once he got talking he kept going in quick, nervous way. "One of my bunkmates knows a marksman who was there when it happened. He said the girl ordered a bear to rip his musket out of his hands. Then the girl, the bear, and the dao fora warrior flew over the village wall and escaped."

Ash glanced at Puppy who was busy sniffing stones. He paused mid-sniff. *Am I the bear?*

Ash winked at him.

"That's ridiculous. No little girl ordered a bear about," countered the older soldier.

"The marksman saw it. So did others," replied the younger soldier. "They said she's an evil willer."

"You can't tell me you believe that horse swill."

"Look, I don't care what you believe," interrupted Tavan. "I just want to get my reward and be on my way." He tried to hand the end of Telltale to the younger soldier. "Are you gonna take her or not?"

The soldier looked at the rope warily. Then he looked at Ash. She gave him a calm, wicked grin.

"You... uh... need to speak with the watch officer," said the younger soldier.

"Where's he?"

"He won't be here 'til morning."

"Fine. I'll leave her with you. I want to be as far from her as possible when night falls." Tavan tried again to pass the soldier the rope.

The younger soldier stepped back. "I'm not taking her. What if she puts a curse on me?"

"Don't be a coward," said the older soldier.

"I'm no coward. I just don't want to take her. Why don't you take her?"

The older soldier grimaced. Tough as he tried to seem, he wouldn't take the rope either. "Come with me. The commander's assistant can sort this out."

The soldier led them through the gates and up several steps to a rectangular plaza that stretched before a long, white building. From the shape of the building, Ash figured this had to be the "I" part of the I.C. initials Tavan had mentioned.

While the soldier talked with two guards at the entrance to the building, Ash surveyed the plaza. Because the Capitol stood on a hill, when she looked back she could see over much of the city. The brick buildings and houses oozed across the land like a broken egg. The further from the Capitol, the smaller and more run-down the structures appeared. Around the outer edges stood mostly rickety shacks, punctuated by smokestacks of various sizes. Beyond these stretched a patchwork of jujube fields.

Far off in the distance, Ash noticed something else—a cluster of towers that reflected the light of the setting sun. The towers looked like polished white teeth jutting out of the earth. Several specks hovered around them, appearing small as flies.

More airships.

Ash glanced at the airship tied to the Capitol mooring mast. The airship shaded half the plaza. Gold letters on the side of the boxcar strapped to the belly of the airship spelled out *Ocras Industries.*

If the four or five airships hovering around the white towers in the distance were the same size as this airship, then the towers must have been enormous—even bigger than the Capitol!

"Is that where Lord Ocras lives?" asked Ash, keeping her voice low so the guards wouldn't hear.

Tavan followed her gaze to the white towers in the distance and nodded. "They call it the House of Ten Thousand Rooms."

The soldier returned a moment later. "The commander's assistant says you'll need to talk with the commander himself, and he's in a meeting with the governor right now. You can wait here for him. Just don't cause trouble."

He led them into a long hall and gestured to a bench where they could sit. Then he hurried out. Three other soldiers occupied the hall—one sat behind a desk, and two stood guard outside a door at the end of the hall.

They waited for half an hour, but no one came out to talk with them. Muffled rumbles of voices leaked through the door at the end of the hallway. Ash figured that's where the governor had to be. They were so close. If the governor left she'd miss her chance. She had to speak with him today.

She fidgeted and glanced at Tavan. Fortunately, he shared her sense of urgency. He tied Telltale to the bench and approached the soldier at the desk.

"Return to your seat," said the soldier.

"No, sir," replied Tavan. "I'm owed a reward and I intend to collect it. Now where's the commander? I demand to speak with him."

The desk soldier signaled to the door guards, and one came to deal with Tavan. Fen added to the ruckus by asking the desk soldier if his uniform was comfortable, and why they had to wear brown, and what the different patches and buttons stood for.

While all the questioning and arguing was going on, Tavan glanced at Ash and winked. This was her chance.

"Want to play a game?" she asked Puppy.

Always! said Puppy. *What's the game?*

"Tug."

With what? Puppy cocked his head at her bound hands.

"Boots," said Ash. "See that soldier guarding the door over there? I bet you can't tug his boots off his feet."

That's easy! Puppy bolted toward the soldier standing guard outside the governor's office. He bit the laces on one boot and tugged so hard the soldier's feet flew out from under him. But Puppy didn't stop there. He dragged the soldier halfway down the hall before the man's boot finally slid off his foot.

The soldier scrambled to his feet, stunned. He tried to grab his boot and Puppy dodged out of the way.

"Get that dog!" shouted the soldier. He chased after Puppy, awkwardly running on one boot and one dirty sock.

The other soldiers moved to grab Puppy.

Chase! exclaimed Puppy. *I love playing chase!* He dodged the soldiers while carrying the boot in his mouth.

With all three soldiers distracted, Ash slipped her hands out of Telltale and hurried to the door at the end the hall. She threw her shoulder against the wood and shoved open the door.

Inside, a man and a woman sat before a large, polished desk. They both turned, startled by her entrance.

"What's the meaning of this?" barked the man. His thick mustache puffed up when he talked. Dozens of medals decorated the front of his brown uniform. "We gave orders not to be disturbed."

Ash yanked the door shut behind her, hoping the guards in the hall hadn't heard mustache man's complaints. "Are you Governor Castol?" she asked.

It was clear from mustache man's expression that he was not.

"You're not allowed in here," said the woman sitting beside mustache man. She wore a gray uniform that matched her silvery hair.

"I need to speak with Governor Castol." Ash scanned the room. A young woman sat behind a desk off to the side. She appeared to be taking notes.

Ash considered who the governor must be. Mustache man was probably the commander. At least he acted like a commander, giving orders and telling others what to do. And the silver-haired woman next to him had even more medals on her uniform. She could have been a general or an admiral, but Ash didn't think she was Ivo Castol. So where was the governor?

"The governor doesn't meet with rude little girls who interrupt," said the silver-haired woman.

"Please. I came a long way to see him."

"Then make an appointment. We have work to do," said the man. His mustache puffed out with each word. It reminded Ash of the wide, stiff broom her dad used to clear the porch after a dust storm.

"I have to see Governor Castol today."

"Officer Jessup!" called mustache man.

A soldier threw open the door behind Ash. His shirt was untucked, and he was missing one boot.

"Escort this child out."

The soldier grabbed Ash's shoulder and tugged her toward the door.

Ash stomped on the soldier's bare toes and squirmed free. "He's here. I know he's here. Why is he hiding from me?"

"I'm not hiding," replied a gruff voice. "I don't hide from little girls."

Ash looked around, but she still didn't see who was speaking. "Then where are you? I thought you were supposed to be a big important person, and big important people are easy to find. That's why you put your house on top of a hill, isn't it? So everyone will know where you are."

"I can't argue with her logic." The voice seemed to be coming from the far side of the desk.

A short, stocky man stood and stretched his arms over his head. Ash wondered if he'd been sleeping behind the desk. He picked up a wide-brimmed hat—the sort of hat that farmers wore to keep the sun off their necks—and pressed it onto his messy-haired head. Then he slumped into the desk chair and thumped two dirty boots on the polished wood.

"Just stretching my back," he said with a sheepish grin. "You wouldn't think that sitting at a desk all day would be harder on a man's back than riding a horse, but it is."

"Mr. Castol?" asked Ash. This wasn't at all how she'd expected the governor to look. His clothes were plain, his cheeks were scruffy, and there was something else about him that refused to come into focus. Ash didn't know what to make of him.

The man tipped his hat. "Call me Ivo. What can I do for you, young lady?"

Ash drew herself up, recalling her father's number one rule for negotiating: make sure the customer wants what you're selling more than you want to sell it. "It's not about what you can do for me," she said. "It's about what I can do for you. I came here to help you. Sir," she added, remembering her manners.

The governor raised his bushy eyebrows. "Take note, Commander. This is what it means to be bold. Let her be, Officer Jessup."

The soldier, who'd been standing right behind her with arms out, stepped back.

"So, young lady, what are you going to do for me?"

"I know how to stop the dao fora from attacking frontier villages."

"Oh?"

"Sir, we need to get back to business," interrupted mustache man.

"Is that a fact, Commander Chandley?" Governor Castol slid his boots off the desk and leaned forward, causing both the commander and the silver-haired woman to sit up straighter. "Sounds to me like this is our business. You two haven't found a way to stop those savages and their dratted monsters from attacking outposts. Heck, an illwen even attacked here two nights ago. Messed up my roof. So, if this young lady has a solution, I want to hear it."

Commander Chandley's face reddened and the silver-haired woman looked down at her lap.

"Go on, young lady," said the governor. "Let's see if you have better ideas than these two fopdoodles."

Ash swallowed. Her mouth had become painfully dry. She tried to look Governor Castol in the eyes, but her gaze drifted past him to the shelf behind his desk. Several fancy items decorated the shelf—a glass pitcher, silver trophies, brass plaques—but one thing caught her eye. It was a white crystal with a streak of green in it. Something about it appeared familiar.

"Where'd you get that?" She pointed to the crystal.

Governor Castol spun in his chair and picked up the green and white crystal. "This little doodad? This is one of a kind. It was a gift from Lord Ocras. He sent it to me in one of his personal airships. You've heard of Lord Ocras, right? I reckon he owns half your village, along with half of all the frontier villages. Most of those webworm plantations out there belong to him. The man's a blasted hero. His patented crystal cloth is the only thing that *actually* works against illwen." He shot Commander Chandley and the silver-haired woman a stern look. "I need a lot more of that stuff, but my accountants tell me it's dratted expensive."

He held the crystal up before him and peered into its greenish center. "Fetching, isn't it? Sometimes it almost seems to glow." Governor Castol set the crystal back on the shelf. "Well, it's been nice talking with you, but now I've got to get back to work."

"Talking with me? You hardly let me speak," said Ash.

Mustache man gasped. Ash kept going before they could kick her out. As quick as she could, she told the governor about how she'd met with one of the leaders of the dao fora and arranged a meeting outside her village to negotiate a peace treaty. While she talked, the governor grinned. It annoyed Ash that he didn't appear to be taking her seriously, but this only made her state her case more forcefully.

"If people stop burning the cloud forest, the dao fora will teach them to grow plenty of crops in the trees," she finished. "It'll be good for everyone."

The governor chuckled. "I like your gumption, young lady. You're a real go-getter. I could use more people like you. But I can tell you right now your plan won't work. Farmers are creatures of habit. I'm a farmer myself, and I can assure you that farmers like the crops they grow. Why would they want to grow new things?"

"Because they can't keep cutting down and burning the cloud forest," said Ash. "The trees bring the rain, and without rain people won't be able to grow anything."

Commander Chandley snorted. "Poppycock! There'll always be rain. It's got nothing to do with a few trees."

"It does," said Ash. "I've seen it. The trees collect water from the clouds and send it to the ground. Where there aren't enough trees, the ground gets hot and dry. Then the air becomes hot and dry too, which makes it harder for clouds to form and bring rain. Like here, and in my village—there's a drought."

"Droughts come and go. There are plenty of rivers and streams for irrigation."

"The rivers and streams are drying out," said Ash. She couldn't understand why they weren't more concerned about this. It was already happening. Crops were failing. Even in Governor City people were going hungry.

"The rivers have run forever, and they'll keep running," argued Commander Chandley. "Cutting down a few trees won't change anything,"

"It already has changed things. You know it has. Why won't you admit it?"

"That's quite enough!" snapped the silver-haired woman. "You had your chance to talk to the governor, now be on your way. We have work to do."

"Here you go, young lady." Governor Castol slid a tray of cookies and fruit across his desk toward Ash. "Take a sweet for the road and tell your folks to vote for Ivo Castol."

Ash plucked a small red fruit off the tray, but she was too upset to eat it. They acted like it was all just an amusing story—as if she'd made up the dying forest and dried-up streams. Didn't they see how amiss things were?

The soldier by the door reached for Ash's shoulder to guide her out. This time he kept his bare foot out of stomping range. Ash clenched her fists. Red juice from the fruit she'd taken leaked between her fingers. She opened her hand and looked at the crushed mess.

It was a ruby fruit. She hadn't recognized it before because the ones she'd been eating were much redder and plumper than this pitiful withered fruit, but now that she saw the seeds inside, she knew that's what it had to be.

"Wait! I brought something for you." Ash dug into her leather pouch for the last of the ruby fruits that Suma had given her. Maybe seeing the fruit would convince them that the things she'd said were true.

Commander Chandley straightened as she held out four plump, perfectly ripe ruby fruits. "Who did you steal those from?" he demanded.

"No one. No one in Governor City has ruby fruits this good."

The governor leaned across the desk to investigate.

"Taste them," said Ash.

The governor, commander, and the silver-haired woman all glanced at each other. No one moved to take a bite.

"They won't hurt you," said Ash. She bit into one herself to show that they were safe. "They're delicious."

The commander took a small bite of one, then greedily devoured the rest until his mustache glistened. The governor and the silver-haired woman ate the other two.

"Wherever did you get these?" asked the silver-haired woman.

"I told you, the dao fora grow them in the cloud forest. They have loads of them, and other crops too." Ash got out the yellow fruit and slices of black fig bread that she had left. She set them on the tray for the adults to taste.

"The dao fora showed you where they grow all this?" asked Governor Castol, admiring a slice of black fig bread.

"Yes. And they can teach others how to grow it."

Governor Castol took off his hat and brushed his fingers through his messy hair. Then he asked her to explain again where he could meet the leader of the dao fora that she'd mentioned. Only this time he actually listened to her.

As they talked, Puppy wandered into the room and several guards gathered in the doorway. A couple of the guards were missing boots and their uniforms looked rumpled, but no one interrupted her. The governor asked Ash questions about the dao fora, which Ash answered as best she could.

Finally, Governor Castol rubbed his chin and nodded. "You're a very resourceful young lady. What's your name?"

"Ash."

"Is that all. Just Ash?"

Ash thought of the wanted poster and decided to keep her last name to herself. "Yes, sir."

"Well, Ash," said Governor Castol, "I believe thanks are in order. You've done your country a great service today."

23

The Governor's Peace Treaty

Miss Vance, the lady who'd been taking notes during the meeting, was put in charge of seeing that Ash, Tavan, and Fen were taken care of. She led them to a C-shaped building with a flower garden in the center—the "C" for Castol that stood behind the "I" for Ivo.

Ash was given her own room, with a huge bed and an attached bathroom that had a white porcelain tub big enough to lie down in. Gas chandeliers and wall sconces illuminated the room instead of candles and kerosene lanterns. Ash marveled at how expensive things must have been. Her mother would have loved it.

Puppy complained that the place smelled too sweet, but when servants in blue uniforms brought them trays of food, including a roast chicken, Puppy stopped complaining and started drooling.

After a warm bath, Ash snuggled into bed. Despite all the comforts, all she could think about was how much she wanted to go home.

Miss Vance knocked on Ash's door early the next morning and told her to eat breakfast and prepare to leave. Ash was already wide awake. She'd spent the better part of an hour cleaning Wayfarer and Kiki in the bath. It didn't seem right that she should get to be clean and not them. She offered to clean Puppy, too, but he refused to get wet.

When Ash was done, the ironwood stick shined like new pewter and Wayfarer had lost a pound of dust.

Miss Vance frowned upon seeing the dirt-stained towel Ash had used, but she didn't say anything as she hustled Ash out to a carriage waiting in the road.

"What about Fen and Tavan?" asked Ash.

"They'll ride in another carriage and meet us there. Governor Castol wanted to make sure you traveled in style. It'll be just us girls in this carriage."

"And Puppy," said Ash.

"Of course. Your puppy can come too. Now let's be off. Your village is quite a distance away. If we're going to make it to this meeting in time, we need to hurry."

The carriage had padded seats, gold-rimmed windows, and polished wood doors. Ash had never ridden in anything so fancy. The strangest thing was that no horses pulled it. Instead, a driver sat atop the front and steered it with a wheel, while another man, called a stoker, fed coal into a boiler fire to make steam. It was like one of Lord Ocras's steam engines, only it ran on rubber tires and dirt roads instead of a metal track.

Once they got going, Miss Vance undid a latch and flipped down a window so they could see outside. Puppy liked to stick his head out the window and sniff the breeze, but black smoke from the boiler fire began to drift into the carriage. Miss Vance coughed and snapped the window shut.

It got hot in the carriage after that. Ash asked if the governor was traveling in a horseless carriage too.

"I doubt it," said Miss Vance. "The governor is extremely busy, but don't fret. He won't miss this meeting. Ending conflicts with the dao fora is a top priority for him."

By the time they reached Ash's village it was, according to the gold pocket watch Miss Vance carried, almost noon. "No time to waste," chirped Miss Vance. She told the driver to continue through the main road to the far side of the village.

Ash peered out the side window. People stared at the horseless carriage as it rumbled past. She wondered if anyone recognized her. If so, did they still think she was a traitor, or did they see her as someone who'd done her country "a great service," like the governor had said? She kept an eye out for her mother and father, but she didn't see them. Instead, she saw soldiers ordering people back to keep the road clear.

Far more wall soldiers bustled about the village than she remembered. Ash even saw two horseless carriages parked off to the side of the main road, only instead of looking fancy like the one that she was in, these carriages were plain and windowless, with the crossed musket symbol of the army painted on the sides.

"Let's make you more presentable," said Miss Vance. She tugged the curtain closed and tilted Ash's face toward her. "There'll be time enough to wave to your friends later. Right now, you need to prepare for the meeting. The governor is counting on you to introduce him to the dao fora leader. It's a very important job. Do you think you can handle it?"

Ash clenched her jaw. She hated when adults treated her like a feckless child. "Have you ever seen a mistcat?" she asked.

"A what?" Miss Vance fussed with Ash's hair.

"They're big enough to eat a full-grown person in two bites. You'd be terrified of them. Puppy and I can handle things. Isn't that right, Puppy?"

Can we open the window again? asked Puppy. *It smells like crushed flowers in here.*

"That's Miss Vance's perfume. It's very expensive," said Ash.

You mean she wants to smell like that? Why would anyone want to smell like that?

"Puppy wants to know why you want to smell like crushed flowers," said Ash.

Miss Vance stopped touching Ash's hair and frowned. It was the same look villagers gave her when they called her daft for talking to herself, but Ash didn't care. If Miss Vance thought she was crazy, maybe she'd leave her hair alone.

Ash tugged the curtain back and looked out the window again. They passed through the forest gate on the far side of her village. The driver steered the carriage onto the dirt road that ran between the rows of jujube trees in the webworm plantations.

At last, the carriage stopped and the driver opened the door. He'd been wearing a clean uniform that morning, but now he was covered in dust. The stoker looked worse. Soot blackened him from head to toe.

The noon sun blazed overhead. They'd stopped in the middle of a webworm planation, about an equal distance between the village wall and the cloud forest. Ash didn't see anyone else there—not the governor, nor the dao fora.

Her throat tightened. Suma had said she'd meet Ash outside her village on the third day. Where was she? And where was the governor? The air felt oppressively hot and still.

Ash glanced at Miss Vance. She'd put on a sunhat—the sort ladies wore in Governor City—and she'd pulled down her crystal cloth veil.

"No need to fret. He'll be here any minute," said Miss Vance. "The governor is very punctual." Although her words were reassuring, her voice sounded strained. A rainbow sheen from the crystal cloth danced across her face.

Puppy stayed close to Ash's side. *There's a bad smell in the air.*

"Perfume?" asked Ash.

It's like that but more... wrong. His muzzle twitched, and he didn't bound off to sniff things like he normally did. Rows of jujube trees, shrouded in webworm tents, grew on both sides of them. Puppy hated webworms.

"It's probably just rotting jujube fruit," said Ash.

Miss Vance gave her another perplexed, frowny look.

A low humming sound caught Ash's attention.

"There he is." Miss Vance pointed to something in the sky beyond the village.

Ash cupped her hands over her eyes. What looked like a fat fly soon grew into the shape of an approaching airship. Gray smoke from the ship's engines trailed behind it. They were the only clouds in the blue sky.

The airship didn't stop over the village. It kept coming toward where Ash stood, growing ever larger until it blotted out the sky overhead.

A hatch in the bottom of the airship opened and a long rope unfurled. The soot-stained stoker grabbed the end and looped it around an iron ring at the front of the horseless carriage. With the driver's help, they pulled the slack out of the rope and tied it fast, anchoring the airship to the heavy carriage engine. Then a rope ladder dropped down from the back of the airship and two soldiers with muskets descended, followed by the silver-haired lady Ash had seen in the governor's office.

Both the musketmen and the silver-haired lady wore crystal cloth spectacles for protection against an illwen attack.

A pang of unease struck Ash. How was she supposed to get Suma to talk with the governor if he was surrounded by soldiers expecting an attack?

Fear, thought Ash. That's what had been straining Miss Vance's voice, and that's what she saw on the soldiers' faces. *Fear ruins trust. If they're too afraid to talk, they'll never make peace.*

"Admiral Kash," said Miss Vance, bowing to the silver-haired lady.

Admiral Kash ignored Miss Vance and scanned the area. The two musketmen knelt on each side of her and aimed their muskets toward the forest, while the driver and the stoker held the ends of the ladder steady.

Once the ladder was secured, Governor Castol began to descend. Ash drew a relieved breath when she saw him. He wasn't wearing crystal cloth spectacles or any trace of the shimmering cloth. In fact, he looked the same as he had the day before—beat-up field hat, brown pants, and a blue farmer's shirt buttoned all the way to the top.

"Good day, Miss Vance. Ash." He tipped his hat to each of them. "Where's this dao fora leader I'm supposed to converse with?"

Ash peered beyond the webworm-infested branches of the stunted jujubes around her to scan the edge of the cloud forest. She didn't see any dao fora.

A familiar trilling broke the silence. This was followed by another call, and another. The governor and his soldiers probably thought birds had made the noise, but Ash knew better. She cocked her head to pinpoint the sound. Then she spotted them—two mistcats in the trees with dao fora on their backs.

"They're in the forest, Governor Castol," said Ash. "They're waiting for you."

"You see them?"

"Yes, sir." Now that she knew where to look, Ash saw several more dao fora standing near the base of the trees. No wonder dao fora thought her people were blind. The dao fora were standing in plain sight among the trees, but none of the soldiers had noticed them. "They're straight ahead."

"Sir, I must advise against going any closer. It could be a trap," said Admiral Kash. "If they want to talk, they need to come out in the open where we can see them."

Governor Castol nodded. "The admiral has a point. It's one thing to ride a wild bull. Quite another to stand in front of it with your britches down."

Ash stepped closer to the cloud forest. She had to get them to trust each other. "Suma, this is Governor Castol," she called in her loudest voice. "He's here to discuss a peace treaty with you, just like I promised."

A few leaves rustled and several dao fora emerged from the forest. Suma came empty handed, but the warriors beside her carried bows and quivers full of arrows. Ash recognized Ipé, Jerrah, and Caihay among seven or eight others in the group.

"They're armed!" snapped Admiral Kash. "Ready muskets."

"No! They're coming to talk," said Ash.

"Then why the poison arrows?"

"Suma, put your weapons down!" called Ash.

Suma paused. "Tell your people to do the same."

The governor raised an eyebrow. "She speaks better than I thought she would," he said. Then he told the soldiers to set down their muskets.

The soldiers looked terrified, and Admiral Kash clearly disapproved, but they did as the governor ordered. In return, the dao fora warriors set down their bows and arrows, and the tight feeling in Ash's chest began to ease.

"You're the leader of the dao fora that this young lady told me about?" asked the governor, stepping forward.

"I'm the one who's been chosen to speak for the people of the trees," replied Suma. She moved closer as well.

"And your tribe has been attacking this village?"

"We've been protecting the cloud forest," corrected Suma.

"The forest where you grow ruby fruits and other crops?"

Suma nodded.

Governor Castol removed his hat and mopped the sweat off his brow. "I'm glad that you came to this meeting," he said. "I'm glad we finally have a chance to end this conflict and create a lasting peace."

"As am I," replied Suma.

The governor pressed his hat back onto his head. His other hand closed into a fist behind his back. Seeing the gesture, Admiral Kash stepped behind the horseless carriage and waved a red kerchief, as if signaling to someone far away.

Ash wondered what Admiral Kash was doing. She glanced back at the wall surrounding her village. Soldiers moved behind the sharpened posts of the gate towers. Dread coursed through Ash as she realized what was happening.

"Suma," she yelled. "Run!"

24

Flames and Arrows

The ground in front of Suma exploded, throwing dirt and rocks into the air. A split second later, Ash heard the boom of the shots. The sound kept coming—a relentless barrage of musket fire pelting the area where a dozen dao fora had stood only a heartbeat before. Branches splintered and leaves fell as shots tore through the trees.

Ash spotted a dao fora warrior lying in the tall grass. He crawled toward the forest, dragging an injured leg. She looked for Suma, Ipé, Jerrah, and Caihay, but couldn't see them.

At last, the thunderous barrage stopped. Black smoke from the muskets cloaked the village wall. The dark haze swirled as the forest gate swung open. Then a horseless carriage—one of the brown army ones—rumbled into the field. Several soldiers lay on top, muskets ready. Another army carriage followed.

The carriages smashed through rows of jujube trees while the soldiers on top fired muskets.

The dao fora warriors who'd been hiding in the brush fled toward the forest. Once the carriages reached Admiral Kash, they stopped and soldiers wearing crystal cloth spectacles and carrying muskets marched out from the carriage backs. They lined up and fired at the fleeing dao fora. A warrior wearing a yellow skirt staggered and fell.

"Caihay!" yelled Ash.

He fell in a patch of tall grass. Ash didn't see him get up.

She screamed Caihay's name, but everything had become so loud, she could barely hear herself. Her ears rang from all the musket fire.

Someone tugged her back. She whirled around to see it was Tavan. He pulled her behind the fancy horseless carriage where Fen stood, pressing his hands to his ears to block out the deafening gunfire. They must have followed the army carriages out of the village.

Tavan said something to Ash, but she couldn't hear it. "Stay here!" he yelled into her ear.

"But Caihay…" Ash turned toward where she'd seen the warrior fall.

"You can't help him." Tavan kept a firm hand on her arm.

Soldiers with muskets advanced toward the forest. They were met by a flight of arrows from the distant treetops. Dao fora warriors hidden in the branches unleashed wave after wave of deadly arrows.

Suma expected this! thought Ash. *She'd prepared for an attack.*

The soldiers retreated behind the army carriages. A few cried out and staggered, arrows protruding from their bodies.

After that, more rounds of musket fire and arrows were exchanged, but little changed. The soldiers couldn't see who they were shooting at, so they shot blindly into the trees until musket smoke clouded the air. Anytime one of the officers tried to get the soldiers to advance, arrows pierced through the smoke and forced them back.

"Cease fire!" ordered Governor Castol. "Cease, you fopdoodles!"

At last, the officers got the panicked soldiers to stop shooting. The booming echo of muskets faded and the smoke began to clear.

Governor Castol strode down the line of soldiers gathered behind the parked carriages. Ash hoped he'd stop the attack. The wide-eyed soldiers looked mad with fear. Maybe the governor would send them back. He could end this.

"Burn them out!" ordered Governor Castol.

"No! You can't do that!" shouted Ash, but no one listened to her.

Soldiers emerged from the backs of the army carriages with bottles full of kerosene. They used a torch to light fuses near the bottle tops and threw the burning bottles at the forest. Where they landed, bright orange fireballs flared. Ash could feel the heat of the flames fifty paces away.

This was her fault. She'd convinced Suma and the dao fora to come here, and she'd brought Governor Castol here. She had to make them to stop.

She ran to the governor and grabbed his shirt.

"Get off me!" snarled Governor Castol. He threw her back, but she didn't let go. Buttons popped and his farmer's shirt ripped. Beneath the plain blue cloth was another shirt. It shimmered in the sun with the unmistakable sheen of crystal cloth.

Ash stared, confused. A whole shirt of crystal cloth! It must have cost a fortune. Governor Castol tried to seem like a simple farmer, but he wasn't that at all. It was just a costume he wore.

"You never intended to sign a peace treaty," she said. "You only wanted to get the dao fora out in the open so you could kill them. It was all a trap."

"Arrest her," ordered Governor Castol.

A soldier grabbed Ash. She thrashed and kicked but couldn't get free.

Other soldiers surrounded Fen and Tavan and forced them into the back of an army carriage.

"Guard the door," said the soldier holding Ash. He started to shove Ash into the back of the carriage when Puppy gave one of his boots a fierce tug.

The soldier yelped as his leg flew out from under him. Puppy tossed the soldier's boot aside and bowled out the legs of another soldier. Then he bit the pants of a third, tugging so hard the pants ripped down the middle.

At first the soldiers had no idea what was attacking them. They stumbled, tripped, and struggled to hold their pants together. Finally, one aimed his musket at Puppy.

"Look out!" yelled Ash.

Puppy darted behind a carriage right as the soldier fired. The back tire of the carriage exploded. Other soldiers raised their weapons to fire back.

"Don't shoot!" cried the first soldier. He held his hands up in surrender.

"What the blazes are you firing at?" asked Admiral Kash.

All three soldiers tried to explain that a puppy had attacked them. The more they said, the crazier they sounded.

In the confusion, Tavan, Fen, and Ash slipped out of the army carriage. They weren't able to get very far before another squad of soldiers charged through the village gates toward them.

Ash searched the field for a way to escape. "Over here!"

She led Fen and Tavan to the fancy horseless carriage she'd arrived in. Miss Vance huddled in the plush interior while the driver and stoker took shelter behind the carriage. No one guarded the rope ladder leading to the airship.

Ash grabbed Wayfarer from the carriage and slung the bag onto her shoulders. Then she held the ladder steady and told Fen to climb. Tavan followed him.

"You're not allowed up there. That's the governor's airship!" called the driver from his hiding spot, but he made no move to stop them.

"Puppy! Bite the anchor rope," said Ash.

This rope? Puppy gave the rope tied to the iron ring a few test bites. *It tastes terrible.*

"Pretend it's deer meat."

Worst. Deer. Ever, grumbled Puppy as he chewed through the rope.

It snapped and the airship shot upward.

Ash gripped the bottom rung of the ladder. Already she dangled several feet off the ground. "Puppy, jump to me!"

Puppy bolted along the roof of the carriage and launched his tiny body into the air. He landed on Wayfarer and scrambled up the carpetbag to her shoulders.

They kept rising. Black smoke from the muskets shrouded the ground, mixing with gray smoke from the forest fires and the orange glow of the flames. Most of the soldiers were too focused on the spreading fires and dao fora arrows to pay attention to the departing airship.

Ash looked down at the scene below, stunned by how amiss everything had become. Among the smoke, she spotted a dao fora woman running from a cluster of trees. The woman grabbed a yellow-skirted body in the grass and dragged him back into the cloud forest. Then smoke stung Ash's eyes.

She climbed the rest of the way by touch, unable to see anything more.

25

Pilot

The airship drifted as it rose, pushed by a breeze.

Now that she was out of the smoke, her eyes began to clear. Compared to the deafening sounds of the battle below, it seemed oddly quiet in the cabin. The windows at the front of the airship presented a full view of the fire and fighting on the ground. It felt strange to see things from such a perspective—peacefully floating above a scene that wasn't peaceful at all.

Except not everything in the airship was peaceful. Tavan stood near the front controls, holding a soldier in a headlock. The soldier's face reddened as he struggled to free himself from Tavan's arms, but he didn't make a sound. Perhaps he couldn't.

Seeing Tavan choke the soldier sickened Ash. She wanted to escape the violence. Only she couldn't escape it, just like she couldn't escape the sense that it was all her fault.

Ash slumped to the cabin floor. Every time she tried to fix something she made it worse—first in the village when people thought that she was a traitor, and now with the peace talks that became a battle. What if Rosa was right and there was something wrong with her? Everyone else knew the peace talks wouldn't work. Why didn't she? If only she could be more like other people and see things the way they saw them, then maybe she'd stop messing everything up.

Puppy licked her hand. *You okay?*

"It's all wrong."

What's wrong? We're still together. We didn't let them catch us. The only thing that seems wrong to me is that I'm belly empty.

"You're always hungry."

That's true. It's what makes eating so nice. Puppy nuzzled her hand.

The soldier Tavan struggled with wheezed and gasped for air.

"Tavan, stop! You're hurting him!" yelled Ash.

Tavan hesitated. The soldier he held didn't fight back any-more. Tavan told Fen to bring him some rope so they could tie the soldier up. Ash heard the fear sharpening his voice as he ordered Fen about. Fear was what made the violence spread. And fear was what made people distrust each other. Maybe fear was the reason she kept messing things up, too.

She closed her eyes and *listened.* Several whispers bubbled up from the well of names within her to describe Tavan and the soldier. Most of them were harsh, angry whispers, but beneath these she sensed other whispers suggesting other possibilities.

"Tavan." She put her hand on his arm. "Let him go. He won't hurt us."

"You don't know that," snarled Tavan.

"I do," she said, trying to sound more confident than she felt. "Isn't that right? You won't hurt us?"

The man grunted and did his best to nod with Tavan's arm wrapped around his neck.

"You better not try anything," grumbled Tavan as he released the man.

The soldier clutched his neck and took several wheezing breaths. He looked older than most of the other soldiers, with a gaunt face and scruffy cheeks.

"We can't trust him. He's a killer," said Tavan.

"I'm no killer," stammered the man.

Tavan drew the knife from his belt. "Then why were your people shooting muskets at dao fora who came to talk peace?"

"Those *peaceful* dao fora sure brought plenty of weapons with them," argued the man. "There must have been fifty or more of them shooting arrows from the trees."

"*They* didn't shoot first. Your people did."

"Stop!" said Ash. "No. More. Fighting."

Tavan grunted and slowly lowered his knife.

"Look," said the man, rubbing his neck, "I reckon I don't like what happened down there anymore than you do, but don't blame those soldiers. They're not a bad lot. They're just a bunch of scared kids following orders."

"Then who should I blame?" asked Tavan.

"I suppose that would be the ones giving the orders," said the man. "'Course, the officers will just say they're doing what the governor tells them to, and the governor will just say he's doing what he has to do to protect his people. That's how it goes around. Everyone loses."

"Not everyone," said Ash. She brushed her fingers across the brass Ocras Industries logo on the airship control panel. The motorized carriages the soldiers had arrived in were made by Ocras Industries too. And the crystal cloth that the soldiers, Governor Castol, and others wore came from Lord Ocras's factories. The more people fought, and the more afraid they became, the more

Lord Ocras profited. All this fear and fighting actually helped him.

Lord Ocras wasn't the hero that the governor claimed. He was the opposite. He only pretended to be a hero while he manipulated people and brought out the worst in them for his own gain. Images from the vision Ash had when she drank from the Pool of Memory came back to her. All at once it seemed clear to Ash who Lord Ocras must be, and what she had to do to make things right.

She turned to the man Tavan had struggled with. "You're the pilot, right?" she said, speaking aloud one of the whispers she'd heard. The name kept repeating in her head. "No… you're *Pilot*."

The man gave Ash a curious look.

"That's your name, isn't it?" A different name was stitched into the breast pocket of his uniform. Captain Mason. But that wasn't his true name. "Pilot," she said again.

"No one's called me that in years. Did someone tell you to call me that? Was it Rui?"

Ash shook her head.

"Was it… my dad?"

Ash shook her head again.

"He's the one who nicknamed me Pilot, on account of my head always being in the clouds. Who told you?"

"No one did," said Ash. "It's just who you are. We need your help, Pilot."

"Is that why you're taking me prisoner?"

"We're not taking you prisoner. I'm asking you to help us. None of us know how to fly an airship."

"Why would I help you? My orders are to stay here."

He sounded angry, but Ash knew that wasn't him. He just needed to remember what it meant to be Pilot. "You don't have to follow those orders," she told him. "You can do whatever you want now."

Pilot scoffed. "No one gets to do what they want, kid."

Ash closed her eyes and focused again on the whispers she'd heard. An image of Pilot as a young man, sitting on a rooftop and watching birds soar past, arose in her mind. "You used to dream of flying like a bird. You weren't afraid then. Nothing could hold you back."

Pilot's scowl softened. Then he shook his head. "Those were the dreams of a child. The Sky Navy owns me now."

"But you're Pilot. You can fly this ship anywhere you like," said Ash. "This is your chance. You can tell the Sky Navy that we forced you to fly us somewhere. Or tell them we tied you up and flew the airship ourselves. All I'm asking is that you take us one place, then you can do as you please."

Pilot peered out the front window. The soldiers far below looked like dots in the dry fields. Even the fires and the horseless carriages looked small, but the smoke didn't. It had become a huge black cloud.

Pilot sighed and sat in the captain's chair. "If I get caught, I'm gonna tell them you and your savage friends knocked me out and stole this airship."

"Tell them what you like," said Ash. "I don't think they're gonna catch you."

"No. They won't." He chuckled. "Why, if you ain't the most bricky girl I've ever met. Where do you want to go?"

Ash looked out at the fire, smoke, and fighting. There was one place she had to go, and she couldn't avoid it any longer.

"There." She pointed to the white towers rising like teeth in the distance. "To the House of Ten Thousand Rooms, where the Shadow Namer lives."

Part 3

The Spear Tip

An enormous green leaf being devoured by webworms—that's what Ash thought the cloud forest looked like from high above. The rivers and streams were the veins of the leaf, flowing from the hills to the ragged edges of the cloud forest where the bright green gave way to the dusty brown fields of web-worm plantations.

Ash moved around the airship cabin, trying to see as much as she could through the windows. The front of the cabin resembled the bow of a ship, and the two main windows Pilot peered through angled downward to show the ground below. Ash climbed onto the wooden panel next to all the brass levers and dials to get a better view. She would have pressed her face to the glass, but Pi-lot warned her not to.

"The glass ain't that thick, and it's a dodgast long way to fall," he said.

Ash leaned back, but only a little. All her life she'd lived on one small patch of the quilted land below. Frontier villages like the one she grew up in were small enough to cover with her hand. Several of them dotted the landscape near the edge of the forest, or where the forest had once been. And around every village, webworm plantations and squatters' fields ate into the forest.

People talked about the cloud forest as if it went on forever. "The green sea" some called it. Everyone acted like it would always be there, but for the first time Ash saw how false that notion was. The forest kept retreating while the roads and plantations kept advancing.

This was why Suma wanted her to face the Shadow Namer. Things hadn't only changed in her village. They'd changed everywhere. For as far as she could see, the forest was disappearing. Even if she succeeded in bringing peace to her village, it wouldn't last because everyone's needs and fears were tangled together. From high above, the roads looked like an immense web spread across the earth, and Lord Ocras, the Shadow Namer, waited at the center of it all.

Tavan peered out the window next to her. "The poor are the spear tip of cloud forest destruction," he said.

Ash furrowed her brow, not understanding what he was talking about. Then she noticed how some of the triangle-shaped clearings looked like spear tips jabbing into the forest.

"I've known squatters," continued Tavan. "Some helped me and Fen after the doa fora exiled us. They gave us food and medicine. They're not bad people. At least, most of them aren't."

"But they're destroying the cloud forest," said Ash.

Tavan nodded. "Burn or starve."

Pilot raised an eyebrow. "That's not something I ever thought I'd hear a dao fora say."

"Because we're heartless savages?" replied Tavan.

"That's one way to put it."

Tavan grunted. "The dao fora weren't the ones throwing firebombs back there."

"Ain't that a fact," said Pilot. "I didn't like that. Fire quickly gets out of hand—believe me, I know. I grew up on a farm. Most of the soldiers back there did too. I hate to see things burn. I'd rather help things grow."

"Then why are you a soldier? Why not be a farmer?" asked Ash.

"Why indeed," said Pilot. "It's a common enough story. My parents were promised land if they moved to the frontier, so they sold everything and went. But when they got here, there wasn't any farmland left. They were too poor to travel elsewhere, so my folks had no choice but to clear a few acres of the cloud forest to plant. Burn or starve," he added, repeating Tavan's words. "That first year we barely ate at all. My dad went in debt for seeds and supplies. He was no scobberlotcher, though. He got up with the sun and worked hard every day to make crops grow. When the rains didn't come, I helped him carry water to the field. We trudged miles each morning to keep those crops alive. I used to think it would all be worth it once the beans and potatoes came in and we got to eat our fill, but I never got to taste a single bean or spud."

"Why not?" asked Ash.

"Soldiers came," said Pilot. "They arrested my dad for clearing the cloud forest without a permit. Then they took the farm and fined him. 'Course, he couldn't pay the fines. Everything he owned was tied up in the farm, so he and my mom had to work on a webworm plantation to pay off their debts. They worked in the jujube fields from sunrise to sunset, but their debts kept growing. That's how it goes. The governor sends folks to the frontier knowing that they'll have to clear the forest to survive. Then he fines them, takes their land, and forces them to work on webworm plantations. That's why I joined the Sky Navy as soon as I could enlist. It was either that or spend my life harvesting silk on one of those plantations down there."

Pilot's gaze grew distant. "You know what the funny thing is?" he continued. "The balloon that holds this airship up is made of webworm silk. Mind you, it's not the fancy crystal cloth kind. Still, webworm silk is the only thread that's both strong enough and light enough to fly. Airships like this wouldn't be possible without workers like my mom and dad. They might have harvested the silk that's holding us up here now. Even so, I know they'd rather be growing food. You spoke true about the poor being the spear tip of cloud forest destruction. Thing is, a spear doesn't get to choose how it's used. Or who it hurts.

Ash couldn't sleep. She spent most of the trip trying to figure out what she'd do when she got to Lord Ocras's towers.

The idea of facing the Shadow Namer terrified her. She was only beginning to understand her naming abilities while he had complete command over two fierce illwen. All she had was Puppy, and she could only get him to play fetch and tug.

She considered everything she knew about Lord Ocras—it wasn't much. People called him a "brilliant titan of industry," yet Ash couldn't recall a single person ever claiming to have met Lord Ocras, or to have seen him in public. She'd never even seen a photograph of him in a newspaper.

Ash recalled how the Shadow Namer had looked in her vision. The red-hot chain he'd wrapped around his head must have burned him terribly. That might be why he avoided the public spotlight. The things he'd done to gain power…

Maybe she didn't have to face him. If she could sneak into the House of Ten Thousand Rooms and find the illwen he'd enslaved, she could free them without being seen. Then the illwen would stop attacking her village and the fearful spell would lift. People might even forget that she'd helped Fen escape. She could go home.

It wasn't much of a plan, but it was the best she could come up with. She mulled it over awhile before explaining it to Fen and Tavan.

Tavan didn't say anything at first.

"We'll help," said Fen, breaking the silence. "It's wrong to keep illwen in chains like that. They need to be free."

"This isn't ours to do, Fen," said Tavan.

"Why not?" asked Fen. "We can't let Ash do it on her own."

"It's too dangerous for us to go in The House of Ten Thousand Rooms."

"Isn't it dangerous for her?"

"Ash is a villager. Lord Ocras will treat her differently than he'd treat us," explained Tavan. "If she's caught, he might have her arrested and sent away, but I doubt he'll harm her. I can't say the same for us. We'll see you to the towers, Ash. That's as far as we can go. Once Pilot drops you off, we'll return to the cloud forest."

Fen protested.

"I'm sorry," said Tavan. "This is how it has to be. I wish you luck, Ash Narro."

27

Shadows in the Tower

The sun was beginning to set as the airship neared The House of Ten Thousand Rooms. Red and orange light reflected off the polished marble sides of the towers.

The beauty of the structures surprised Ash. Six white towers rose above the plantation fields, surrounding a taller tower in the middle. Windows encircled the upper levels of the central tower, glistening like jewels on a crown. The colorful sunset reflecting off the spires enthralled everyone in the airship, except for Puppy. He scampered around the airship cabin grabbing lengths of rope and shoving them at Ash and Fen, trying to get someone to play tug with him. When he wasn't doing that, he sniffed the floor of the cabin like he needed to pee.

Are we there yet? he asked Ash for the tenth time.

"Almost there." She scratched Puppy behind his ears. He spun and gnawed her hand playfully.

I need out, out, out, out!

"Almost there," repeated Ash.

Pilot steered the airship toward a plaza near the base of the towers. An enormous brick building with massive sliding doors lined one end of the plaza. Three airships were tied to mooring masts in the plaza, like horses tied to hitching posts. Workers carried potted jujube trees up ramps that led to the cabins of the anchored airships.

"What's that?" Fen pointed to the brick building with the gigantic doors.

"That's the airship factory," said Pilot. "Every Ocras Industries airship was made there."

"Have you been here before?" asked Ash.

"'Course. I used to fly here a couple times a week to pick up cargo. That was my job before I got assigned to the governor."

"What sort of cargo? Jujube trees?"

"Not just any jujube trees," said Pilot. "Ones with Lord Ocras's patented Miracle Crystal Cloth Webworms on them. Their silk is the finest. Every plantation owner wants them. That's why Lord Ocras is so rich."

"This is where all the webworms come from?"

"All the expensive ones," said Pilot. "Folks say he's got a special webworm queen in one of those towers who lays the eggs for every single Ocras Industries Crystal Cloth Webworm he sends out. She's his most prized possession. Hard to imagine how one little webworm could be all that special, but if it's only her offspring that spin crystal cloth silk, she must be."

Ash studied the towers. Dozens of fancy bridges and covered walkways connected the towers to each other. No wonder the place was called The House of Ten Thousand Rooms. Inside, there must have been a maze of halls, stairs, and rooms. "Which tower does Lord Ocras live in?"

"Beats me," said Pilot. "I've never seen Lord Ocras. He doesn't dawdle on the docks with ship rats like me."

Pilot steered the airship toward an open mooring mast. Two workers below hurried to grab the anchor line at the front of the airship.

"Wait! Go higher," said Ash.

"But we're almost down. I thought you wanted me to let you off here."

"Not here," said Ash. "Up there." She pointed to the central tower. Instead of a spire on top, it had a flat roof with a mooring mast at one corner. "Someone like Lord Ocras would never leave from the ground floor. He has airships. He'd come and go from up there—that's why no one down here sees him. There must be a way in up there."

"If you say so." Pilot pushed a lever and the engines roared. He cranked the steering wheel to turn away from the mooring mast, only to head toward one of the anchored airships. "Hold on. It's gonna be dicey."

The massive airship continued to descend for several seconds before the engines caused the front to tilt upward. They started to rise, but the anchored airship in front of them loomed large. If they kept going at their current trajectory, they'd crash.

"We're not rising fast enough. We need to be lighter!" said Pilot. "Toss out anything that's not nailed down."

Fen opened the bottom hatch and they tossed out everything they could: a few boxes of supplies, the rope ladder, some blankets. It barely made a difference.

"Go to the back of the cabin!" ordered Pilot.

Tavan, Ash, and Fen did, and the shift in weight tilted the cabin up toward open sky. The side engines roared, propelling the airship higher. Through the open floor hatch, Ash saw the gray top of the other airship pass only a few feet beneath them.

"Close shave," said Pilot. "Now we're climbing."

He turned the airship and headed toward the tower with the flat roof. As they ascended, the area on top came into view—a rooftop garden with potted jujube trees arranged around the edges.

"I'll do my best to slow down, but I won't be able to stop. There's too much wind up here," said Pilot, his forehead wrinkled in concentration. "Unless a ground crew miraculously appears to belay our anchor rope, we're gonna drift past. You'll have to lower yourselves on the ladder and step off quickly."

"What ladder?" asked Fen. "The one I threw out?"

Pilot frowned. "Well, that complicates things."

"I can jump out," said Ash.

"And fall to your death?" Pilot scoffed. "No way I'll let you do that, no matter how bricky you are. No one's getting off this ship without at least a rope."

Ash, Tavan, and Fen searched the cabin, but all the ropes were gone. Except one.

"Will this work?" Ash pulled Telltale out of Wayfarer.

"If it's long enough," said Pilot.

Ash secured one end of Telltale to the center cabin post and lowered the other end out the hatch. Fen tugged the rope, checking her knots.

"Get ready." Pilot steered toward the rooftop garden. Wind gusted against the side of the airship. "With this wind I won't be able to hold us over the roof for long."

Puppy leapt onto Ash's shoulders and nudged out a place between her back and Wayfarer. Ash made sure Kiki was secure, then she adjusted Wayfarer's straps so they wouldn't slide off.

"Take care of Telltale," she told Pilot.

He gave her a confused look.

"The rope. He's special," she explained.

"Good luck, bricky girl. I hope you know what you're doing."

"Thank you, Pilot."

"*Pilot,*" he said, savoring the name. "This is the first time I've truly felt like one in a dizzy age. You ready?"

Ash reached for the part of the rope Fen held.

"Now!" shouted Pilot.

Fen jumped out the bottom hatch.

"Fen!" yelled Tavan.

"I didn't think he was going," said Pilot.

Ash's heart skipped. Fen swung near the bottom of the rope, then dropped onto the roof.

"Come on! What are you waiting for?" he called.

Tavan bellowed an impressive string of curse words as he slid down the rope after his son.

"Now or never, bricky girl," said Pilot.

The roof below was drifting further and further away. Ash swallowed her fear and lowered herself through the hatch. Puppy's paws trembled against her neck as she climbed down the rope. When she reached the end, her feet dangled high above the roof. A gust of wind pushed the airship sideways. Soon she'd be dangling over open air.

"Drop!" yelled Tavan.

Ash closed her eyes and let go.

She hit the stone tiles with a jolt that sent her crashing into a potted jujube. Both Ash and the tree tumbled over the roof edge. Luckily, Fen snagged Wayfarer, and Tavan grabbed Fen.

When Ash came to a stop, half her body hung off the roof. Only the straps of Wayfarer kept her from falling. The jujube tree was still plummeting toward the ground far below.

Tavan hoisted her back onto the roof. Ash checked to make sure that Wayfarer, Kiki, and Puppy were all with her. Puppy licked her chin.

"What were you thinking, Fen? You scared the life out of me!" said Tavan.

Fen shrugged. "I wanted to see what it felt like to drop out of an airship. Besides, we can't let Ash go in alone." He looked at Ash and winked.

Ash winked back. As dangerous as Fen's last-minute stunt had been, she felt grateful to him for staying with her. The airship they'd dropped out of was already a couple hundred feet away.

"Dodgast it," grumbled Tavan. "We're in it now."

They found a door set into a square-shaped structure at one corner of the roof. It wasn't locked. Why would it be? To even get up here someone would need an airship, and Lord Ocras owned most of those.

Ash, Fen, and Tavan hurried through the doorway, while Puppy sniffed around the roof looking for a suitable place to pee. He kept his distance from the jujube trees since they had web-worms on them.

The door in the square structure opened onto a plush waiting room with a glowing kerosene chandelier. At the far end of the room a stone staircase spiraled downward. Ash headed toward it. She expected there to be guards in the tower, yet none appeared.

They took the staircase down to a hallway with several rooms branching off it. Puppy trotted ahead so he could warn Ash if he heard or smelled anyone. Each room looked finer than the fanciest parlor in the Wombley's mansion, with polished wood walls, plush velvet couches, and glowing chandeliers.

After doing a quick search of all the rooms and finding no one there, they took the spiral staircase down to the next level. The rooms on this floor contained paintings and stone sculptures, but still no people.

"Let's find the illwen and get out of here," said Tavan.

They continued searching rooms. On the next floor, several of the rooms had floor-to-ceiling bookshelves, with fancy ladders on rollers so people could reach the books on the top shelves—if ever someone entered the rooms.

Not only were there no people, the rooms looked immaculate. Not a single dirty cup, stray plate, or open book left behind to show that anyone had ever been there.

They searched two more floors before they arrived at a room that must have taken up a whole level of the largest tower. Unlike the other rooms, the only light in this room came from the fading glow of the sunset through the windows. A marble fountain, trickling pleasantly, occupied the room's center. Ash had never seen a fountain in a room before. She was so intrigued that she started walking toward it.

Someone's here, warned Puppy. His fur was bristling. *And something else. It smells like... wolves.*

Ash hadn't noticed the man standing near the windows with his back to them. Two enormous creatures sat beside him. The sky outside had faded from red to dark blue. Even in the dim light, she recognized the man.

Lord Ocras stood with the same regal posture he'd had in her vision of the Shadow Namer. If she'd had fur on her back like Puppy, hers would have pricked up as well.

Tavan and Fen stiffened beside her. No one said a word. Ash considered running for the stairs before Lord Ocras saw her, but the lower levels of the tower would certainly be guarded.

"Beautiful, isn't it?" said Lord Ocras, making it clear that he knew they were there.

Ash swallowed. So much for finding and freeing the illwen without being noticed.

"I hope you'll forgive the darkness," continued Lord Ocras. "I had the chandeliers on the other floors lit so you wouldn't have any trouble finding your way here, but I didn't want to spoil the view on this floor. Watching the sun set from up here, one can see both the fading light of day and the first stars of night."

He turned and lit a candle. The flickering yellowish light illuminated his face. He looked at once thinner around his eyes and plumper around his jaw than he had in her vision. When he smiled, he appeared handsome. A ribbon of crystal cloth shimmered on his forehead. The fine cloth had been woven through the links of the chain crown.

What Ash could see of the skin beneath the chain looked wrinkled and scarred—burn scars from when he welded the chain closed with dragon fire. It must have been incredibly painful. She almost felt bad for him, until she remembered what he'd done to the illwen with the other sections of the chain.

"I'm glad you received my invitation," said Lord Ocras. "You've arrived just in time for dinner."

"What invitation?" asked Ash.

Lord Ocras gestured to the room. "What do you think these towers are, but an invitation that only the worthy are able to reply to? If what I've heard is true, that includes you, Ash Narro. After all, you found your way in here. That's no simple task." He stepped toward her.

Puppy growled at Lord Ocras.

In response, the two creatures next to Lord Ocras bared their teeth and produced much deeper growls.

Ash startled. The creatures had been so still she'd thought they were statues. Now she recognized them as the wolves from her vision. They appeared larger in person than they had in the cave, with teeth the size of carving knives and eyes full of malice. No doubt they could tear her to shreds before she could take two steps.

"Eagla! Anobaith! Sit!" commanded Lord Ocras.

The wolves immediately sat, although their teeth remained bared. A silver lock dangled from the chain around each wolf's neck.

"These are guests, and we won't harm our guests." Lord Ocras opened his arms and nodded to Ash. "Please, be welcome. Don't let my pets scare you. Not everything is what it seems. A namer should know that—even a young namer like yourself, who still doesn't know who she is, or where she belongs."

Named and Unnamed

Servants set an elegant table near the windows along one side of the room. All the servants wore crystal cloth veils, and Ash had trouble telling them apart, but Lord Ocras seemed to have no such difficulty. He spoke to each servant by name, thanking them for their assistance. It wasn't at all like how the Wombleys ordered their servants about.

"You must be hungry from your journey. Please, eat," said Lord Ocras. "After dinner Zeera will show you to your rooms. It's my honor to have you stay here as my *guests*."

Tavan and Fen immediately sat.

Ash hesitated. The word "guest" echoed in her head, urging her to go along with things and not make a fuss, but something didn't feel right. She'd come here to free the illwen Lord Ocras had enslaved, not have a fancy dinner with him.

She *was* hungry, though. Her mouth watered as the servants set out plates of steaming potatoes, bread, fish, chicken, and other foods. It would have been rude to refuse to eat. She was a guest, and guests were supposed to be polite.

Tavan and Fen were already eating. That was the proper thing to do. Lord Ocras had welcomed them and offered them food. A guest shouldn't question such a kind host.

No, thought Ash. *Lord Ocras isn't a kind host.*

This was the man who'd stolen and enslaved three illwen. Not only that, he'd taken over so much farmland to grow web-worm silk for his factories that squatters were left no choice but to cut down and burn the cloud forest to grow food. He was the reason the forest was being destroyed, which meant he was the reason the dao fora and illwen kept attacking villages. Even the drought could be traced back to him and the crystal cloth he profited from. She couldn't trust him. He'd only called her a guest to distract her.

Ash remained standing.

Lord Ocras raised an eyebrow. "I see the rumors of your abilities aren't overstated. Good. I would have been disappointed if you weren't clever enough to sense my influence and resist it."

"Influence?" asked Ash.

"There's no point lying to me. I know why you came here, Young Namer. You want to take my illwen." He gestured to the wolves at his sides. "Perhaps I should introduce them to you properly. Let me present to you Anobaith and Eagla, my loyal companions."

The word "companion" echoed in her head. A companion was a partner. A friend.

Before the word could take root, Ash knew she had to change it. When talking with a namer, a great deal depended on what things were called.

"They're not your companions. They're slaves," she said.

"Ah... now you're being honest with me." Lord Ocras grinned. "That's much better. It's hard to have an interesting conversation without honesty. Don't you agree?"

"What about you? Are you being honest?"

"Of course. I have nothing to hide."

Tavan and Fen stopped eating. They both looked up from their plates, bewildered, as if they'd only now realized where they were and what they were doing. The effect of Lord Ocras's influence over them must have been wearing off.

"I know what you did," said Ash. "I saw it when I drank from the Pool of Memory. You're the Shadow Namer. You stole the Heart of the Forest, melted it down, and used it to capture and bind the illwen."

"Yes. I'm sure the dao fora you've met have told you many terrible stories about me." Lord Ocras leaned back and looked at Fen and Tavan. "I won't deny that I've had to do some unpleasant things. But do you know why I did such things? *That's* the question you should be asking."

Ash frowned. "It doesn't matter why. The illwen are wild forest spirits. They need to be free."

"And you've never captured and bound an illwen?" He glanced at where Puppy lay on the floor, gnawing a hambone that one of the servants had brought him. "Your puppy has quite an appetite. He must be very *spirited*."

Puppy paused, sensing everyone's gaze on him. *What? I was hungry. Villain or not, his food's still good.*

"Perhaps we should discuss this after you've had a chance to rest," added Lord Ocras. "Your friend doesn't appear to be enjoying our conversation."

As if in response to Lord Ocras's words, Fen swayed over his plate. His face was pale and sweaty.

Tavan put a gentle hand on Fen's shoulder. "Son, are you okay?"

"Yeah. Just... dizzy."

"Let's take a walk." Tavan helped Fen stand.

Ash considered going with them to make sure that Fen was okay, but Tavan seemed to want time alone with his son.

"The forest outside my village is burning right now," she said after Fen and Tavan left the table. "Governor Castol and his soldiers started the fire. They were supposed to have a peaceful meeting with leaders of the dao fora. Instead, the governor tried to kill the dao fora."

"I heard about that. Such an unfortunate incident," replied Lord Ocras.

Ash dug her nails into her fists. She knew Lord Ocras must have had something to do with the fighting. He profited from it. Just like he profited from having hungry squatters cut down the cloud forest. With the trees gone, there was more land for webworm plantations.

"The governor works for you, doesn't he?"

Lord Ocras shrugged. "*I* didn't send him to your village if that's what you're suggesting. And I'm not the one who convinced the dao fora to go there. It seems to me that whoever arranged the meeting is responsible for its results."

Ash clenched her jaw. As much as she wanted to blame Lord Ocras for everything, she couldn't deny her role in bringing the governor and the dao fora to her village.

"A namer who doesn't know her own name is a very dangerous thing," continued Lord Ocras. "I don't blame you for your mistakes. You had no guidance. That's why it's good that you've come to me. I can help you. However, it would be best for us to discuss these matters later." Lord Ocras looked toward Tavan and

Fen, who were walking around the fountain in the center of the room. "Your friend seems to be feeling better."

"How does all this water get up here?" asked Fen. He still looked tired, but at least he'd recovered enough to ask questions.

"It's quite a feat of engineering," replied Lord Ocras in a jovial voice. "There's a windmill on the back side of this tower that pumps the water up. The more the wind blows, the stronger the water flows. When it's gusty, that fountain nearly reaches the ceiling." He beckoned for them to return to the table. "Let's eat, before the food grows cold."

Ash stirred potatoes around her plate. Eating made her feel better, but no less confused. The things Lord Ocras had said kept swirling about her head, muddying her thoughts.

Why did he say she didn't know her own name? Was it because she didn't know why her parents had named her Ash? A true name hinted at what something could be and where it belonged, but she wasn't sure where she belonged anymore. Her home had changed so much.

Nothing seemed clear to her, not even why she'd come here. Lord Ocras wasn't at all how she'd expected him to be. What if he wasn't the villain she'd thought?

Ash stared out the windows of the tower. A sprinkle of stars shimmered in the dark sky.

Something nudged her leg beneath the table. At first she thought it was Puppy, until she saw him on the floor gnawing the hambone. The nudge came again, pressing against her knee. Ash reached down and touched the large, bristling muzzle of one of the wolves.

A jolt of fear shot through her. She nearly yelped, but she forced herself to stay calm. Slowly, carefully, Ash looked down.

The wolf had to crouch to fit under the table. Its jaws stretched wider than her chair and its enormous forepaws encircled her feet. It sniffed her hand then pressed its nose to her palm.

Ash tensed. If the wolf wanted to, it could snap off her hand in one bite. Instincts urged her to get away from the creature. The illwen seemed the essence of fear itself—a nightmare in the shape of a wolf. But when she met its gaze, she saw a faint flicker of something else. Something she hadn't sensed before.

Courage.

She took a deep breath and stroked the illwen's head, her fingers reaching for the same spot behind the ears where Puppy liked to be scratched. Touching the wolf both frightened and emboldened her. Where there was fear there was also courage. There had to be. One gave rise to the other, the same way there couldn't be light without dark, or stars without night.

The second wolf crawled closer under the table and nudged her other leg. This wolf's touch filled her with a deep, crushing sadness. Her shoulders slumped beneath the weight of the emotion. She wanted to give up.

Despair, she thought, naming the feeling she got from this illwen. And yet, as the wolf rested its head against her leg and gazed at her, Ash sensed something else in its form too.

Hope.

She put her hand on top of the wolf's head. The fur was prickly and stiff, but not entirely unpleasant.

Despair and hope were connected, just as courage and fear were.

The wolves kept looking at her. They appeared to be asking her for something. They even whimpered—a low, pitiful sound.

Ash glanced at Lord Ocras. He was busy cutting a piece of meat. The chain crown on his forehead gleamed in the candle-light. Among the silver links and crystal cloth, a few beads of sweat dotted his brow. Although he was powerful, he didn't have complete control over the illwen. Other names still lurked beneath the names he'd given them.

Lord Ocras heard the wolves' whimpers and looked up abruptly. "Eagla! Anobaith!" he snapped.

The wolves immediately scooted out from under the table and trotted to him.

"Forgive them," said Lord Ocras. "They're terrible beggars. I gave them cheese once and now they won't stop pestering people. I'm afraid I've spoiled them."

Lord Ocras took two squares of cheese off a plate and gave one to each of the wolves, ordering them to sit beside him.

They sat and snapped up the pieces of cheese with mechanical precision, as if they didn't want to obey, but they had no choice.

Restless

After dinner, the servant named Zeera led Ash and Puppy to a room on the floor below the one with the fountain. Tavan and Fen were taken to a room at the other end of the hall.

Zeera lit the lanterns in the bedroom then left. Puppy darted about Ash's feet, trying to interest her in a game of chase, but she felt too tired to play. She sank into the alluring softness of the bed. Puppy jumped back, growling.

"What is it?" asked Ash.

Get away from there!

Ash turned to see what had spooked him. She expected there to be a spider or snake crawling out from under the bed, but everything looked fine. It was a far nicer bed than her own thin mattress. Nicer even than the bed she'd slept on in the Capitol. The quilted blanket had red and purple flowers stitched into it, and the pillow was stuffed with tiny feathers.

"It's just a bed."

It smells bad. Puppy bit a corner of the flower quilt and thrashed his head.

"Puppy!" Ash worried that he'd tear the quilt. It probably cost a fortune.

The heart-shaped locket tied around Puppy's neck jangled as he tugged and pulled the quilt completely off.

The sheets of the bed were made of pure crystal cloth. They shimmered in the light, reflecting a myriad of colors. Ash reached to touch them.

Puppy nipped her hand. *Don't!*

"Why not? It's beautiful."

It's bad.

"But why is it bad? I don't understand. And don't tell me it smells bad. It smells perfectly fine to me."

Puppy sat back and scratched his ears. *You think mint and oranges smell fine, and they're both awful.*

"See, that's my point—mint and oranges are delicious."

This is worse than mint. Or oranges. This smells like a friend who snarls and bites when he should wag and play. Whatever it touches smells bad too. I don't want you to smell like it.

"Then where am I supposed to sleep?"

Puppy dragged a blanket to the corner of the room, as far as possible from the crystal cloth bed. Then he turned in a circle on the blanket, nudging it until it was tangled into a nest on the floor. Satisfied with his work, he plopped down in the middle and yawned. *This is a perfect bed.*

Ash had to smile. "All right. I'll try it your way." She took Kiki and Aisling out of Wayfarer and arranged the carpetbag as a pillow. Then she curled up next to Puppy on the floor.

Puppy yawned and stretched his paws. *Perfect,* he said again.

In only a matter of minutes, Puppy was fast asleep. His whiskers twitched and legs trembled as he dreamed.

Ash wondered what he dreamed about. Was he chasing squirrels through the forest or fetching a ball? He seemed more puppy-like now than ever.

During dinner Lord Ocras had suggested that naming Lost Heart Puppy was no different from what he'd done to the illwen he'd enslaved. She'd even put a collar on Puppy, like he'd done to Eagla and Anobaith. But was it the same? Puppy wanted to be a puppy, and he wanted to be with her, didn't he? She was his family now. Or had he simply forgotten about being a wild, stormy illwen? And if he did forget, would that be such a bad thing?

Thoughts like this kept her awake, despite how tired she felt. She eventually gave up on sleeping and got up, careful not to disturb Puppy. As long as she was awake, she might as well explore the towers. After all, she'd only found two of the illwen Lord Ocras had bound. The third illwen—the cocoon-shaped one that he'd taken—had to be somewhere.

Ash brought Kiki with her and slipped into the hall. She considered going to Fen and Tavan's room but decided not to wake them. Tavan wouldn't approve of snooping around the towers, and Fen needed rest.

She tiptoed down a flight of stairs to a floor with rooms full of shelves. Instead of books, these shelves held rocks—hundreds of rocks, humming with energy and potential. Some looked plain and some looked like gems or crystals. She couldn't tell much else about them, since it was dark and she was afraid of being caught in the room. The only illumination came from moonlight trickling through the windows.

A breeze tickled her face. Two glass doors at the end of the hallway stood open. Ash passed through them to a balcony with an ornate stone railing.

It felt good to be outside. She inhaled the cool night air and started to relax, until she realized she wasn't alone. Lord Ocras stood at one end of the balcony, gazing at the stars.

Ash raised Kiki for protection. Luckily, the wolves weren't with Lord Ocras.

"You too," he said. He didn't seem surprised or upset to see her there, just amused. "Everyone dreams the dreams we give them, while we lie awake. It's one more thing we have in common."

Ash scowled. "I'm nothing like you."

Lord Ocras straightened his dinner jacket. As he did this, his fingers tucked a necklace with a skeleton key into his shirt.

"I see you brought a friend." He nodded to the stick Ash held. "I bet she has a name."

"She does. I'm not telling it to you."

"Good. True names should be kept secret. To hear the whispered names of what something can be is a powerful gift."

"What makes you think I hear whispers?" asked Ash. She'd never told anyone how objects whispered their names to her.

"Because that's how it works for me. We're more alike than you think, Young Namer. I probably understand you better than anyone you've ever met. And, like you, I hear the whispered names of things."

"What sort of things?"

"Well, my slippers," he said. "The table we ate dinner at. I've even named a few of the tiles in my favorite room. This whole house is full of elemental objects that I've named, and they're all precious to me. I built these towers to hold them. I have room after room of such priceless objects. Tomorrow I could show you my collection if you like."

Ash stood, uncertain.

"Ah… I see you still don't trust me. Would it help if I let you see into myself?" He held his hands out before him.

Ash stared at his hands, perplexed. She had no idea what she was supposed to do.

"Don't tell me you've never used your abilities to see who someone is?" said Lord Ocras. "Namers like us can do far more than simply hear whispered possibilities for things. With people, we can see the memories that shaped them. I'll show you. Rest your hands on mine and look into my eyes."

Ash hesitated.

"You don't need to be afraid. It's simple. I thought you would have explored your abilities more by now. When I was your age, I was seeing what memories shaped people all the time."

Ash considered how she'd known that Pilot had loved watching birds soar when he was a child. Perhaps she had done something like this before.

She lightly placed her hands on Lord Ocras's palms, ready to pull away if he tried to grab her. Then she looked into his eyes.

Only, instead of simply seeing his eyes, she saw colors—brown, blue, and green wisps swirling about. It was hazy at first, but the more she focused on the colors, the more they resolved into images, like when Balance Keeper had shown her images of the cloud forest.

Ash saw two workers hauling items out of a small house. Some nicer items went into a black carriage parked in the street, but most things were tossed into the yard. Chairs, dishes, clothes, and books piled up in the dirt while a boy—maybe six or seven years old—gathered what he could.

The boy stuffed several books and other knickknacks into a suitcase. Nearby, his mother grabbed clothes and dishes, and his father watched with a lost look. All the while, workers continued tossing items out of the house.

People stopped to observe this curious scene. A few onlookers helped themselves to hats, scarves, and other items strewn about the yard.

The mother fought with one of the workers over a jewelry box. He tore the box from her and carried it to the carriage.

"You can't do this. Please…" begged the father. "We have nothing left."

The workers ignored the father's pleas.

Desperate, the father charged the carriage and tried to force open the side door. One of the workers came up behind him and thumped him with a club. The father slumped to the ground, clutching his head. Blood seeped between his fingers.

A constable arrived wearing a blue uniform. He talked with the two workers. Instead of arresting them for hitting the father, the constable hoisted the father to his feet, cuffed his hands behind his back, and shoved him into the back of a wagon. Then the constable dragged the mother across the street, away from the house.

Once the man was removed, the workers continued throwing items out until the house stood empty and everything valuable had been loaded into the carriage. At last, one of the workers approached the boy.

"Come on, boy," he said. "Your father owes more than this house is worth. The bank wants it all."

The boy stared at the man, refusing to give up the suitcase.

That's when Ash realized she was seeing the man from the boy's perspective. It must have been Lord Ocras's memory of something he'd experienced as a child. The feeling of powerlessness she got from the scene disturbed her.

With grim resignation, the man pried the boy's fingers from the suitcase. Then the man tossed the suitcase into the black carriage and the workers departed, leaving the mother and boy in the road.

The scene faded as Lord Ocras lowered his hands. He drew a deep breath and straightened his jacket.

"You see, I know what it's like to lose my home," he said. "That day, I swore I'd never be powerless again. I applied all my faculties to studying people and how power works. A few years later, while watching crowds in the marketplace, I saw that people flow like water. Without direction, they run rampant and cause problems. But with direction, people can be guided into creating great things."

Lord Ocras looked out from the balcony at the other towers. Lanterns far below illuminated the roads leading to his crystal cloth and airship factories. "I did all this to create a better world," he said. "One in which everyone has their place and purpose in the greater design."

"What about my village?" asked Ash. "Things aren't better there. They're worse. No one trusts anyone else. Everyone's fighting. How is that better?"

"Do you want to know why the governor attacked the dao fora outside your village when he could have made peace with them?" asked Lord Ocras. "Why people keep acting the way they do?"

Ash nodded.

"If you truly want to understand people, then you must see things the way they do." Lord Ocras reached into the inner pocket of his dinner jacket and pulled out a pair of crystal cloth spectacles. "You cannot name what you do not understand." He offered the spectacles to her.

They were the finest crystal cloth spectacles she'd ever seen—far fancier than the ones the soldiers wore. Along the front the cloth was long, like a veil without a hat, while the shimmering ribbons of crystal cloth that held the spectacles in place in the back were lacy and elegant. The cloth appeared so finely woven it was nearly invisible, yet it reflected light like the wings of a dragonfly. Her mother would have loved them. Ash reached for the spectacles, then hesitated.

"I see. You're still too timid to face the truth. So be it." Lord Ocras started to slide the spectacles back into his pocket.

"Wait." Ash reached for the spectacles again.

"Are you sure?" asked Lord Ocras. "I don't want you to feel obligated…"

Ash took the spectacles and backed away. "It's late. I need to get some sleep," she said.

"Of course," replied Lord Ocras.

Once Ash was safely back in her room upstairs, she studied the spectacles. How harmful could they be? Everyone wore them, or at least everyone who could afford crystal cloth did. And everyone else wanted crystal cloth. She was sick of not knowing what all the fuss was about.

The shimmering cloth felt cool to the touch. It reminded her of something, but Ash couldn't put her finger on what. Maybe she did need to wear them—just for a little bit—to understand how other people saw things. And if she didn't like them she could always take them off.

She put the spectacles on and glanced around the room.

The crystal cloth cast a slight haze over things, but other than that nothing looked or felt different. Puppy was still Puppy, sleeping on a tangled blanket in the corner. The moon was still the moon, shining through the window. The bed was still a plush, inviting bed.

She tied the long ribbons of crystal cloth around her head to hold the spectacles in place. The finely woven cloth made the tips of her fingers tingle. Why had she been frightened of this?

Ash lay on the bed and fell into a deep, dreamless sleep.

The Power of Naming

Puppy's growls woke her.

"What's wrong?" asked Ash.

The fur on Puppy's shoulders bristled as he glared at her.

Ash checked the room but no one else was there. Didn't he recognize her? "It's just me, Puppy." She brushed her hair back from her face and her fingers touched the smooth silk of the crystal cloth spectacles. She must have fallen asleep with them on.

Looking around, she noticed that the spectacles softened the bright morning sunlight and made things appear much easier to deal with.

Why are you wearing those? snarled Puppy. *And why did you sleep on the bed?*

Ash stretched, ignoring Puppy's growls. "It's nothing to get upset about. I just wanted to see things the way others see them."

Puppy edged back. *You don't smell good.*

"Well, sometimes you roll in things that I'm not very fond of."

That's different.

"Not to me."

I was afraid this would happen. You're changing.

"Don't be such a worrywart. Look, I can take them off anytime." Ash removed the spectacles and set them on the bed. "See? I'm still me." She reached to pet Puppy behind his ears. He sniffed her hand warily.

"You're probably just hungry," she teased. Her eyes watered from the harsh sunlight pouring through the window. After giving Puppy a few quick pets, she put the spectacles back on.

Puppy growled again.

"Trust me. I know what I'm doing," she said. "Now let's get some breakfast."

Ash stuffed her feet into her boots and packed Aisling and Kiki into Wayfarer so she could take all her things with her. If she didn't, someone might steal them. With Wayfarer strapped to her shoulders, she headed down the hall to find some food. An anxious, needy sensation gnawed at her, and hunger seemed the best explanation for it.

She went upstairs to the fountain room where they'd eaten the night before. Platters of eggs, ham, bread, and fruit covered the table. Ash poured herself a hearty glass of fresh-squeezed sunfruit and loaded her plate full of eggs. She even took a slice of ham. She didn't usually eat ham—every pig she'd known had a name and eating a named creature had always felt wrong to her—but the ham smelled so delicious she couldn't resist it.

Puppy watched her as she ate. He still seemed upset. It wasn't until she'd devoured most of the food on her plate that she realized he didn't have any food. She loaded up a second plate and set it on the floor for him.

He sniffed it once and backed away. *I'm not hungry.*

"That's a first." Ash took a second slice of ham for herself.

Tavan and Fen wandered in not long after. They must have smelled the food, but they both stopped before they reached the table and gaped at her.

"What?" asked Ash, annoyed.

Fen pointed to her crystal cloth spectacles. "Why are you wearing those?"

"Everyone wears them. They're very fashionable."

Fen frowned. "Since when do *you* care about being fashionable?"

"Why shouldn't I care? I can be fashionable. I'm just as important as all those fancy ladies strutting around Governor City."

"I didn't say you weren't important. I just thought you didn't like that fancy stuff," said Fen.

"Well, now I do. I think they look good on me, and if you were polite, you'd say so too."

Fen looked perplexed.

"Let it go, Fen." Tavan set his hand on his son's shoulder. "There's no point arguing with her. We need to leave this place. It's not safe here."

"It seems perfectly safe to me. The food's much better here than anything you cooked," said Ash.

Tavan stepped closer to Ash and lowered his voice until he was nearly whispering. "Do you remember why you came here? What you were going to do?"

"Of course."

"And…?"

"And I'm working on it. Not everything is what it seems."

"What does that mean?"

"It means that things are more complicated than you think. Lord Ocras…" Ash hesitated and glanced at the entrance to the room. "Lord Ocras had good reasons to do the things he did."

Tavan opened his mouth, but before he could say anything else, Lord Ocras strode in, followed by his wolves, Eagla and Anobaith.

"I'm glad you found your way to the food," he said. "I trust you slept well. Ash, if you've finished your breakfast, I'd be honored to take you on a tour of the collection I mentioned."

Ash glanced at Tavan and Fen. They were both giving her dark looks. "That would be splendid," she answered.

She stood to go. Puppy moved to go with her, but Lord Ocras muttered something and Eagla and Anobaith blocked Puppy's way. "I'm afraid the invitation is for Ash alone. Don't worry. I'll make sure you're all well taken care of."

He gestured and two servants, wearing crystal cloth veils, stepped forward to attend to Fen, Tavan, and Puppy.

"Shall we?" Lord Ocras offered Ash his arm.

"Ash, wait!" Fen slipped past one of the servants to get to her.

"You can't stop me from going," she said.

"Don't trust him. He's up to something," whispered Fen.

"I can take care of myself."

"I know. But if there's one thing I've learned, it's that taking care of yourself isn't enough. You have to take care of others too. And sometimes you have to let them take care of you."

"I don't have to do anything."

Fen frowned. "The wolves, Eagla and Anobaith—do you know what their names mean? Tavan looked it up in a book he found. In another language, Eagla means fear and Anobaith means despair."

Ash shrugged. She'd already sensed as much from touching the wolves. "So?"

"So that's how he controls things. He brings out the worst in them."

"Why are you telling me this?"

"Because I don't want him to do the same to you. Don't let him tell you who you are. Don't let him name you."

"What do you know about who I am?"

"I'm Friend of Strangers, remember?" said Fen. "That's what you called me. To be someone's friend, you need to understand them—or at least try to."

Ash shook her head. "You don't know me. Not truly."

"I know that you always try to see the best in people. You're the opposite of him." Fen nodded to where Lord Ocras stood by the door, watching them. "Even though you're acting strange right now, I'm still your friend—because I'm Friend of Strangers, and friends help each other, especially when they lose their way."

Ash narrowed her eyes. "I'm not the one who's lost."

She turned and left with Lord Ocras.

The tour Lord Ocras led her on spanned several towers. They crossed bridges, climbed stairs, and wound through halls and tunnels. Everywhere they went, servants silently followed.

Along the way, Lord Ocras showed Ash dozens of rooms brimming with treasures he'd collected. Some were obviously valuable—gold cups, jeweled eggs, sparkling gems. Others appeared ordinary. One room had only acorns, sticks, and the shiny carapaces of dead beetles. Another room was full of dried flowers and animal teeth.

Several of the objects Lord Ocras showed her seemed to hum with energy when Ash approached them. Some practically buzzed in the cases and jars that contained them. Even plain-looking objects, such as pieces of wood and bone, had a subtle hum that set them apart.

Lord Ocras watched Ash carefully as he shared his collection with her. At one point she touched a stone on a shelf. He immediately moved it a hair to the left, setting it back exactly how it had been before she'd touched it.

"Everything has its place," he said. "Few people truly understand how precious these things are. Most people think I'm simply an eccentric old man who collects rocks and feathers. But you know these things are more than that, don't you?"

"Did all of these objects speak to you?" asked Ash, amazed that one person could have so many named objects.

Lord Ocras laughed. "Yes, I suppose they did. Do you know what these objects are, Young Namer? Why it is that they contain so much energy and potential?"

Ash studied the feathers, bones, and carvings on the shelves. Although she could feel their energy, she still had no idea why some objects whispered to her and others didn't.

"It's because they're elemental objects," continued Lord Ocras. "Do you understand what that means?"

"Maybe," said Ash, although it wasn't a term she'd ever heard before.

Lord Ocras strode toward a pair of plush chairs arranged around a side table. He gestured for Ash to sit, then settled in the chair across from her. A servant brought them glasses of water.

Lord Ocras raised his glass and took a sip. "Thank you, Zeera. This is refreshing."

The servant glided back to her post by the door.

"Now, where were we?"

"Elemental objects," prodded Ash.

"Right. The world around us is made of form and energy. Or, if one were to speak more poetically, form and spirit. Form refers to things that are solid and fixed. Spirit is formless and constantly changing. Together, form and spirit make up everything, but they're not as separate as people tend to think."

Lord Ocras took another sip of water and gazed at the liquid remaining in his glass. "All forms contain some spirit energy, and it's this spirit energy that enables forms to shift and change. Even, sometimes, to come alive. The more spirit energy a form has, the more changeable and alive it is. Some forms contain so much life—so much spirit energy—that they're barely able to stay in one form for long. Their vast energy makes them volatile and unstable, so they constantly shift and change their shape."

"Like the illwen," said Ash, recalling the night she'd named Puppy. Although the illwen she'd faced had appeared solid, it kept shifting its form, swirling like black smoke.

"Yes," said Lord Ocras. "The illwen are the elemental energies of life embodied. They contain so much spirit energy that when they pass through other forms, they leave traces of their energy behind." He drank the rest of his water and held the glass up before him. Beads of water ran down the sides and collected in the bottom. "You see? Even when you pour the water out, the glass still contains a few drops." He set the glass on the table before her. "That's how elemental objects, like the ones I've collected here, are created. An illwen has passed through each of these objects, infusing it with some of its spirit energy. Energy that makes the object a little more alive. A little more… changeable."

Ash thought of the illwen she'd seen in the cave, passing through the objects on the shrines. What Lord Ocras said made sense. The objects that the illwen passed through hummed and glowed with spirit energy. This even explained why she'd found Kiki in the square the day after an illwen attack. The illwen that had attacked her village must have carried the ironwood stick there, infusing it with some of its energy.

"Is that the only way elemental objects are created?" asked Ash. "By illwen?"

"It's the most common way," said Lord Ocras. "People can infuse forms with small amounts of spirit energy too, if they spend enough time with an object and care about it a great deal. But people can't infuse things with nearly as much spirit energy as illwen can. Illwen are the elemental powerhouses of creation. Nevertheless, as powerful as they are, they have their limitations. Spirit can only know itself through form, which is why illwen sometimes like to take on certain forms. And it's why illwen can be controlled through forms."

He picked up a feather from the shelf beside him and brushed the soft end against his cheek. "The dao fora understood that illwen needed to know themselves through forms. They built shrines to honor the illwen, and they filled those shrines with objects that reflected the qualities they admired in various illwen—just as we might honor someone we admire by giving them pretty things."

Ash thought of the sacred objects she'd seen on the shrines in her vision of the Cave of Illwen. Had all of them been given to honor various illwen? That made sense for most of the objects she recalled, but one object—the silver Heart of the Forest—had seemed different. Instead of glowing with the spirit energy of a single illwen, it glowed with energy from all the illwen in the cave, as if all the illwen she'd seen in her vision had passed through it.

"What about the Heart of the Forest?" asked Ash. "It's not an ordinary elemental object, is it?"

Lord Ocras raised an eyebrow. "No, it's far from ordinary. There are certain rare objects that contain energy from many elemental spirits. The Heart of the Forest was one such object. I believe there may be others. After all, there are illwen elsewhere—the elemental spirits of the mountains, plains, deserts, and oceans. If illwen exist elsewhere, it stands to reason that heart stones exist elsewhere, too. One day, I intend to find them."

Ash shuddered to think what Lord Ocras might do with other heart stones. "It's… an impressive collection," she said.

He smiled, appearing pleased that she understood the value of his objects. "You know, *you* could have a house like this someday, with rooms to keep all of your elemental objects safe. Would you like that?"

"Yes," replied Ash. But as soon as she said this, she felt ashamed. The small, modest rooms she'd grown up in weren't even as big as a single floor in one of Lord Ocras's towers. And he had several towers here, each with dozens of floors. To have a home like this was beyond her wildest dreams. And what would she fill it with?

Ash touched the straps of Wayfarer. The lightness of the bag made her chest ache. Once these straps had squeezed her shoulders like a hug. Now she barely felt them. "I used to have several elemental objects that I'd named, but I had to give them up."

Lord Ocras nodded. "The world will keep trying to take what's precious to you. That's why you must take what's yours and guard it carefully. To keep what you care about, you must become more powerful than those who'd steal from you."

"I don't want power."

"I said the same thing when I was young. Then, as you know, I lost all that I cared about. What you cannot protect will be taken away. It's only a matter of time. However, you have the ability to keep that from happening."

"How?"

"By using your abilities to shape things," said Lord Ocras. "That is, after all, why you name things, isn't it? To make things be what you want them to be."

Ash furrowed her brow. Was that why she named things?

"I see you doubt me," said Lord Ocras. "You still know so little of the world. I bet you think that naming is merely a matter of listening to what others cannot hear. But listening is barely even half of it, Young Namer. The real trick is *telling* something what to become. When you hear names, you're hearing possibilities. Forms don't have one true name. They have several names—several possibilities for what they might be. Each name is a lever you can use to shape something into what you want it to be. Watch."

He held the feather up before him and examined it.

Ash sensed spirit energy humming within the feather.

"*Seta!*" said Lord Ocras. With a quick snap of his arm, he threw the feather at the wall.

Only it wasn't a feather anymore. It blurred and changed, becoming a sharp-tipped dart that stuck into the wood paneling.

"Is this a trick…?" asked Ash.

She examined the dart lodged in the wall. The wispy tuft on the end had the exact same spots on it that she'd seen on the feather moments before, and the long shaft of the dart looked like a natural quill that had grown into a straight, deadly point.

"Hearing possibilities and telling something what to be—*that's* what naming truly is," said Lord Ocras.

"That's not possible. Things can't simply change like that."

"Things change all the time. Water can be liquid, ice, mist, or steam, depending on its energy. An object infused with spirit energy has the elemental energy of change within it. I'm simply telling these objects what to change to." He walked over to another shelf and picked up a small stick.

Lord Ocras examined the stick closely. "*Chama*!" he said.

The wood ignited into flames. It burned so quickly that he had to drop the stick and snap his hand back. By the time the stick reached the ground, it was only ashes.

"Is it the word that makes things change?" asked Ash.

Lord Ocras chuckled. "It's my will that makes things change. The words are simply tools I use to focus my will. Any word in any language can be a binding word of power with enough will behind it. However, I've learned that it's best not to use one's ordinary language for words of power. Too many mistakes happen that way. That's why I prefer to use words from other languages to shape elemental objects."

"Why are you showing me this?" asked Ash.

Lord Ocras brushed his fingers along his vest. "Because I see what you can become, and I may be the only one who sees it. You're not the first namer to find your way here, but you are the youngest. That speaks to your potential. Your parents, your friends, the people in your village—none of them understand what you might be. They think you're merely a strange girl who talks to herself. But you could be the ruler of a kingdom bigger than a hundred villages. Bigger than a thousand."

"What if I don't want to be a ruler?"

"You do," he said. "You might not realize it yet, but eventually you'll see that this is the only way to protect all that you care about. Naming is a great gift. What I do helps people. I tell them who they are and what to want. I give them aspirations and things to work for. Even these towers provide a shining example of what to strive for. I give them purpose and direction. Industry and jobs. Order and meaning."

Ash could feel the influence of his words pulling on her as he spoke. Everything Lord Ocras said seemed true.

"Being a namer is your purpose," he continued. "Shaping the world into what you want it to be is what you were born to do. There's no need to fight it anymore, Young Namer. All I want is to help you develop your potential. It would be a crime to let such a gift go to waste."

31

The Stolen Illwen

Ash didn't see Fen and Tavan that afternoon, but she found Puppy curled up on the blanket in the corner of her bedroom.

"Hey, I'm back."

Puppy startled awake. The fur on his shoulders bristled. *You don't smell like yourself.*

"Stop being silly. Nothing's changed." She moved to pet him, but he avoided her hand.

Don't come near me with those things.

Ash stood, perplexed. Then she caught sight of herself in the mirror and her heart skipped.

At first glance she thought she was looking at her mom. The crystal cloth spectacles covered most of her face. She tilted her head from side to side to make sure it really was her reflection. The brown-haired girl in the mirror with the shimmering veil covering her eyes tilted her head as well.

The crystal cloth spectacles felt so much a part of her that she'd forgotten she was wearing them. Ash didn't want to take them off, but Puppy kept watching her. For his sake she untied the ribbons that held the spectacles in place and slid them off her head.

Immediately, the bright, harsh light in the room struck her. Her head ached, and she wanted to put the spectacles back on.

What's wrong with you? Are you okay? asked Puppy.

"I'm fine." Ash forced her lips into a tight smile and moved to set the spectacles in a dresser drawer. Still, she didn't want to let them go. What if someone took them?

Instead of leaving the spectacles, she swiftly tucked them into her pocket. Puppy was being overly cautious. It would be foolish to leave such valuable things behind. She might need them later.

"See. I'm still me," she said, turning back toward Puppy. She held out her hands to show that they were empty. "No more crystal cloth. I was just wearing those silly things to trick Lord Ocras."

Puppy cocked his head. *Trick him?*

"Yes. I wanted him to think that I was going along with him."

Why?

"So that he'd show me around."

Puppy's tail thumped the wooden floorboards once, then stopped. *You mean, you were only pretending?*

"Of course," said Ash. "You didn't actually think I'd choose stinky crystal cloth over being with you, did you?"

Puppy's tail thumped the floor a few more times. He edged forward, sniffing the air, then stopped. *You still smell strange.*

"It'll pass," said Ash. "In the meantime, I found the room."

What room?

"The room where Lord Ocras is hiding the third illwen."

On the way, Ash explained to Puppy how she'd found the room. She knew Lord Ocras must have had a secret room somewhere—why else would he hide the key he wore around his neck? When he took her on the tour, she kept an eye out for any rooms he avoided showing her.

She'd almost missed it. Lord Ocras had been very clever. He'd gone up and down the stairs in some of the smaller towers, then crossed back on sky bridges to the main tower. But Ash counted the steps whenever they went up or down. That's how she discovered a whole floor in the main tower that Lord Ocras had skipped.

Unfortunately, the door to the secret floor was locked. Ash doubted she'd be able to get the key from Lord Ocras without him noticing, but there was another way in.

She led Puppy to the balcony she'd found the other night. When she leaned over the edge, she could see a smaller balcony jutting out from the floor below—the floor that Lord Ocras had avoided showing her. If she could get from the upper balcony to the lower one without falling to her death, she might be able to enter the secret room that way.

Since Ash didn't have Telltale with her, she had to make her own rope. For this she used a pair of velvet curtains that she swiped from the hall. She twisted the curtains and tied them together, then tied one end of the makeshift rope to a balcony pillar. With Wayfarer strapped to her back and Puppy huddled on her shoulders, she climbed over the railing.

Her stomach lurched as she immediately slid downward. The velvet curtain rope was so smooth, she could barely grip it. Luckily, she'd tied a knot at the end. Her hands caught the knot, and she came to an abrupt stop.

That's a long way down, said Puppy. *I can't even smell the ground from here.*

"Look out, not down," she replied. Nevertheless, she couldn't keep herself from glancing down. She shuddered when she saw how high above the stone plaza they dangled.

She had to swing back and forth to reach the lower balcony. After several attempts, Ash managed to hook her leg over the railing and clamber onto solid ground.

Puppy hopped off her shoulders and sniffed the potted jujube trees that lined the balcony. For once, he didn't complain about their smell.

Unlike the jujube trees she'd seen in plantation fields, these didn't have any webworms on them. Their bright green leaves looked shiny and healthy. A few of the jujubes had small white flowers on their branches. Without the webworms and their sticky silk tents, the jujubes actually looked pretty.

While Puppy investigated the balcony, Ash peered through the glass panels in the balcony doors. The secret room had a similar size and layout to the fountain room two floors above. Only, instead of a fountain, this room had a stone pedestal in the center. Upon the pedestal lay the chained cocoon of the third illwen.

Ash reached to open the balcony door, then stopped. A figure moved in the room. She ducked behind a potted jujube to avoid being seen. Through the tree's branches, she watched Lord Ocras approach the pedestal with silver tweezers. Using the tweezers, he carefully unwound a strand of silk from the cocoon-shaped illwen.

What do you see? asked Puppy. He was too short to see through the glass door panels himself.

"Shh… Lord Ocras is in there."

Doing what?

"I'm not sure," she whispered.

The silk thread Lord Ocras unwound from the cocoon glowed with a warm yellow light. While Lord Ocras worked, the cocoon writhed and bulged in places, as if something inside wanted out, but the silver chain kept it bound in its current form.

Lord Ocras snipped off several pieces of the glowing silk thread. As soon as the scissors cut the thread, the glow dimmed. He carried the cut pieces to a table near where one of the wolf-shaped illwen lay. From the black streak of fur running down the wolf's forehead, Ash recognized him as Eagla.

Eagla's name might have meant fear, but the wolf didn't look very terrifying right now. He appeared to have given up, resting his head on his paws. The wolf didn't even twitch when Lord Ocras snipped a tuft of fur from his shoulder.

Lord Ocras took a piece of cocoon thread, no longer than an inch, and twisted it around a strand of wolf fur. Holding the inter-twined strands near his mouth, he whispered something. Immediately, the twisted strands merged and wriggled.

Ash gasped. Just as he'd turned a feather into an arrow and a stick into flames, Lord Ocras turned the twisted strands of cocoon silk and wolf fur into a webworm.

What is it? asked Puppy.

"Nothing," she said. If Puppy got excited, he might give them away.

Lord Ocras set the wriggling webworm in a bowl and re-peated the process with several more pieces of cocoon silk and wolf fur. Then he carried the bowl of newly created webworms to the potted jujube trees in the room and placed two on each tree.

Ash's mind raced to make sense of everything she'd seen. This was how Lord Ocras cast his spell over people. His patented Miracle Crystal Cloth Webworms didn't come from a special webworm queen like people thought. They came from the illwen he'd enslaved. He was cutting off pieces of illwen and using the spirit energy they contained to create webworms that devoured the forest. It seemed both cruel and unnatural. No wonder Puppy was repulsed by webworms and crystal cloth.

Lord Ocras pulled a cord hanging beside the main door. Two servants, faces veiled in crystal cloth, appeared in the doorway. They carried the jujube trees he'd infected with webworms out of the room. Lord Ocras followed them, calling both wolves to him as he left.

"He's gone," said Ash. She pushed open the balcony door.

Puppy trotted into the room. When he saw the glowing cocoon chained to the stone pedestal, he froze and his tail curled between his legs.

I don't like that silver chain. It's as bad as crystal cloth.

"I'll try to get rid of it," said Ash.

She grabbed the silver chain and attempted to pull it off the cocoon. The chain wouldn't budge, so she tried lifting the cocoon from the pedestal. The moment she touched the silky cocoon, an intense sensation of hunger struck her. She stumbled back clutching her stomach. The empty feeling wasn't only in her belly. It was in her head too—a sharp, painful yearning.

Gradually, the yearning sensation passed. Ash circled the pedestal, not wanting to touch the cocoon again. Even if she had been able to lift it, the chain around it was locked to the pedestal.

To move the cocoon she'd have to break the chain, and the chain was named Unbreakable.

The padlock that held the chain shut looked similar to the one her father had used to lock Fen in the rabbit cage. Ash slid Kiki out of Wayfarer and worked one of the ironwood twigs into the keyhole. The first twig was too thick, and the second too thin. It jangled about, doing nothing when she turned it.

"If your name means two keys, then why won't you open the lock?" she said, glaring at the ironwood.

Ash sighed and searched the room for something else to open the padlock with. A cabinet shrouded in crystal cloth curtains stood along the wall. She lifted one of the curtains and peeked in.

The interior of the cabinet was lined entirely with crystal cloth. Bones, rocks, a beaded necklace, and several intricate animal carvings sat on the cabinet shelves. The objects hummed with spirit energy, like Lord Ocras's elemental objects had done, only stronger.

These are from the Cave of Illwen! thought Ash, recognizing the objects from her vision. They were all things that the thieves had taken from the illwen's shrines. That explained the crystal cloth lining the cabinet—it would keep any searching illwen from finding their stolen objects.

Only a few of the stolen objects appeared to be on the shelves. Seeing them reminded Ash of some of the other sacred objects that had been taken. Objects like the green and white crystal she'd noticed in the governor's office.

Ash recalled how the governor had boasted about Lord Ocras sending him the crystal. She hadn't thought it important at the time. Now, though, it occurred to her that Lord Ocras must have sent the stolen crystal to the Capitol for a reason. If illwen could sense the hum of spirit energy coming from their sacred objects, just as she could sense it, then they might come looking for what had been taken from them. That would explain why illwen kept attacking the Capitol. And if Lord Ocras sent stolen objects to other frontier towns and villages, illwen would attack those places too. It was like scattering bait to attract bears. But why would Lord Ocras want the illwen to attack villages?

What's in there? asked Puppy. *Can I see?*

Ash tugged the thick crystal cloth curtain shut, fearing what Puppy might become if he saw all these reminders of what he'd been before. "It's just stuff," she said.

Puppy sniffed at the curtains then scampered back, repulsed by the crystal cloth.

"Let's see if we can pry that lock open." Ash returned to the cocoon chained to the pedestal and wedged Kiki into the top loop of the padlock. "Help me with this."

"Here you are, right on schedule," interrupted a voice.

Ash turned to find Lord Ocras standing in the doorway. The wolves sat beside him, and servants lingered in the hall beyond.

"There's no need to be frightened. I knew if I didn't show you this room, you'd find it yourself and sneak in here," he said. "It was a test. You claimed you weren't interested in power, yet here you are, going to great lengths to steal my most powerful illwen. What do you make of that?"

"I'm not stealing it. I'm freeing it," said Ash. "You have no right to keep the illwen here."

"Who are you to speak of freeing illwen?" Lord Ocras gave Puppy a look. "What some bind with chains, others bind with a ribbon and a heart."

Puppy growled at the wolves, but Eagla and Anobaith didn't move. Their dark eyes stayed fixed on Lord Ocras, awaiting his next command.

Instinctively, Ash's hand went to her pocket to touch the crystal cloth spectacles hidden there. The more frightened she became, the tighter she gripped the protective cloth.

"Tell me, do you even know the name of that illwen you wish to free?" asked Lord Ocras.

Ash glanced at the cocoon. She could sense vast amounts of spirit energy churning within the silk cocoon, but she couldn't make out the illwen's whispers. It was like hearing a raging waterfall through a locked door.

"Go on, touch it," said Lord Ocras. "I won't stop you. If you want to free it, don't you think you should at least know what you're releasing into the world?"

Ash gritted her teeth. As much as she didn't want to touch the cocoon again, she had to admit that Lord Ocras had a point. She summoned her strength and stretched her hand toward the chained cocoon. The instant her fingers brushed the glowing silk, an overwhelming sensation of hunger struck her.

This time, Ash didn't pull her hand back. She let the hunger course through her.

The sensation soon changed to yearning. She wanted to be home, in the safety of her room. Only she wanted her home to be different. She wanted her room to be bigger, with shelves like the ones Lord Ocras had. And she wanted the shelves to be full of all the objects she'd lost, along with more things—her own collection of named objects. She wanted her mother to get over her fearful illness and be attentive and loving again. She wanted her friends to apologize for being mean to her, and she wanted everyone in the village to listen to her and do what she said. She wanted to be older, taller, and prettier. She wanted everything to be the way she thought it should be…

"*Want,*" she said.

"That's a crude name for it, but it will do," replied Lord Ocras. "Want. Desire. Yearning… It's the hunger that causes a caterpillar to eat and eat. I know what you want, Young Namer. It's control. That's why you're here. You don't like that I have control over these illwen. You want things to be different. That is what's motivated you all along, isn't it? You thought things were amiss, so you set out to change them. You wanted your mother and father and everyone else to act differently. You wanted them all to behave exactly the way you thought they should."

Ash drew back.

Lord Ocras grinned. "Did you think you only saw *my* memories the other day? Oh no. Among namers, such visions are a two-way street. I know everything about you, Young Namer. I know how your friends shunned you. Your mother abandoned you. Your neighbors called you a traitor. I even know how you like to organize your room and keep everything in its place."

Lord Ocras strode around the room as he spoke. Ash kept a wary distance from him, and from the two giant wolves who sat by the door, blocking her escape.

"I know all the things you did that brought you here," continued Lord Ocras. "It's a tragic story, actually. So far, almost every action you've taken has made things worse. You tried to help your village. Instead, people saw you as helping their enemy. You tried to make peace between the governor and the dao fora. Instead, you caused a war. And now you've come to take my illwen, thinking that I'm the villain, but I'm not the villain in this story. If anyone's been the villain, it's you." Lord Ocras held her gaze. "You're the one who keeps causing problems. But fear not, Young Namer. I can help you change that. The reason you keep messing up is because you fail to understand how the world actually works."

"I understand enough," said Ash. "I know that what you're doing is wrong. Keeping the illwen in chains is wrong. Using them to make crystal cloth is wrong. And destroying the cloud forest for your webworm plantations is wrong!"

"Such conviction. Sometimes I forget how young you are. Once you've seen more of the world, you'll see that right and wrong are simply names given by those in control to things they like or don't like. Most people like crystal cloth. They think it's stylish and beautiful." He touched the crystal cloth woven through the chain links of his crown. "Such a beautiful, useful thing can't be wrong."

"It only appears beautiful," said Ash. Now that she'd seen how crystal cloth was made, she knew what it truly was. "It's just *want* and *fear* twisted together."

"*Want* and *fear*." He shook his head and sighed. "I do hope that you'll learn to speak more elegantly when you name things. However, you're not entirely mistaken. Initially, I tried weaving crystal cloth only out of what you call 'want,' but people wanted so many different things, it wasn't a very effective means of control. To direct their wanting I needed fear to be woven into the cloth as well. The more people wear crystal cloth, the more fearful they become. And when people are afraid, they become much easier to control. All I have to do is direct their fear toward a common enemy."

"The dao fora," said Ash.

"For a time, but they were too easily contained. I needed something more terrible and unpredictable. Something people could fear but never defeat. Something," he waved his hand in the air, "dramatic."

"The illwen! That's why you want the illwen to attack cities and villages!"

Lord Ocras nodded. "Now you're getting it. The illwen are the perfect enemy. The more people fear the illwen, the harder they'll work to buy crystal cloth for protection from an enemy they can never defeat. Keep people afraid, and keep them wanting, and they're easy to control. It's the perfect system. Even you have fallen under its spell."

"That's not true," said Ash.

"Your actions suggest otherwise." He glanced at the crystal cloth spectacles in her hand. When had she pulled them from her pocket?

Ash's stomach fell as she realized that the want and fear woven into the cloth had influenced her too. She recalled how she'd refused to leave the spectacles behind earlier. She'd even lied to Puppy about them, and she'd gotten angry at Fen because of them.

"There's no need to hide it," continued Lord Ocras. "You're afraid and you want control. That's nothing to be ashamed of. In fact, it's something I understand quite well. As I said before, we have much in common. I can teach you how to use your abilities to harness the power of the illwen so that you can shape the world into exactly what you want it to be. In time, if you prove yourself, you might even take over some of what I've begun."

She started to say no, but Lord Ocras cut her off.

"Before you speak, think about what I'm offering you. Once I've trained you, things can be arranged any way you like. You'll have the power to make the world a better place. You could even create your own House of Ten Thousand Rooms and fill it with all that you desire. You'll never have to lose anything again. With your illwen and mine, we'll have an empire like none in history. All you have to do, Young Namer, is say yes."

Young Namer. He kept calling her that. Each time he did, the name sank a little further into her, molding her into what he wanted her to be. Not Ash, but someone young and impressionable. Someone who'd become exactly like him.

"I won't let you tell me who I am," she said.

Lord Ocras shrugged. "Those who want control never like to submit to control themselves. Are you sure you don't want to rethink your answer?"

"I'm *not* like you. I'll never be like you."

"We'll see." All the friendliness fell from Lord Ocras's face, revealing a cold, cruel expression. He reached into his coat pocket and pulled out a white feather. Then he held the feather close to his lips and whispered a quick name.

"*Poison seta*!"

Chains

In a blink, the feather changed into a poison-tipped dart. Even while Ash saw this, she sensed another name beneath the one Lord Ocras had spoken. Another possibility that could still be taken. The image of a quill pen flashed in her head.

Lord Ocras threw the dart at her.

"*Quill,*" she said, focusing all her will on making the name fit the dart.

Something in the dart pushed back, but Ash kept willing the name to be true. Like pressing a needle through thick cloth, she felt resistance until the new name pierced through the name Lord Ocras had spoken and took hold.

The dart became a harmless feather quill. It drifted to the ground, landing at Ash's feet.

Ash sucked in a breath, amazed.

"You learn fast, Young Namer," said Lord Ocras. "That's good."

He uttered another word, one that Ash didn't hear. Chunks of rock fell from the ceiling, big enough to crush her. Luckily, Puppy nudged her out of the way. He dodged the falling stones and shook the dust off his fur.

Ash glanced at the hole in the ceiling, wondering how Lord Ocras could have made the ceiling crumble like that. The whole room, from floor to ceiling, must have absorbed traces of spirit energy from the illwen that had been kept here. She focused on the clay tiles Lord Ocras stood upon and sensed spirit energy humming within them. Ash searched for another name to shape their essence.

"*Sand!*" she said, levering the word into the tiles with a surge of her will.

The floor beneath Lord Ocras's feet fell like grains of sand through an hourglass. Lord Ocras plummeted downward. He grabbed the leg of one of the wolves.

Eagla tensed but didn't move. With a spat word, Lord Ocras made the tiles stop crumbling. As he heaved himself out of the sandy hole, Ash caught sight of the skeleton key around his neck. In a flash, she knew—it wasn't a key to the room like she'd first thought. It was the key to the padlocks that held the illwen's silver chain collars shut. To free the illwen she had to get the key from him.

Lord Ocras regained his footing, and the wolves crouched by his sides. "You're clever, but don't get cocky. Telling elemental objects what to be is just the beginning." He tore a handful of fur off of each wolf. "Let's see how you handle this." Lord Ocras whispered to the fur he'd grabbed, then threw it at Ash.

Giant claws from an enormous vulture slashed through the air toward her. Ash yelped and dove, hitting the ground so hard she skinned her knees.

"Ash! It's okay. I've got you," said her mother.

Essa was here! Her mother had come to save her. Ash's heart soared.

A soft hand grabbed her arm and helped her up. Ash looked at the hand, only to find it covered in rotting skin. Her mother's bones showed beneath her dress sleeve, and a skull lurked behind her dirty veil.

Ash jerked her arm back, causing the skeleton to collapse beside her.

She tried to scream, but she had no breath. The vulture lunged at her again, its hooked beak opening to pluck out her eyes.

Ash clenched her eyes shut, but no vulture struck. It was just fear, causing her to see things. Fear and despair.

Eagla and Anobaith, thought Ash. Lord Ocras had changed their fur into terrifying visions of fear and despair.

"*Illusions*," said Ash, renaming what she'd seen. "*Harmless illusions*."

The attacking vulture and her skeletal mother vanished.

Lord Ocras clapped. "Well done. Are you sure you don't want to become my student?"

"Never."

"Such stubbornness." Lord Ocras's brow knotted. "It's a shame to destroy someone as gifted as yourself, but you leave me little choice. Eagla, Anobaith, kill her."

The wolves charged. Unlike the illusions that had been made from their fur, Ash couldn't make them disappear. Nor could she change them. Their forms were bound to the names Lord Ocras had given them by the chain collars locked around their necks.

Puppy darted ahead of her. Although he was pitifully small compared to the wolves, he was faster. He nipped at Anobaith's paws, tripping the huge wolf. Then he jumped and grabbed Eagla by her ear. The wolf shook her head, but Puppy had already moved on, leaping from Eagla's head to Anobaith's back. He moved faster than Ash had ever seen him go—jumping, dodging, and nipping to keep the wolves distracted.

While the wolves lunged and snapped at Puppy, Ash fended off Lord Ocras. He changed a handful of stones into knives that he threw at her. Ash barely managed to duck behind a table, which she changed into a shield to protect her. A moment later, Ocras commanded the wooden shield to ignite into flames, and she had to drop it.

Ocras grabbed a pair of scissors from his workbench and whispered a command. The scissors stretched and gleamed, becoming a deadly sword. Then he turned the tile she stood upon into muddy clay. Her feet sank up to her ankles.

Ash couldn't think fast enough to keep up with the changes. Lord Ocras had only been playing with her before—testing her. Now he didn't hold back. Her heart pounded as he strode toward her with the sword.

Ash sensed traces of spirit energy in the ornate plaster work on the ceiling. She focused on it, hearing faint whispers. "*Dust!*" she said, renaming the plaster.

Pieces of plaster fell onto Lord Ocras's head, but this only appeared to enrage him further. He spat and brushed the dust from his eyes while Ash struggled to pull her feet out of the floor. The clay had hardened around one foot, holding her there.

Lord Ocras's eyes narrowed as he raised the sword above him.

"Puddle! Dirt!" gasped Ash, desperately trying to rename the clay that held her foot stuck. None of the names worked. She had to listen more deeply. At the edge of her vision, she saw the sword swinging down.

Puppy streaked toward her—a blur of black-and-white fur. He slammed into Lord Ocras and knocked the sword from his hand. Then Puppy skidded across the tile floor, losing his footing.

Eagla darted in to take advantage of Puppy's bad landing.

"Look out!" cried Ash, but it was too late. The wolf pounced and caught Puppy beneath his paw. Everything else faded from Ash's awareness as the wolf's jaws snapped around Puppy's tiny body.

Eagla thrashed his head and tossed Puppy across the room. The small black-and-white body thumped the wall.

"*Mud!*" said Ash, finally hearing a name that fit. The hard clay that held her foot became soft and slippery. Ash yanked her foot free and scrambled to where Puppy lay motionless by the wall.

"Puppy, get up! Please, get up."

He was still breathing, but his legs collapsed when he tried to stand.

He gazed at her and whimpered, unable to make his borrowed body do what he wanted it to.

Were we playing a game? he asked, sounding dazed.

"Yes," said Ash. "You were protecting me."

Eagla and Anobaith stalked closer. Their fur bristled and teeth glistened as they spread out to cut off her escape. Ash didn't care. All that mattered was Puppy.

Was it a good game?

"The best," said Ash. She stroked the soft, fluffy spot behind his black-and-white ears.

Good. Puppy tried to lick her hand, but he was too weak. *Is the game over now? I'm sleepy.*

"Please don't sleep. Stay with me."

But I'm tired. Puppy's eyes fluttered. *Something's wrong with me.*

"You can fix him," said Lord Ocras. "It's only his borrowed body that's broken. You can make the illwen take on another form. Tell him what to become and bind him to his new name. Make him be your fierce protector."

Ash heard the eagerness in his voice. This was what he'd wanted all along. By making her fight him, he was getting her to become like him. Another Shadow Namer. She looked at the two giant wolves pacing around her with their chain collars.

"Do it! You're running out of time," said Lord Ocras. "It's the only way to save him."

Ash? Are you still there?

Ash pressed her face against Puppy's head and smelled his warm fur. "I'm right here."

I can't keep my eyes open. They're not working anymore.

"I know. I'm sorry."

Was I a good Puppy?

"The best," she whispered. "I'm glad you found me."

She stroked the soft fur behind his ears one last time. Then she slipped her fingers under the ribbon collar. Before she lost her nerve, she tugged the collar over his ears and released him.

Whispers poured out of his body, speaking new possibilities for what the illwen could be. Among the excited whispers, Ash heard one that sounded clearer than the others. It was a name that reflected the other side of the tame puppy she'd known.

"Be free, *Wildness*," she said, speaking the whispered name aloud.

33

The Trouble with Names

Puppy let out his last breath.

Only his breath kept coming, like a storm rushing from his mouth. The sudden gust knocked Ash back and slammed her into the approaching wolves.

The wind darkened, taking on the shape of a six-legged illwen with a sharp, slashing tail. All that pent-up wildness was eager to be free. It raced about the room, kicking up sand and rubble.

"Foolish child! Freeing that illwen won't help you," shouted Lord Ocras. "Unbound illwen don't serve anyone. They don't care about people. They're primal spirits that must be controlled. Eagla, Anobaith, finish her!"

The wolves struggled against the wind in the room. Anobaith slid back while Eagla kept advancing, cornering Ash.

Eagla lunged. Ash barely managed to block his snapping jaws with Kiki.

The wolf bit the ironwood and tugged, but Ash didn't let go. Eagla tossed Ash onto her back.

Wayfarer broke her fall, only now the wolf loomed over her, jaws widening. Ash jammed the end of Kiki into his mouth.

Eagla snarled and snapped at the ironwood twigs. Slobber dripped from his teeth onto her cheeks while the silver padlock dangled from the chain around his neck. Ash wished she could rename the chain and turn it into something else, but she couldn't hear any names for it other than Unbreakable. Somehow, Lord Ocras had bound it to that name, just as he'd bound Eagla and Anobaith to theirs.

If only I had the key.

She glanced at Lord Ocras. He still wore the key around his neck, but he was far across the room. Ash gripped Kiki tighter. It took all her strength to keep Eagla from devouring her.

Kiki! The ironwood stick chanted its name in her head. *Kiki, Ki—!*

One of the twigs snapped off and fell onto her chest. Even Kiki was breaking.

No. Not breaking, thought Ash. *Changing*.

She grabbed the fallen twig with one hand and felt it hum with potential.

"*Skeleton Key!*" said Ash, renaming the twig. As she spoke, she envisioned the skeleton key she'd seen hanging from Lord Ocras's necklace.

The twig straightened, and the bumps and knots on the end took on the shape of the key she'd seen.

Eagla tore Kiki from her grasp. While the wolf tossed the stick aside, Ash seized the padlock dangling from the wolf's chain collar. She shoved the key into the keyhole and gave it a twist.

The lock snapped open.

The chain fell free.

Whispers rushed into the silence surrounding the wolf. Several of the whispers called to Ash, but one name sounded a clear, familiar tone.

"Be free, *Sinach*!" said Ash.

It was a dao fora word—one that Caihay had taught her. *Keep sinach here*, he'd told her, pointing to his heart. Even if he'd never told her the word's meaning, she would have known it from the way it made her feel. *Courage.*

Eagla instantly changed, becoming a larger, brighter creature. Instead of attacking Ash, the illwen galloped about the room. Unbound, Sinach's form was less fixed and more fluid. He moved in graceful leaps, his once dark coat shining silver. The six-legged illwen that had been Puppy ran with him and the two playfully chased each other, tearing things up like a tornado trapped in a house.

The rollicking illwen barreled into Anobaith, knocking her onto her belly. Sinach clamped his jaws around the metal chain on his sister's neck and dragged Anobaith toward Ash. The padlock that held the illwen's collar shut jutted to the side. Sinach looked at Ash, making it clear what he wanted her to do.

"Don't!" shouted Lord Ocras. "She'll turn on you. She'll destroy you. Illwen must be controlled!"

Lord Ocras kept yelling, but his voice sounded hollow. Empty. Ash slid the key she'd created into the lock on Anobaith's chain and turned it. The lock clicked open. Ash pulled the lock off the chain and Anobaith burst free.

Only the illwen wasn't simply Anobaith anymore. As had happened with Sinach, Ash heard other whispers for the unbound wolf—other possibilities she could call forth.

"Be free, *Va-Tay!"* she said, speaking the dao fora word Suma had taught her. *Va-tay. Last Hope.* Where despair had been, hope now surged. You couldn't have one without the other.

Va-Tay raced about the room with Sinach and Wildness.

In their raucous, exuberant celebration, they shattered pots, smashed open the balcony doors, and broke parts of the balcony railing. They were destructive, but they were also beautiful.

"Eagla! Anobaith!" snapped Lord Ocras.

The running wolves stopped and turned toward him, becoming what he'd called them. Sinach darkened, growing fearful again, and Vay-Tay became as heavy and menacing as despair.

Lord Ocras's face paled when he realized his mistake. Although he could name the illwen, now that they were free of their unbreakable chain collars, he couldn't command them. Both wolves growled as they stalked toward him. Lord Ocras's eyes widened. He shuffled back onto the balcony, terrified.

Ash didn't know what he saw. He'd called the wolves Eagla and Anobaith—fear and despair—so perhaps he saw his worst nightmares stalking toward him, along with a complete loss of hope.

She wanted to tell him to name the wolves differently. That's what she'd done, and there were plenty of other names for the illwen that would bring out other possibilities in their spirits.

But before she could say a word, the wolves charged. Lord Ocras scrambled back, tripped over the broken balcony railing, and tumbled through the air toward the plaza far below.

Transformations

The six-legged illwen that had once been Puppy kept bounding about the room. It seemed too shifting and complex to fix to any one name now. It was wind, claws, and smoke—at once playful, fierce, and wild.

It tossed the table into the cabinet that held the illwen's stolen objects. The cabinet shattered and splinters of wood, shelves, and crystal cloth scattered in various directions. The illwen snapped up the stolen objects in its jaws. Then it galloped to the balcony and leapt into the air.

Instead of falling, it changed shape and soared on enormous wings. The two wolves leapt off the balcony after it, becoming as light and fluid as gusts of wind. The darkness that Lord Ocras had called forth in the illwen when he'd named them Eagla and Anobaith receded into the silver and gold they'd become when Ash had renamed them Sinach and Va-Tay. But there were other colors in them as well, along with other names. They looked far more magnificent than they'd ever been while bound.

From the balcony, Ash watched the three illwen chase each other around the spires and towers. They tore off shingles and crashed through archways before shifting again and blowing like fast-moving storm clouds toward the distant forest.

Tears blurred Ash's vision as the illwen left because they were beautiful and because they'd gone without once looking back.

Ash had hoped that the illwen that had been Puppy would at least give her a sign it remembered her—a backward glance or other gesture of farewell. But it hadn't. Perhaps Lord Ocras had been right and illwen didn't care about people. Even so, she felt lucky to have seen such beautiful spirits run free.

When she finally left the balcony and stepped inside again, her gaze settled on the small, black-and-white body in the corner. It was a limp, empty thing, like a discarded piece of clothing. Beside it lay the ribbon that had once held the heart-shaped pendant around Puppy's neck. The pendant was gone. Ash picked up the ribbon and tucked it into her pocket. It was all she had left to remember Lost Heart Puppy by.

Tavan and Fen burst into the room.

"Are you all right?" asked Fen. "The whole tower shook. We saw guards running up the stairs."

Tavan locked the door behind them. Then he studied the room, taking in the collapsed ceiling and the hole in the floor. "Lord Ocras?"

"He's gone," said Ash.

"What about Puppy?" asked Fen. "We thought he was with you."

"He's gone too."

Fen followed her gaze to the body on the floor. "Oh."

He hugged Ash and tried to comfort her, but there was no time to mourn. Already, guards pounded on the door, demanding that they open it.

"That door won't hold them long. We need to get out of here," said Tavan.

"This way!" Fen pointed to the hole in the floor that Ash had made when she'd changed a tile into sand. "We can climb down to the floor beneath this one and escape."

"There's something I need to do first." Ash approached the cocoon chained to the pedestal in the center of the room.

The pounding on the door grew louder as guards attempted to break it down. With each blow, the door shook in its frame and the wood started to crack.

"There's no time," said Tavan. "If they catch us, they'll arrest us."

Ash used the skeleton key she'd created to open the padlock on the chain. Then she lifted the chain from the cocoon, being careful not to touch the cocoon again. She didn't want to be struck by the painful wanting she'd felt the last time she'd touched it.

The cocoon glowed bright yellow for a moment before fading to a dull brown.

"There. It's free. Now let's go." Tavan stuffed the remaining lengths of the silver chain into a sack.

The pounding from the guards continued. A crack ran down the center of the door. With every blow from the guards the crack widened.

"Something's wrong," said Ash. The illwen should have burst free. She should have heard its whispers rushing out like she had when she'd freed the wolves from their chains. But the only whispers she heard were faint, and the illwen's glow kept fading.

Ash put her hand on the cocoon's silky exterior. A hungry wanting rushed into her, only the sensation wasn't nearly as strong as it had been before. Beneath it, she sensed a new whisper. A reason for the hunger.

"Go on. You're free," she said. "*Change.*"

Something in the cocoon nudged her fingers. The silk on the outside had become a dull, lifeless shell, but whatever was inside felt very much alive and it wanted out.

A tear opened along one side of the silken cocoon. Through this, Ash glimpsed a bright white-and-brown-striped body. A thin limb pushed through the silk and the tear spread.

Fen stepped toward the cocoon, as if magnetically called to it. "What is it?"

Tavan pulled Fen back.

A second white leg emerged, then a third, and a fourth. At last, the head, covered in brilliant white fur and topped with two feathery brown antennae, wriggled out of the top of the cocoon. This was followed by two more legs, a furry white-and-brown-striped body, and four folded-up wings.

Soldiers broke through the door and piled into the room. Instead of confronting Ash, Fen, and Tavan, they stopped and watched the creature emerge from the cocoon in stunned silence.

The illwen's body pulsed as its wings unfurled. Each wing became hundreds of times bigger than any moth wing Ash had ever seen. They shimmered, reflecting more colors than the finest crystal cloth.

No one spoke. Everyone was held in awe by the sight of the giant moth emerging.

Several soldiers took off their crystal cloth spectacles to see the radiant creature better.

The four wings trembled, reflecting rainbows of light. With a powerful beat of its wings, the illwen rose off the pedestal and hovered. It seemed to be testing its wings out. Then it circled the room and fluttered out the balcony doors.

Ash and Fen ran to the balcony. The giant moth wasn't alone in the sky. Tens of thousands of small fluttering moths swarmed around it. Every webworm made from pieces of the illwen must have transformed as well.

Across the land, moths fluttered into the air from every plantation and jujube tree for as far as Ash could see. Their wings caught the light of the sun and sparkled like crystal fragments in the sky. Together they formed a shimmering cloud that stretched toward the forest where the other illwen had gone.

"I feel like jumping into the air and flying with them!" said Fen.

Tavan gripped Fen's shoulders and tugged him back from the edge. "Don't be silly. You're a boy, not a moth."

More soldiers removed their crystal cloth spectacles to better see the countless shimmering moths flying toward the forest. Only a few noticed that the crystal cloth had lost its luster. It was dull, ordinary cloth now—as drab and lifeless as the discarded husk of the cocoon.

After the illwen receded into the distance, the soldiers blinked and rubbed their eyes. They looked like they were waking from a dream. Some dropped their weapons. Others buried their faces in their hands and wept. None of them tried to apprehend Ash, Tavan, or Fen.

In fact, they couldn't even explain to themselves why, only a few minutes ago, doing such a thing had seemed important.

It took several minutes for Ash, Fen, and Tavan to descend all the flights of stairs to the plaza at the base of the tower. Many other workers and servants headed there as well. By the time they made it out, hundreds of workers from the Ocras Industries airship factory had gathered, along with dozens of guards. Some people still wore their crystal cloth veils and spectacles, but most had taken off the dull cloth.

People were oddly quiet. Ash feared she'd have to tell someone that Lord Ocras was dead, but people appeared to already know. They didn't seem upset or happy about the news. Instead, everyone looked confused. For so long Lord Ocras had directed them. Now that he was gone, people wandered the plaza, unsure of what to do.

Only one airship was still tied to the mooring masts in the plaza. Tavan, Fen, and Ash headed toward it.

Ash recognized the figure struggling with the airship's anchor line.

"Pilot! You came back for us!" she said.

"Well, I'll be," replied Pilot. "I suppose I did, although that wasn't my intention."

Pilot went on to explain that, after he'd dropped them off on the roof of the tower, he had to refuel. And since they'd thrown all his other lines out the bay doors, he had to use the rope she'd left him as an anchor line. But when he tried to leave, the rope wouldn't come undone. "It was the dodgast strangest thing," said Pilot. "Every time I untied one knot, another formed. I couldn't puzzle it out until just a few minutes ago the line started to come undone. If I didn't know better, I'd say that rope was waiting for you."

"Telltale's a very special rope," said Ash.

"That it is. I'm guessing you want to come aboard?"

"If you're willing to take us."

"Far be it for me to disagree with a rope. We best get going, though. This crowd looks a bit sparksome."

Tavan and Fen made their way up the gangplank into the airship cabin. Ash followed, pausing halfway. Several servants from the tower had gathered around the airship, along with factory workers and soldiers. They were all gazing up at her and whispering to each other.

"What is it? What do you want?" asked Ash.

The people glanced at each other. Finally, an older woman stepped forward. Ash recognized her from her clothing as Zeera, the servant from the tower. She'd never seen Zeera's face before because of the crystal cloth veils Lord Ocras had made his servants wear. Seeing her now, Ash was surprised by her thin, hollow cheeks. Zeera had served them heaping plates of food at every meal, and yet she looked like she'd barely eaten a morsel herself in months.

"You're the same as Lord Ocras was, aren't you?" asked Zeera.

"I'm not like him at all," replied Ash.

"But you're a namer of spirits. An *Ainm Dhilis*—that's what my grandmother called ones like you back in the old country."

"Anyone can name something," said Ash. "You just need to listen closely."

"No… you're different. Lord Ocras was different. People listened to him."

The people kept looking at Ash expectantly.

"I'm *not* like him," she repeated.

"Child, we saw what you did in there. We know what you are. Just because he used his abilities for selfish reasons doesn't mean you can't use yours for good."

"He thought he was doing good," said Ash.

"No… he knew otherwise," said Zeera. "I served him breakfast every morning. I watched him when he thought no one was looking. He tried to convince himself that what he did was good, but when something's truly good, you don't need to convince yourself. Lord Ocras deceived himself, same as he deceived us. It's wrong to pretend what you're doing is other than what it is. Just as it's wrong to pretend you're not what you are. You could take over here."

Everyone kept looking at her. Ash heard several whispers rising from the crowd—nervous, anxious, uncertain whispers.

"I just want to go home," said Ash. "You should go home too."

"We don't have homes. Not anymore. We had to leave our homes to come here." Zeera gestured to the white towers. "This is all we know."

Ash studied the somber faces in the crowd. Most of them seemed to be immigrants, like her mother and many of the squatters who came to her village—people who risked everything to find a better life.

"This could be your home," said Ash.

"*Live? In the towers?*" Zeera sounded hesitant, as if even speaking such a thought was preposterous.

"Why not? You built it," said Ash. "Lord Ocras lied to you when he told you this was his. It's your work. Your land. This belongs to all of you."

"What a thing to imagine." A nervous smile made Zeera's eyes crinkle. "Thank you, *Ainm Dhilis*."

35

Home

It took two days to fly back to Ash's village on the airship because the wind blew against them and they had to stop to refuel. On the way, Ash thought constantly about her parents, friends, and anyone else who might have gotten hurt in the battle she'd caused.

Now that the spell Lord Ocras had cast with his crystal cloth had lifted, she wondered if things would return to how they used to be in her village, before everything had gone amiss. She imagined her mother welcoming her home with open arms, her father lifting her up, and her friends being grateful to see her again.

But when the airship finally got close enough that she could see her village, it wasn't the peaceful, welcoming scene she'd imagined. Smoke clouded the air, and the fields beyond the wall appeared burnt and lifeless.

The fires that the governor's soldiers had set must have spread out of control. Not only did parts of the cloud forest look burnt, most of the jujube trees were gone and the plantation fields smoldered. Pillars of black smoke rose from within the village too.

Pilot flew over the village, but it was hard to see the square or the houses and barns through the rising smoke. It wasn't safe to land near flames, so Pilot landed in a blackened field outside the wall.

Tavan climbed down Telltale and anchored the airship to the remains of a horseless carriage. All the wooden parts of the carriage had burned away, along with the rubber tires, but the heavy steam engine remained.

Fen and Ash climbed down after Tavan. The governor and his soldiers appeared to have gone, leaving the scorched fields deserted.

Ash tried to stay optimistic. The wall surrounding her village still stood, so maybe the buildings and homes beyond it stood as well. She ran toward the gate.

"Hello!" she called. "I live here! Let me in."

The forest gate stayed closed. No soldiers moved along the parapet walkway or watchtowers. Smoke stung her throat. Had everyone, including her parents, left? Or were they simply ignoring her? Maybe they all hated her for freeing Fen, and for bringing the governor and his soldiers here.

Ash pushed such thoughts aside. "Is anyone there?"

She wished Puppy was with her so she wouldn't feel so alone. Several times each day, she stumbled into painful reminders that he was gone, along with almost all of her named objects. Wayfarer hung nearly empty on her back. The only thing that kept her going was the thought of coming home, and now her home looked empty too.

Ash heard voices in the distance.

"Fetch more buckets! Hurry!" called a woman on the far side of the wall. Someone else shouted back, but Ash couldn't make out what they said.

The smoke grew thicker. A building must have been burning—that's why no one was at the gate. They were still putting out fires!

Ash tried to shove the gate open, but the wood felt hot. She pulled her hands away with a gasp. Flames danced along the top of the guard tower overhead, and a few of the gate timbers smoked.

She listened again, only this time she listened more deeply.

The dry, thirsty wood baked in the leafless sun. Timbers cracked, calling out for moisture. A few timbers even hummed with spirit energy and whispered names to her. It didn't surprise her that some of the timbers held traces of spirit energy. Illwen had climbed this gate several times. What did surprise her was that some of the timbers whispered names like *Scorch, Burn*, and *Blaze.*

Lord Ocras had once changed a stick into flames with a single word. Ash wondered if she could do the opposite. She focused on a section of the gate that smoked and buzzed with excited whispers. "*Be calm*," she said. "*Be wood.*"

A few timbers stopped smoldering, but most of the posts in the wall continued to sizzle and smoke. There wasn't any moisture—not in the air or the ground. Burning parts of the guard tower split in the heat, sending off sparks and embers, and the shooting embers spread their fiery whispers to the gate.

It was too much to hold back. The wood wanted to burn. Despite Ash's efforts, flames soon spread along the gate.

Among the raging whispers, Ash heard another name. Her own.

"*Ash?*" It sounded like a question at first. Then louder. "Ash!"

She turned and peered through the thickening smoke. "Suma?"

The dao fora woman tugged her back from the flames. Already the heat had singed Ash's hair.

Ash coughed and struggled to return to the gate. "The village…" she said. "I have to help them. My parents are in there."

"They can escape through the far gate," replied Suma.

"But it's my home. It's burning."

"I know." Suma gave Ash a long look—a look that said she knew what it was like to see her home burn.

The watchtower near the gate collapsed, causing the warning bell inside to clang as it hit the ground. Ash's eyes watered and lungs ached.

Suma pulled her further from the smoke to where Ipé and Jerrah waited by Tavan in the field. Fen stood slightly apart from the group, inspecting the scorched remains of the horseless carriage.

"Where's Caihay?" asked Ash. "Is he…?"

"He's recovering, along with several others." Suma explained how they'd escaped the fires that the soldiers had set by carrying the wounded to the river. But when they got to the river, barely a trickle of water remained.

"I thought we were trapped," said Suma. "The flames spread quicker than our mistcats could run. Then the wind switched and blew the fire toward the village. Ipé and Jerrah saw soldiers try to put it out, but the flames kept spreading. After two days, the soldiers gave up. They left yesterday. Some of the villagers left with them. Others stayed to protect their homes."

“They’ve been trying to put the fires out ever since,” said Jerrah. “Every time they extinguish one area, another starts up.”

Ash watched the burning gate. It was just like the vision she’d had of her village burning. She hadn’t changed anything. “We have to help them.”

“We tried, but they were too afraid to open the gate for us,” said Jerrah.

“They need water.”

“There’s no water left. The streams have all run dry,” explained Suma. “Even the river is dry. The drought has gotten worse. Everything’s out of balance.”

Balance Keeper, thought Ash. “What about the mistcats? They could help us.”

Suma shook her head. “There’s not enough mist to form them.”

“But I did what you said. I faced the Shadow Namer. I freed the illwen. You said if I freed the illwen, then things would get better.”

“I thought they would.” Suma gazed at the village. Flames engulfed the gate from top to bottom.

“You did what you could,” continued Suma. “There simply aren’t enough trees left anymore. The sky river has stopped flowing. Without rain, the fires will keep spreading.”

“But I freed the illwen,” repeated Ash. “I gave up everything—even Puppy. I let them all go.”

“Not all. There’s one more illwen that needs to be released.” Suma looked to Tavan. “I’m sorry, old friend. It’s time.”

“*Mabh falsa,*” grumbled Ipé.

“You called Fen that before. What does it mean?” asked Ash.

"It means false face," explained Suma. "It's what we call a body possessed by an illwen. My people believe that it's wrong to keep an illwen bound in one form. Such spirits must be free."

Fen was still off in the burnt field, playing on the charred remains of the horseless carriage. He didn't seem to have heard them.

Ash looked at Tavan. "That's why you were exiled, isn't it? Because of Fen. He's not really your son."

"He is," replied Tavan. "And he isn't."

"You lied to me."

"No. Everything I told you was true. My son got sick with fever when he was young." Tavan lowered his voice so Fen wouldn't hear. "I prayed to the gods and forest spirits to heal him, but nothing worked. His breathing weakened until he didn't breathe at all. Still, I prayed. For hours I stayed by his body and prayed. Then my prayers were answered. A spirit passed into him and he got up from bed. I knew he was a *mabh falsa*—a false face. And I knew that to treat such a spirit as human was forbidden, but none of that mattered."

Ipé made a hissing sound, clearly disapproving of what Tavan had done.

"The spirit that inhabited his body needed me. And I needed him," continued Tavan. "So I held him and called him my son. I protected him and promised to be his family. It's a mighty thing, heartbreak. We speak of it as something bad, but the truth is hearts break open. I lost my son that day, and I found a son."

"Do you think he remembers what he used to be?" asked Ash.

Tavan gazed at Fen, playing on the burnt remains of the carriage. "I think he knows he's not a boy. He keeps asking me where he belongs."

"It's time," encouraged Suma.

"I can't," said Tavan. "Let me talk with him first. Let it be his decision."

Suma nodded and Tavan went to the burnt remains of the carriage where Fen sat. Ash couldn't hear what he said, but she watched him hug Fen and kiss his forehead.

"Go on," he said to Ash when he returned. "See if he wants to remember."

Ash slid Wayfarer off her back and pulled Aisling, the small blue bottle, from the empty bag. She carried the bottle to where Fen sat in the driver's seat of the carriage. He was pretending to drive, wrenching the wheel from side to side.

"It won't go anymore," said Fen. Soot from the carriage stained his hands black. "Funny, isn't it? Fire made it go, and fire made it stop." Fen squinted at the bottle she held. "What's that?"

"Water from the Pool of Memory," said Ash. "Have you heard of it?"

"It sounds familiar, but I'm not sure why. May I see it?"

Ash passed him the bottle. Only a tiny bit of liquid remained—enough for one or two sips.

"Careful. It's special," said Ash. "One sip will cause you to remember. Two sips will cause you to forget."

Fen held the bottle up and swirled the remains around. "There's something I need to remember, isn't there?"

"Maybe there's something you need to forget."

"Is that what you and Tavan were talking about?"

Ash nodded. "Why do you call him that?"

"Tavan? That's what I've always called him."

"Never *Dad*?"

Fen pulled the cork off the top of Aisling and sniffed it. "It smells like water. Do you think anything is ever truly forgotten?"

"I don't know," replied Ash. "I know that people try not to remember things that are hurtful to them. But I think forgetting hurts more in the end."

Fen held the bottle close to his eyes and peered through it. "Finding your name is a strange adventure. Every time you try to become one thing, you find out you're actually something else."

He tilted the bottle back and drank, taking only one sip.

36

What Fen Became

Fen's brow scrunched and his mouth twitched, as if he was recalling something painful. Then his face relaxed. He gazed at the orange-tinted sky and pulled off the leather hair band he always wore. With a sigh, he let out his breath, only his breath didn't stop. It became a gust of wind rushing from him, stirring up dust and soot.

The wind made a howling, mournful noise as it swirled around the field, blowing Ash's hair back. She struggled to see what happened to her friend, but the wind was too strong. It pulled up so much dirt and smoke that the sky darkened.

The howling whirlwind kept spiraling upward, growing as it rose. It stretched above the airship and treetops, expanding into a massive cyclone.

Illwen often brought storms with them, but this soon became the biggest storm Ash had ever seen. Distant clouds streamed from the forest to join the spiraling cyclone, and tufts of mist lifted from the trees, drawn into the darkening clouds.

In the swirling procession of shifting clouds, Ash glimpsed several familiar figures.

A monkey.

A moth.

Two wolves running side by side.

A hawk.

A snake.

A tortoise.

A hummingbird.

A squirrel.

A coati.

A puppy.

A dragon.

All the illwen from the cave reunited in the sky.

Lightning flashed among the churning clouds, followed by rumbles of thunder that shook Ash's chest. A few cool raindrops fell. They splashed against the ground and sizzled when they met flames. It was only a little rain at first. Then the sky opened and the rain became a downpour.

Steam rose from the burning wall. Ash raised her head to the clouds. "Thank you, Friend of Strangers."

The cool drops washed the dust and soot off her face. It washed away her tears too. She'd never felt so sad, and so grateful for it to rain.

One blackened side of the forest gate still stood. The other had collapsed, but the flames had mostly gone out. Ash stepped over the burnt remains of the wall littering the road.

As she walked, she listened to the rapidly changing whispers around her. Rain pattered the stones of the square and the dry, packed dirt. Each drop was a voice, calling out to other voices in the ground. There were more whispers than she'd ever heard before—more than she'd ever let herself hear. Trees whispered for water. And fires whispered a new name. To those stubborn flames that refused to give in, Ash whispered it herself. "*Ash*," she said. "*Be ash.*"

The flames she whispered her name to sputtered and went out.

Seeds dropped from the rain-struck trees and dry grass into the blackened, ashy earth. "*Grow*," she said to the seeds. "*Sprout. Be plants. Be trees.*"

The seeds let go of their shells and drank in the water, beginning their own miraculous transformations. Ash marveled at how strange it was that, even while her heart ached, she could feel the joy of so much life awakening around her.

She found most of the villagers gathered at the far corner of the square, near the remains of Mr. Rotterberg's barn. Everyone appeared to be staring at the sky.

Ash searched the soot-stained faces for her parents. At first, she didn't recognize her mother—Essa's eyes looked different without the pitiful scrap of crystal cloth covering them.

Her mother didn't see her approach. No one saw her. The old, familiar fear of being rejected caused Ash to hesitate. What if they didn't want to see her? They might still be angry at her for running off, or for helping Fen. For so long, she'd wanted her mother to hold her, and for so long she'd been disappointed.

But now she couldn't wait any longer. She tugged on her mother's shirt. When Essa turned, Ash wrapped her arms around her mother and pulled her close.

Essa stiffened.

"Hello, Mom."

Essa let out a soft cry and folded her arms around her daughter. "Ash. You came back."

"I missed you," said Ash.

Her father wrapped his arms around them both. He seemed to be crying, but it was hard to tell with all the rain. Every time her mom or dad stopped hugging her, it was only for a second. Then they pulled her close again, as if to assure themselves that she really was there.

Other villagers, including Rosa and Raffi, welcomed Ash. Amid all the excitement and cheers for rain, no one seemed to mind that three dao fora had come with her. Suma, Jerrah, and Ipé offered people food from the satchels slung over their shoulders.

People's eyes widened when they ate the black fig bread and ruby fruits. Between bites, villagers raised their heads to the stormy sky and drank the rain.

Ash raised her head too. She caught cool, sweet drops on her tongue, admiring the clouds her friend had gathered.

Only one person wasn't celebrating.

Tavan stood by the far side of the square. Ash waved for him to come closer, but he made no movement toward her. In his arms, he held what looked like a bundle of sticks wrapped in a moss cloak.

He nodded to Ash, then turned and walked out through the burnt forest gate to bury his son.

Epilogue

One morning, a few weeks after the rain came and put out the fires, a blue jay with a black feather-crested head squawked on Ash's windowsill.

"Shh…" she muttered.

The jay kept squawking.

Ash rolled over in bed and pressed her pillow to her ears to block out the sound. The jay pecked at her window.

"What do you want?" grumbled Ash, finally sitting up.

The jay cocked one silver-rimmed eye at her, then the other. Ash got the peculiar sense that the bird wanted to tell her something.

She slid her boots on and went outside. As soon as she stepped out from beneath the porch roof, a pebble thumped her head.

"Ow!"

The jay flapped into the air while making a chuckling sound, as if laughing at her. Then it landed on top of one of the new greenhouses that farmers had built with glass from the abandoned army carriages. The jay cocked its head and fixed its gaze on her.

"Cree! Cree!"

"Hold your horses, I'm coming," said Ash. Clearly, the jay wanted her to follow it.

A few farmers, up early to get their work done before the heat of the day, gave the girl running down the road in her nightgown an odd look, but Ash paid them no mind. She was used to curious looks, and they were used to seeing her do peculiar things while whispering to herself. No one called her strange anymore.

The jay left its perch when Ash approached. It flew to one of the charred forest gate posts. The gate itself was no longer there, so the posts looked like two lonely figures standing in a field. Most of the wall that hadn't burned had been taken down so that the timbers could be used to rebuild houses lost in the fire. The bell from the gate watchtower had been moved to the school yard where children rang it to signal when school ended for the day. Instead of causing people to freeze with fear, the sound now caused children to run and play.

When Ash reached the blackened gate post, the jay flew again. This time it flapped and soared across the field to a sapling near the cloud forest. The branch it landed on bent beneath the bird's weight. It was a funny sight. Most birds would have known better than to land on such a skinny branch, but this jay seemed to like the way the branch dipped and bobbed. It flapped its wings, see-sawing up and down.

Ash chased after the jay. Although the field had been nothing but burnt jujube trees and blackened ground a few weeks earlier, it teemed with green seedlings now. All the ashes from the fire made the soil very fertile, and since crystal cloth had lost its luster, few webworm plantation owners wanted to grow jujube trees. Instead, the farmers who remained planted fruit trees and cloud forest seeds that Suma shared with them. Where before there'd been rows of jujube trees, now parts of the cloud forest were coming back, and villagers were helping it return.

Ash recognized the thin tree the jay had landed on. It was one of the yellow-fruit saplings Caihay had brought them. He'd visited the village several times lately, always wearing Nester as a skirt.

"You better not hurt that tree!" said Ash.

The jay bobbed up and down again, then plucked a small yellow fruit from the tree. It flapped into the air above her and dropped the fruit, barely missing her head.

"Hey!" Ash grabbed the fallen fruit and threw it at the bird. She missed.

The jay chuckled and flapped into the forest.

"Well, if that's how you want to play," said Ash. She went to one of biggest trees still standing near the edge of the forest. The bark was burned black from the flames, but the tree was old enough, and the bark thick enough, that it had survived the fire. Ash pressed her palms against the blackened bark and closed her eyes.

She focused on the life flowing like a river through the roots to the other trees in the forest. Into this living river, she sent a vision.

It was early enough in the day that mist still swirled near the edge of the forest. The mist stirred and thickened into the shape of a jaguar.

"Good morning, Balance Keeper. Do you feel like running?" asked Ash.

The mistcat knelt and Ash hopped onto her back. She pictured the area of the forest where she'd last seen the jay.

Balance Keeper sprang into motion, leaping onto a low branch, then up to a higher branch in a neighboring tree, and up again until they reached the canopy where the branches spread so wide they touched other trees. They bounded from tree to tree as if galloping across the ground.

Ash spotted the jay through a gap in the trees. It perched on a lower branch and cocked its head to watch the forest floor. The mistcat moved so quietly that the jay didn't notice them above it. Ash gathered a wet clump of *tun'ka* moss and dropped it right onto the bird's back.

"Cree!" The startled bird tumbled off the branch and took flight.

"Got you," said Ash.

The jay croaked indignantly and flapped through a tangle of branches. It circled where Balance Keeper crouched, then swooped closer and grabbed the mistcat's tail in its twig-thin feet.

Balance Keeper spun around, surprised. Most animals knew better than to taunt a mistcat, but the jay kept flapping and pulling at the jaguar's tail.

Ash's heart sped. There was only one creature bold enough to tease Balance Keeper like that.

"Puppy?"

Took you long enough to figure it out, replied a familiar voice in her head.

"Puppy!" said Ash.

The jay let go of Balance Keeper's tail, flew higher, and spiraled in a clumsy display of aerobatics before crashing onto a branch near Ash.

Do I look like a little dog to you? The jay puffed out his bright blue feathers.

"No. But you play like one," said Ash.

The jay shrugged his wings. *Still getting used to this form. Did you know that flying makes you hungry? And the more you eat the harder it gets to fly.*

"I can see how that might cause problems for you," said Ash.

Flying isn't as easy as it looks. It takes concentration. Oh, but the games birds play... They have wonderful games. Did you miss me?

"You mean, do I miss you chewing my shoes, tugging my laces, stealing my blankets, and eating everything in reach?" asked Ash. "Of course I do!"

Good. Because I think I'll wake you every morning right before the sun rises. That's my favorite time of day now.

"You better not!"

The jay made a low, chuckling sound. *Why not? Your mother gets up then.*

"How do you know?"

I saw her this morning. The jay cocked his head toward the forest floor. *She's right there.*

Ash squinted in the direction the jay indicated. She could barely see a woman kneeling near the edge of the cloud forest. Her mother seemed to be using a stick to dig small, round holes. "What's she doing?"

Planting seeds. They're delicious!

"You've been eating them?"

The jay shuffled back and forth guiltily. *Only a few. She plants them too close together. I'm helping her.*

Ash urged Balance Keeper closer to where her mother worked. The jay swooped ahead and landed on the ground in front of Essa.

This was a part of the forest that the fires had passed through but hadn't completely destroyed. The jay pecked at the ground a few times, gulping down several seeds.

Essa gasped, startled by the silent approach of the mistcat. "Ash! You scared me."

"Sorry." Ash slid off Balance Keeper's back.

Over the past few weeks, Ash had begun to understand her mother better. Although Essa wasn't as fearful as she'd been when she'd worn the crystal cloth, she was still a very jumpy, sensitive person. Part of being sensitive meant being more aware than most people. Essa frequently noticed things that others overlooked. It was something Ash felt she had in common with her mother—something not unlike hearing the whispered names of things.

Ash placed her hand on Balance Keeper's shoulder and thanked the mistcat. Balance Keeper nodded in return, then bounded into the forest, fading into mist.

"What are you doing?" asked Ash.

"Planting," said Essa. "Some seeds grow best in the shade, but that dratted bird keeps eating them. Shoo!" She waved her hands at Puppy.

The jay flapped past her and landed on a canvas bag full of seeds. He pecked at the bag, eating more seeds as they spilled out.

"Puppy!" said Ash.

What? They're yummy. You should try them.

Her mother watched the exchange with a curious expression. She couldn't hear what the jay said, but she knew Ash was hearing something.

"You named the bird *Puppy*?" asked Essa.

"Doesn't he look like a playful puppy to you?"

Essa studied the jay. Puppy puffed out his chest feathers and squawked proudly. Then he scooped up another beak-full of seeds and took off, flapping clumsily through the branches.

See you tomorrow, bright and early, he said.

Ash watched Puppy go, wondering what new forms the illwen might take on.

"I'm glad you came here," said her mother. "There's something I want to show you."

Essa led Ash to a small sapling growing in a patch of sunlight between a few trees that had burned in the fire. The sapling looked healthier than most of the trees around it, with several arrow-shaped leaves sprouting from its spindly branches. Its shiny young leaves practically glowed.

"Do you know what this is?" asked her mother.

"A sapling," replied Ash, but she knew that wasn't what her mother meant. She stilled her breathing and *listened.* Whispers surrounded the tree, as they did many growing things.

Ash had gotten better at hearing whispers. All forms had spirit energy in them, even if only a tiny bit. Instead of holding on tightly to a few special things, she was learning to see something special in almost everything. Everything whispered with possibilities. It was like Tavan had said—hearts break open. The more open she was, the more whispers she heard.

Several whispers came from the little tree her mother had indicated, but the only word Ash could make out was her own name, which made no sense.

"Ash?" she finally said, speaking the name aloud.

"That's right. It's an ash tree," said her mother.

"Is that why you named me Ash? After a type of tree?"

"I didn't mean to," replied her mother. "When you were born, I didn't know what to call you. Your father and I couldn't decide on a name. Then, one morning, you looked up at me and I heard the name *Ash*. It seemed to me that you were telling me what you wanted to be called. That sounds odd, doesn't it? A baby coming up with her own name?"

"I hear names like that sometimes."

"I think I did, too, when I was young," said Essa. "Then I stopped hearing the names of things. Until I had you." She squeezed Ash's hand. "Anyway, that's why I named you Ash."

Ash looked at the sapling growing out of the blackened, ashy earth. Her name was what survived fires, and it was what grew afterwards, forming a new forest. "It's a good name," she said. "It fits me."

She closed her eyes and listened to all the whispers rising around her. There were several young ash trees, whispering her name—a chanting forest of whispers, welcoming her home.

Author's Note

“I don't know if you know this, but trees are like us. They talk like us. This is why I'm very careful about cutting them down. People hurt them a lot. If I cut down a tree, the kin will ask, 'Why did you kill my brother?”
—Ntoni, leader of the Kisêdjê people

“Climate is a judge that knows how to count trees, and never forgets. And never forgives.”
—Antonio Donato Nobre

Although *The Namer of Spirits* is a work of fiction that takes place in an imagined land, several things in this book were inspired by real world events, real places, and real people fighting to save our forests.

The original seed for this book was planted by a fabulous series NPR produced called "The Rain Forest Was Here." In those reports, Lulu Garcia-Navarro said, "The poor are the tip of the spear that pushes civilization forward into the wilderness." That quote, and the complex reality it conveys, grew into this story.

To acknowledge the incredible reporting that journalist Lulu Garcia-Navarro and others have done on deforestation, I included an allusion to Lulu's "tip of the spear" quote in the book. In addition, the saying "burn or starve" is a reference to a farmer Lulu interviewed who said (in regards to slashing and burning the rainforest), "You either burn or starve. It's as simple as that." Sadly, last year there were over 80,000 forest fires in the Amazon rainforest. Almost all of them were set by people.

I also want to thank this NPR series for introducing me to Antonio Donato Nobre, a Brazilian climate scientist whose research into how deforestation causes droughts, and how large forests attract rain clouds to create what he calls a "flying river," deeply influenced this book. Scientists who've studied the Amazon have warned that if even just 10-20% more of the Amazon rainforest is cut down, there won't be enough trees left to create the atmospheric river the ecosystem needs. Once such a tipping point is reached, most of the rainforest could die off and weather patterns around the world would likely shift.

Other thinkers who influenced this book include Garrett Hardin and his essay "The Tragedy of the Commons," Thomas Malthus, and indigenous leaders who have been working for generations to protect forests. You might notice that some names and characters in the book pay tribute to these thinkers and activists, as well as others.

Although reports on rainforest destruction in Brazil inspired this book, deforestation isn't simply one nation's problem. The fictional world in *The Namer of Spirits* reflects many different places where cloud forests and rainforests exist, and where deforestation has taken place. Sadly, the story of deforestation is one that several nations share, and it's a story that often follows a similar pattern. People rarely intend to destroy the forest, and people rarely understand how precious forests are until they're gone.

According to the United Nations, **40 football fields of forest are cut down every minute**. This is something we can and must change. Forests like the Amazon rainforest are not only the lungs of our planet (absorbing carbon-dioxide and releasing oxygen that we breathe), they're the heart of our planet (circulating rain and stabilizing our climate). Protecting forests is a way to protect all life on earth, and to create a more abundant and sustainable future.

If you want to join the many brave, caring people who are working to save forests and protect our planet, visit my website, www.ToddMitchellBooks.com and click on "Do Something Good." There you'll find a list of actions you could take and organizations you could volunteer with or donate to. We're all in this together, and when you work to heal the planet, you're also healing yourself.

Enjoy the adventure!

Todd Mitchell

Discussion Questions

Part I:

1) Ash's dad, Garrett Narro, is described in the first chapter as being someone "who rarely troubled himself with questions he didn't have answers for," but Ash is very different from him. How would you describe her personality? What are some of her character traits?

2) How do Ash's character traits cause problems for her with her friend Rosa? Why doesn't Rosa want to play with Ash anymore?

3) Why did the village of Last Hope put up the wall? What problems did this solve or cause for villagers?

4) Why does Ash leave the longhouse and go out in the storm?

5) Ash says a few times that things feel amiss. What does she mean by this? What are some of the things that feel amiss to Ash?

6) Fen says that something is causing the illwen to come to the village. Ash decides to figure out what it is so she can stop the illwen from attacking. Why is this important to Ash?

7) Why do villagers like Mr. Rotterburg and the wall soldiers treat Ash as an enemy at the end of Part I?

PART II:

8) Although Tavan calls Fen his son, they have an unusual relationship. What seems odd or curious to you about their relationship?

9) Tavan tells Ash not to talk about what Puppy used to be, especially around Fen. Why do you think this is?

10) In the Cave of Sorrows, what does Ash do to keep the Sorrows from eating her? Why is this hard for Ash?

11) After Ash drinks water from the Pool of Memory, she sees why the Sorrows and other illwen from the cave have become angry and lost. What did the Shadow Namer do, and why does this upset the Sorrows?

12) Why does Suma want Ash to face the Shadow Namer? Why does Ash decide to do something different? Do you think Ash's new plan will work?

13) In Chapter 21, Tavan says, "The whole world can change without anyone meaning it to. It doesn't matter what you mean. It matters what you do." How does this apply to the way the cloud forest has changed? What other changes in the book, or in our world, might this apply to?

14) When Ash speaks with Governor Castol, he initially tells her that her plan won't work. What causes the governor to change his mind and agree with Ash's plan to meet the dao fora and form a peace treaty?

15) At the end of Part II, Ash wonders if there was something wrong with her for thinking that the peace talks would work. Do you think Ash is right to blame herself for what happened at the meeting between the dao fora and the governor?

PART III:

16) In Chapter 26, Tavan says, "The poor are the spear tip of cloud forest destruction." What does he mean by this? How might this describe deforestation in our world?

17) Lord Ocras claims that he helps people by giving them purpose and direction. Do you agree with this? Why or why not?

18) In Chapter 31, Lord Ocras says, “Keep people afraid, and keep them wanting, and they're easy to control.” How does he use want and fear to control people? How does he try to control Ash?

19) Lord Ocras says in Chapter 31 that Ash has much in common with him. In what ways does Ash seem similar to Lord Ocras? In what ways is she different?

20) Lord Ocras offers to teach Ash how to use the power of the illwen to “shape the world into exactly what you want it to be.” Do you think Ash should have agreed to become Lord Ocras's student? Why or why not?

21) Ash changes Eagla's name from one that means “fear” to one that means “courage,” and she changes Anobaith's name from one that means “despair” to one that means “last hope.” What connections do you see between apparent opposites like fear and courage, or despair and hope? How does this relate to the different names Ash gives Puppy?

22) To give something a true name, what does Ash need to do? How would you describe the “power of naming” that Ash and Lord Ocras use? Are we able to do something similar when we name things in our own world?

23) Fen tells Ash in Chapter 35, “Finding your name is a strange adventure. Every time you try to become one thing, you find out you're actually something else.” What did Fen try to become, and what does he find out he is? Have you ever tried to become one thing and found out that you're actually something else?

24) In the Epilogue, Ash learns that "her name was what survived fires, and it was what grew afterwards, forming a new forest." How does this describe her character and the things she did in the book?

25) In the end, Ash gets better at hearing the whispered names of things. What do you think helped her get better at this?

26) What connections can you find between events in this book and events in our own world?

Acknowledgements

I'm grateful to all the kind souls who helped this unusual story sprout and grow into a book. I especially want to thank:

Ginger Knowlton, the best agent in the business, for sticking with me all these years. The fabulous and fun Darby Karchut, for showing me what an amazing publisher Owl Hollow Press is. Emma, Hannah, and all the fine folks at Owl Hollow Press, for taking a chance on my weird visions and working to make this story become what it needed to be—you're the dream airship of publishers. Olivia Swenson, for being an incredible editor and a joy to work with.

Asur Misoa, for designing a cover I love. Robert Chang, Jennifer Phang, and Good Neighbors Media for believing in this story so strongly that you optioned this manuscript for film/TV development long before it was even published.

Kate Sullivan, for giving me early feedback on the manuscript. The brilliant, brave, and kind peeps of my stalwart writing coven: Laura Resau, Laura Pritchett, and Karye Cattrell, for being wise, creative, critical, and enthusiastic readers (a rare combination).

My parents and sister, for always supporting my strange endeavors and letting me use your desks when I visit. Juniper, for being my Puppy on this journey. Addison Story and Cailin

Elizabeth, for reading everything and helping this manuscript become what it is—you're each half Ash. Finally, many glowing thanks go to my partner in naming, Kerri. At the end of the day, I always want to share every story with you.

THANK YOU FOR READING!

If you enjoyed this book, please let others know about it. Posting a short review on Amazon, Goodreads, Indiebound, or other sites makes a huge difference for writers like me.

Reviews don't need to be long. Even one sentence helps to spread the word, support creativity, and raise awareness about deforestation. Write on!

30% of all author profits from the sale of this book will be donated to organizations working to preserve the rainforest ecosystems upon which we all depend.

Todd Mitchell is the author of several award-winning novels, including *The Last Panther* (Delacorte Press, Colorado Book Award Winner and winner of the Green Prize for Sustainable Literature), *The Traitor King* (Scholastic Press), *The Secret to Lying* (Candlewick Press, Colorado Book Award Winner), and *Backwards* (Candlewick Press, CAL Award Winner). He created the graphic series *Broken Saviors* (available on Comixology), and co-wrote the graphic novel *A Flight of Angels* (Vertigo, a YALSA "Top 10 Great Graphic Novels for Teens").

When Todd isn't writing, he's often mountain biking, kayaking, surfing, and exploring the outdoors. He's worked several wild jobs, including rescuing injured wolves, rehabilitating hawks, taking care of orphaned bear cubs, building homes for foxes, and teaching every grade except kindergarten.

Currently, Todd serves as Director of the Beginning Creative Writing Teaching Program at Colorado State University. He lives in Fort Collins, Colorado with his wife, dog, and two wise daughters. He loves speaking with readers and writers of all ages, and often does author visits to schools (in-person and virtually). You can visit him at:

www.ToddMitchellBooks.com

#TheNameOfSpirits